Murder in the Forest

Louise Hodkin

Copyright © Louise Hodkin
All rights reserved.
ISBN 13: 9781983121937

For Matt, Hugh and Seb.

Chapter One

*Friday 17th October 1851.
Berry Hill, Forest of Dean.*

Darkness came early that night. Already lights were showing in cottage windows, small pinpricks of light from tallow candles and oil lamps. The sweet smell of wood smoke mingled unpleasantly with the sulphurous aroma of damp burning coal and hung in the air as wisps of mist gathered amongst the tall trees. Mature oaks and horse chestnuts swayed in the wind, shedding their brightly coloured autumn leaves, adding further to the thick mulch strewn across roads and blown into piles in the corners of the yard. The handful of miners and quarrymen's cottages which made up the hamlet of Berry Hill braced itself for the coming storm.

Nesta sat curled in her mother's basket chair watching the leaves bustle around the yard. Despite a thick blanket wrapped around her shoulders she shivered as the keen wind blew in through gaps around the wooden door and ill-fitting windows. The kitchen of the small cottage was cold and dark, the only light coming from the small fire that burned cheerfully in the open grate. Steam swirled from the spout of the battered, blackened kettle which hung just above the flames. Turning from the window to survey the room, Nesta took in the old oak table, scrubbed to a bright white, the centre of her mother's domain. Normally the kitchen would be full of life, as her mother prepared the evening meal surrounded by Nesta and her four siblings. All would be listening out for the sound of Thomas, Nesta's father, arriving home from a long days work in the pit. At the first sound of his heavy footsteps Nesta would rush out to the wash house with a full kettle of hot water, so that he might wash off the coal dust with warm water. Uncles and Aunts would flit in and out, perhaps calling in to drop off a gift of vegetables from their gardens, pass on the latest gossip, or join them for whatever delicious meal her mother had prepared all cooked over the small kitchen fire or baked in the tiny bread oven.

But today the kitchen was empty save for Nesta. Earlier that day, Mary, Nesta's mother, had gone into labour with her sixth child. While the rest of the family had been sent to wait for news out of the way with Thomas' cousin Jane, Nesta had been deemed old enough to stay and help. At sixteen it was the first time that Nesta had been deemed old enough, and she was both pleased and scared in equal measure. For now she had been sent downstairs to keep out of the way. A shout dragged her from her revelry and out into the narrow hallway.

"At last! Come on, we be needing you upstairs. Bring that there kettle of water, an' make sure you don't go scalding yourself on the way up" chided her Aunt as, arms full of clean linen, she eased her considerable bulk up the narrow staircase. Carefully folding a cloth around the handle, Nesta collected the heavy black kettle from the hearth and followed her Aunt upstairs.

"Come on, come on! Where's that there water?" called a voice from bedroom. Nesta took a deep breath and entered the familiar room. There all was awry. The covers from her parents' bed were all piled higgledy piggledly in the corner, and the small dressing table had been swept clear, and covered with cloth upon which stood Agnes' battered bag, some folded clean white cloths, and a very sharp knife.

"Come on, come on! Over 'ere quickly, I'll be needing some hot water to clean these" called the voice from the foot of the bed. There crouched the wiry frame of Agnes the village midwife. A tall, slim woman, Agnes pushed a stray lock of hair out of her eyes, tucking it swiftly behind an ear. Dressed, as always, in a dark brown skirt and clean freshly starched cream blouse she had donned an old, somewhat stained apron in preparation for the baby's arrival. Despite having no formal training Agnes had been assisting women giving birth in Berry Hill and the surrounding villages for many years. Originally she had started out helping her mother, another Agnes, to deliver many of the women she now helped herself. Although she wasn't well liked generally – her abrupt manner meant that Agnes was not often invited to socialise with the villagers – her help was better than nothing. In the presence of Agnes and her calm, detached manner, Nesta felt her fear recede. She gently poured the scalding water into the wash stand, and turned to look at her mother, Mary, for the first time since entering the room.

Propped up with pillows, Mary lay on her bed and groaned. Normally smartly and soberly dressed, her hair always pulled back into a tight bun, she lay with her hair hanging limply across her tearstained face and her nightdress pulled up around her hips. To Nesta her mother had always been strong, calm and unflustered, managing the household with an iron grip which belied her diminutive size. Clutching her sister's hand Mary let out a long, low sob.

"The babes nearly 'ere. Come and hold her hand while I help Agnes" said her Aunt softly. Nesta squeezed through the narrow space between her Aunt Rose and the wall, and gently sat on the edge of the bed. Taking her mother's hand in hers, she carefully swept the damp hair away from her mother's wane face and smiled at down.

Suddenly Mary's face contorted with pain. "It's time. Push, Mary, push!" came the sharp command from Agnes. Mary groaned. Her face becoming redder and redder. She started to pant, and then gasp. Finally, after what seemed like an eternity to them both, an excited shout came from Rose. "It's another girl. Foot first, just like you Nesta! There we go, easy does it, you've done it Mary. You've done it!" Mary squeezed Nesta's hand tight.

"It's all over now Nesta. All done now" Mary's voice was so quiet and whispery that Nesta had to lean in close to hear her, a far cry from the clear, strident voice that Nesta was used to hearing, calling her and her five younger siblings in from the fields and the forest. As Mary smiled wanly up at her eldest daughter, they both became aware of a fierce whispered exchange between Rose and Agnes. "You've got to let her hold her first!"

"No. No, it's best that she don't see 'un, give it to me, I'll take it"

"If you're sure that this is the best way"

"Yes. Yes. Give it to me."

"What's going on? What's wrong? Where's my daughter?" Mary's voice was full of anguish as she began to sense that something might be terribly, dreadfully, wrong.

"I'm sorry, Mary, I'm so sorry" Rose came to stand beside her sister, and holding her hand tightly, tears running down her face "She's gone. She's gone."

"What? What's 'appening? Where's the baby? I don't understand" Nesta looked between her Aunt and mother, taking in the anguished look on both their faces.

Agnes looked up at Nesta from the foot of the bed where she was busily wrapping a small shape in a clean sheet. She spoke softly.

"The bairn didn't make it. It happens, particularly if the mother's older and they come foot-wise. I'm sorry. There was nothing I could do. She never breathed. I'm sorry." Agnes' voice faded away to mere whisper, and a look of true compassion crossed her face as if she knew, and understood, Mary's pain. For a moment Nesta thought that Agnes would go on, would offer some further words of comfort, but the moment passed. The compassion was replaced with a much harder look. "Now Nesta, you run downstairs and put the kettle back on. Hot, sweet tea, that's what your Ma needs now. Go on, be off with you."

Nesta looked down at her mother, who slowly nodded in confirmation. Standing unsteadily, Nesta took a last look around the room and at the small, sad bundle wrapped in a blanket at the foot of the bed, before dashing down the stairs. As she went she heard Agnes continuing in the same soft voice "There's nothing else I can do here. I'll see myself out. You stay 'ere Rose, and take care of Mary" Then more sharply, "No, Mary. I'll take her. I'll take care of everything, tis for the best. Rose, you tell her. Tell her it's best."

Nesta crashed the kettle down on the table, tugging off the lid to refill it as she did so. Grasping the battered earthenware jug which habitually stood full of water on the dresser, Nesta found to her dismay it was empty. Sighing, she picked the jug up, knowing that she would get soaked as she headed outside into the cold to collect fresh water from the well which served the little line of miner's cottages that huddled together on the edge of the village. An almost total darkness had engulfed the little cottages as the storm which had been threatening all afternoon had finally broken. Rain fell heavily, battering at the windows and doors, and blowing into Nesta's eyes and mixing with the tears she shed for her little sister. She pulled the door to behind her so as to keep out the worst of the weather and stumbled across the yard to the well. Pulling on the handle she drew up a bucketful of water and slopped it into the waiting jug. Then, hugging it to her with both hands, carried the heavy jug, and stumbled back to the warm, welcoming kitchen. As she reached the door, she was knocked almost off her feet as Agnes bustled out of the door carrying a large heavy basket. Water splashed from the jug, and onto the bottom of Agnes' skirt.

"Stupid girl! Watch where you are going can't you? Now, you just get that there kettle boiling, and then go back upstairs to your Ma. Your Aunt has already gone to tell your Pa the news. You make sure you bide with your Ma till she gets back. You be taking good care of her mind" and with that, Agnes hurried away into the darkness, heading back to her own small encroachment cottage inside the gloom of the forest.

Nesta did as she was told and having carefully filled the kettle and put it on the stove to boil, she raced up the stairs to her mother. The room was still and quiet. Mary lay back against the head board and stared at the flames in the small hearth. Clasping her mother's hand in her own, Nesta sat on the edge of the bed, and joined her mother in silent tears.

Chapter Two

Monday 26th October, 1851

The next few weeks passed in a whirl for Nesta. The loss of the baby had hit her mother hard. Instead of rushing around constantly busy, Mary had withdrawn into herself. Barely leaving her bed, she had not left the cottage for weeks now. So Nesta had stopped helping out at the little valley school, and instead had taken on all of the laborious household chores herself. Every moment of her day was now filled with scrubbing, cooking and cleaning, mending clothes, soothing hurts, and helping to sort coal. Each morning she rose long before dawn from the bed she shared with her four siblings to stumble in the dark down to the little kitchen. There Nesta would coax the fire back to life, and make sure that the kettle was filled and on to boil ready so that her father could have a hot drink with his bread and butter before he went to start work down in the mine.

Like many of his friends and relations, Thomas was a Free Miner. This ancient right was conveyed on the men born in the Hundreds of the Forest of Dean who had worked a year and day underground. It gave him various privileges, including being able to run his own mine, known locally as a gale, extracting coal and iron ore from beneath the Forest of Dean with limited interference or taxation. As a consequence of this the Forest was littered with small drift mines and mine shafts tapping into the abundant coal and iron seams. Thomas had started work down his own father's small drift mine aged just twelve and there he served his apprenticeship, learning how to hew coal, make props from straight trees, and prop the seams to make the roof safe. After his father's early death, worn out by years of back-breaking toil, Thomas continued to work the mine at Hollow Meadow with his older brother. Long, hard days scratching the coal from seams using nothing more than a hand pick and shovel; pushing it to the surface in small wooden trucks that they made themselves. There the coal was sorted, bagged and sent off for sale in the coal yard in Coleford that was owned by their uncle. However, despite the long hours that the men put into the mine, times were hard. While there was always money to put food on the table and keep a roof over their heads, there was never quite enough, and Nesta and her brother and sisters, while not starving, were always slightly hungry. Nesta was therefore very pleased, when opening the kitchen door to go to collect more water, she found a rabbit tied to the door handle. Looking up and down the frosty yard, there was no sign of who had left this unlooked for bounty – the result no doubt of a friend's nocturnal foray into the forest. But although receiving the poached rabbit could get the family into trouble with the local gamekeepers and Verderers, it was still a most welcome addition to the larder. Picking the rabbit up, Nesta tucked it inside on the kitchen table, ready to prepare on her return.

When Nesta returned to the kitchen, already chilly from her brief trip outside, she found her father, brother, and sisters sat at the table.

"Who's yon coney from?" Thomas asked in a gruff voice.

"No idea Pa, it were hanging on the back of the door when I went out. I thought maybe to have it for tea – make a stew of it?"

"Whatever you think is best. Just make sure you get rid of it quick like, we don't want no trouble with the law and having poached rabbits on the table will only lead to trouble. Now I'm off to the gale." With that, Thomas rose from the table. Pausing to kiss each of his children goodbye he made his way out into the cold morning heading for the mine.

Nesta sighed and began the task of chivvying her siblings through their breakfast. Nesta was the eldest at sixteen, then there was ten year-old Minnie, Lucy at eight, and Anne was seven. At 5, Arthur was the baby of the family. A rather introspective young boy; he'd started school just that September and was still finding it hard. Arthur would much rather have stayed at home playing with his great treasure, a small horse that his father had carved him out of a scrap of wood. All the children attended the small school in the chapel at Christchurch when their parents could scrape together the fees. Then after the day's lessons, they would go on to the mine, helping to sort and bag the coal ready for it to be collected by their Great Uncle. Most children finished their lessons at fourteen, leaving to marry, go into service, or begin work underground or for one of the great foundries. Nesta was unusual in that she had stayed on at the school, helping the Master teach the younger children the basics of reading, writing and maths. However, although she enjoyed the work, it didn't bring in very much money. Sometimes, lying awake in bed at night, she had heard her parents discussing sending her away to work in service at some grand house, where if she was lucky, she might get a position as a housemaid. Then if she worked hard, and showed an aptitude, she might rise through the ranks of servants to be become a lady's maid, or even a house keeper. Nesta dreamed that one day she might be the housekeeper at a great house, with a whole host of servants to do her bidding. For now, that seemed like an impossible dream. The idea of running a great household, and having a small room of her own, with her own bed, and maybe even a dresser with her own things was beyond her wildest dreams. However, with her mother deep in melancholy, grieving for her lost daughter Nesta had stopped going to school, instead she stayed home to take care of the household chores. That day was Monday, and therefore wash day. Nesta would spend the day washing the family clothes in the wash house out the back pounding the sheets and clothes in a heavy tin barrel with the old wooden clothes dolly, before running them through the mangle, and finally hanging them on the line to dry. It was hard, physical work, tiring even on the best of days. Nesta's heart sank as she looked out of the window and saw that there had been a hard frost in the night. It promised to be a long, hard, cold day and Nesta knew that by the end of it her hands would be red and bleeding from fighting with the cold heavy wet clothes. But there was no help for it, so chivvying the younger children out of the door to their lessons, Nesta began the long, laborious task of the washing. By mid morning she had just finished running the last of the clothes through the old mangle, when she heard a shout.

Sticking her head out of the wash house door, Nesta saw a tall, dark man kick the well in frustration. He then started hopping as he'd clearly hurt his foot. Although Nesta tried to suppress a giggle, she didn't quite succeed, and the man turned quickly to see where the stifled snort had come from.

"I suppose you think that this is funny, do you? There's no water in the house. The well is frozen solid, and now I've hurt my foot. How am I supposed to get water with it all iced up? Don't you have any taps? A pump even?" Although he sounded peevish, he had a slightly self-depreciating air, and his eyes sparkled as if he was laughing at himself. His voice was strong, and he was clearly well educated. In fact, his whole appearance made him look out of place in the small shared yard. At close to 6 foot he was taller than most of the local men.

He was also considerably better dressed in a smart dark morning jacket, fresh linen shirt, and shiny black top hat. A bright silk cravat, held with a gold pin, marked him out as being significantly wealthier than any of the inhabitants of the small row of cottages, none of whom had the money to spend on such fashionable extravagances.

Nesta sighed "No sir, there's no taps in the village. But I'll show you how to break the ice, there's a trick to it. Then you can get some water" with that she strode over to the well, and attaching the bucket to the rope, she sent it down the well with a resounding smack. The ice shattered, and with careful swinging of the rope, Nesta managed to fill the bucket and haul it to the well top with the bucket brimful of water. "There. Tis easy when you know how!"

"Hmmm. Yes, well. Ummm thank-you. I'm much obliged to you. I suppose it is a skill I will need to learn for myself if I'm going to work out here." Nesta looked at him quizzically, clearly wondering what someone so well dressed would be doing in the small mining hamlet. The man noticed her look and smiled.

"I'm sorry I didn't introduce myself, my name is Dr Edward James, I've taken over Dr Thomas' practice in Coleford, Berry Hill is now in my 'patch' as it were. And you are?"

"Nesta, Nesta Phillips Sir. I live down at the end cottage" Nesta turned red and gave a small curtsey "We never saw much of Dr Thomas out here. He used to just stay in

Coleford really. There's not much call for a doctor round here" And not much money to pay for one either she thought. When a visit to the doctors cost a shilling, and most people would be lucky to earn 20 shillings a week, a visit to the doctors was an unaffordable luxury. Nesta herself had never visited the doctors, nor did she know anyone who had, except perhaps the Parson. Her friends and family were left with the cheaper, if less skilled, services of Agnes the village midwife cum herbalist. Agnes knew all the traditional treatments for the aches pains, coughs, colds and minor accidents that befell the people that lived in and around the small hamlet of Berry Hill. Yet, here was a doctor trying to draw water from the well.

Dr James seemed to read Nesta's thoughts. "Yes, I know that Dr Thomas didn't treat many people out this way, but I was riding back from a visit to Sir Cyril when I came across a young lad in some distress in the road. It would seem that Mrs Andrews has had a nasty fall and has dislocated her arm. Young Frederick had gone out to fetch help from..." he frowned as he searched for the right name "an Agnes is it? Anyway, he found me instead. I've set the arm for her and I don't think there will be any problems. But if you could keep an eye on them, that would be very helpful. I'll be calling in to check on her on Thursday, however, if there are any problems before hand, perhaps you'd be able to send a boy to Coleford to fetch me? Now I must get on. There wasn't any water in the house to make tea even!" The doctor's words came out in a garbled stream, punctuated with much hand waving. Before he had even finished speaking he was turning and heading back towards the kitchen door. Accustomed to working at St Thomas' Hospital in London, a charitable foundation it treated patients for free and consequently was always busy. Having to rush from patient to patient, he had developed the habit of speaking quickly, imparting as much information as he could in as short a time as possible, before moving quickly on to the next task. Naturally polite, Edward had at first found it very difficult to speak so quickly and abruptly to his patients, but spending time on the large wards, where there was never enough time to see the all the patients, had forced him to develop the habit, and now it was second nature to him. Having moved from London to the Forest of Dean only six weeks earlier, he had yet to adapt to the much slower pace used by all his new patients. As he strode back to the end cottage carrying the bucket of water, Nesta had to run, catching up with him as he let himself in through the back door to the Andrews's kitchen.

It was cold in the small kitchen, the fire still banked from the night before and the heavy shutters still drawn across the windows. An empty mug stood on the scrubbed table, a brace of rabbits hung from a hook on the wall, and a pair of eyes watched their every move from the safety of the stairs.

"Here. I'll do that. Your time is much too valuable to be making tea" said Nesta taking the kettle to fill and put onto boil. Expertly she took the poker and coal bucket she began work bringing the fire back to life, and some warmth back into the house. "Now, I'm sure you need to get back to Coleford. I'll take care of things here."

Dr James quickly glanced at the silent watcher on the stairs, and then looked back at Nesta. "Well, actually, I'm not due back at my surgery until this afternoon, and I'd like to keep an eye on Mrs Andrews. I had to give her a strong painkiller so I could set her arm, and I'd rather like to see how she's getting on as that wears off. I don't want her to be in too much pain so that she can't sleep and may need to give her another dose later. It's no trouble."

Nesta winced, thinking that there would be trouble when no-one could pay the bill. Even if all the neighbours chipped in, the cost of the visit from the doctor, relocating the elbow and medicine would probably be far more than the small family could afford. "I'm sorry Dr James, I don't know if anyone has explained to you..." Nesta's voice trailed off as she saw Dr James grin.

"It's alright Miss Phillips. I am not intending to charge for this treatment. Part of my reason for visiting Sir Cyril today was to discuss the establishment of a charitable hospital for the people of the Forest of Dean. As a principle landowner in this area, Sir Cyril is concerned that his workers often cannot afford even basic medical care, and so we are discussing setting up a friendly society to provide treatment to rate payers in the Forest of Dean. Mrs Andrews is its first case!"

Nesta let out a heartfelt sigh of relief. Now that she was no longer worrying about where she would be able to find enough money for the doctor without worrying her parents any further, her natural confidence returned. She quickly took charge in the kitchen, hunting out the tea, cups, and milk - a quick sniff of which told her it was sour. Walking to the bottom of the stairs, Nesta looked straight up at the small unkempt boy that sat peering down, watching their every move with wide eyes.

"Here, Frederick. This milk 'as turned. Run back to my house and tell my Ma what's happened. Then fetch our jug of milk from the side. There are some biscuits in the tin on the shelf, bring them back for us too. Go on, away with you" kindly shooing him out of door. Watching him run across the yard, Edward felt sorry for him. Frederick was a skinny boy of about eight. Small for his age, he was dressed only in short trousers and an old shirt. Despite the chill of the day, he had no pullover on, and was wearing shoes that looked to be several sizes too big so that they slopped when he ran. However, though his clothes were old and of poor quality, they were all clean, and had been carefully mended. While Frederick looked poor, he also looked well cared for, and clearly loved. Edward suddenly became aware that while he was watching Frederick, he was being scrutinised in his turn.

Nesta looked at him, her eyes narrowed. "Now then Doctor. That's got rid of young Fredrick here, would you care to tell me the real reason why you're still here. I don't believe that it's just to keep an eye on her pain, you could leave a bottle of medicine with me for that!"

An irritated look crossed Dr James's face, before being replaced with a wry smile. "Ah. Yes well. It would appear that you have seen through me. You see, in confidence, I'm not sure that Mrs Andrews fell, so much as was pushed. She's got a lot of bruises, some old, some new. I did rather wonder how she'd come across them, and whether she required any further assistance. I don't suppose you'd have any ideas on that would you?"

"No. No idea." She said thoughtfully "My mother might though; they often used to sit together on an afternoon before the men got home from the gale. If anyone knows anything, it'll be Ma that does. Well, Ma, or Aunt Rose. Nowt happens in Berry Hill that Aunt Rose doesn't know about! Not that she's a gossip like" Nesta added quickly "it's just that people like to talk to her if you know what I mean. Aunt Rose is a good listener. She's good at solving problems."

"And where could I find your mother or Aunt?"

"Well, Aunt Rose'll be at the alehouse, she's married to the landlord. It's the other end of the village. That's if she's not out visiting or helping up at the Gale. Ma is still in bed." Seeing the doctors questioning look, Nesta continued uncomfortably "Ma lost a babe a few weeks ago. She's, well, she's not been the same since. Aunt Rose says she just needs a bit of time, so I'm looking after things at home."

The door crashed open, saving Nesta from making any further comment, and in charged Fredrick. "I've got the milk, but I couldn't reach the biscuits. Not even standing on a chair! I couldn't find your Ma, neither. I called out, I even went upstairs but she's not there." Fredrick carefully placed the milk jug on the table and looked at Dr James. "Can I go up to Ma?" Nesta nodded absentmindedly, slightly puzzled that Fredrick hadn't been able to find her mother.

The door crashed open again, this time with Nesta's father. "Jane! Jane! Come quick! It's your Pete. There's been an accident. Oh!" Thomas stopped to look between his daughter, Fredrick and the strange man. "What's going on Nesta?" he said looking pointedly at the doctor.

"Da, this is Dr James. Jane has had an accident and he's helped her. He says she'll be alright, and there's no charge." Nesta continued quickly as she saw the look of worry cross her father's face. "What do you need her for?"

Doctor James stood up and reaching for his bag said "I really don't think that Mrs Andrew's should be disturbed at this time. If someone has been hurt, perhaps I can be of assistance, Mr Phillips?"

Thomas took a deep breath "Aye, maybe you can." He said ponderously. "Pete's had an accident up at the Gale. He's, well, he's in a bad way. It's a just a short stretch if you'd come, see if there's owt you can do for him." He turned to look at Nesta as she began to move too "No, Nesta, stay here and keep an eye on Jane. Send Frederick to get your Ma and Aunt Rose too. We'll need their help as well"

"Yes Da, but Frederick couldn't find Ma at our house. Do you know where she might be?"

A dark look, a mixture of worry and anger, crossed Thomas' face. "Ah, she's probably just gone visiting. She said she were feeling a bit brighter this morning. She'll be up at Rose's that's all. Fredrick, hurry up to Rose's place, and tell them to come up to the mine. You come straight back here to Nesta mind! None of your wandering off, do you hear me?"

"Yes Mr Phillips." And with that, Frederick ran out across the yard, Thomas watched him go; then turned back into the kitchen with a sigh. "We'd best get on then, Doctor. Before we're too late" and with that he led the way back into the trees towards the mine.

Chapter Three

It was the quietness that struck the doctor first as he reached the mine at Hollow Meadow with Thomas. There was none of the noise of busy industry that he had come to expect from visits to the docklands and industrial areas of London and the busy tin mines near his grandfather's estates in Cornwall. Thomas slowed the fast walking pace that he had set to what could only be described as a dawdle, the quietness clearly affecting him as well. Alerted by the sound of their heavy footsteps cracking the ice that had formed on the frozen mud of the track, the door of a ramshackle hut opened slowly, and two men emerged. Edward stopped walking and took careful stock of his surroundings. The mine, or gale, was much smaller than he had expected - just a few dilapidated timber buildings, some mining apparatus, and a rather half-hearted attempt a low fence to mark the edge of the site. Standing alone in an area of rough moorland a short distance from the village, the mine was surrounded, not by trees as Edward had expected for a forest mine, but rather by low scrub and thick tussocks of grass. A collection of small sheds, most of which seemed to have been inexpertly made from rough sawn timber were the only buildings visible on the site. To one side a line of small empty trucks stood on iron rails, waiting to be unloaded into an old cart. Through the thick coal dust Edward could just make out the name "Phillips & Son; Coleford" on the side. An equally old looking horse stood dozing gently in its traces, covered in a broad blanket.

 Here there was no heavy machinery, no great winding engine like those he had seen at the tin mines near his cousin's Cornish estates. Instead the shaft was simply an opening dug into the side of the hill into which the iron rails disappeared. A pair of battered wooden gates stood closed, held together simply with a loop of worn rope. Edward doubted that they would hold back even a determined child for long. To Edward it looked more like an itinerants' camp than the site of heavy industry.

 The younger of the two men walked up to Thomas shaking his head sadly. He was a large man, dressed like Thomas in stout work boots, rough trousers, thick cord waistcoat and a grimy collarless shirt. The family resemblance was sufficient that without being told Edward could tell that they were closely related. Cousins or brothers, Edward thought, given that they were close in age, the new man probably just a year or two younger than Thomas.

"He's gone Tom. I've sent the boy for the vicar and Agnes." He said sadly "Did you not bring our Jane? Probably best to keep her away 'til we've cleaned him up a bit like." He turned slightly to indicate the doctor with his head, clearly asking who the stranger was, and raised an eyebrow as if questioning why Thomas had brought him to the mine on this of all days.

"This is the new Doctor, he's taken over from old Doctor Thomas in Coleford. He were at our Jane's when I got there. She's had another fall." Thomas' meaningful look drew the older man into the conversation for the first time, a slow nod from Thomas continuing the conversation without the need to elaborate further "Anyways, he said he'd come, see if there was owt he could do."

The older man who had so far not spoken looked up quickly, seemingly taking an interest in the conversation for the first time. "An accident? Again! What happened to her this time?" he started towards the doctor "What's he done to her? The bastard! God rest his soul."

Edward looked questioningly at Thomas, who muttered to him "This is our Uncle William. He's Jane's father."

"Ah. Jane told me she'd had a fall. Her elbow has been dislocated, but I've set that, and it will soon mend. She also has some bruising, some recent, some much older. I take it you think that her husband might have been responsible for at least some of it?"

"Aye, well, he was quick to anger, particularly if he'd had a drink." William shook his head sadly, and continued in a much quieter voice, almost to himself. "I never should have let her marry him. She deserved better than him, but at the time..." William's voice faded away, and he looked beseechingly at the other two men, searching for, and failing to find approbation. He turned towards the shed in which he had been waiting for Thomas. Shaking his head as if to clear it, he continued in a much stronger voice. "Still. Jane needs to be told, and it'll be best coming from me. She shouldn't be alone at time like this. I'm minded to take her and the boy back to stay with me in Coleford. Where I can keep an eye on her. Aye, that'll be best." And with that William climbed up onto the cart and starting the horse with an expert flick of the reins, set off down the track to the village.

Edward watched the horse plod slowly along the track until it was lost from sight.

"So, Mr Phillips, and Mr Phillips, is it?" he said inkling his head in greeting "Would you mind if I had a look at this Pete. Just to be sure there's nothing to be done, you understand?"

The younger man looked at Edward with suspicion. "How'd you know my name? And how'd you come across Jane for that matter? When she's taken a hiding she's always been like to go to Agnes, not go out visiting Doctors."

"I came across young Fredrick as I was heading back towards Coleford from a house call. He darted out into the road from trees. Damned near ran under my horse hooves. Near hysterical he was, grabbing at my stirrup saying there'd been an accident and he couldn't get 'Agnes'. He's lucky my mares calm, otherwise he'd have been trampled. Anyway, Frederick led me back to his house where I found Jane slumped at the bottom of the stairs. It was obvious her elbow was dislocated. Covered in cuts and bruises as well, so I set her arm, cleaned her wounds and was just about to have a cup of tea with Miss Phillips, when Mr Phillips here came in, and here we are!" Edward smiled "As to how I know that you are brothers, well one does not need to be a doctor to see the clear family resemblance. Now shall we get on; I'd like to drop back in on Mrs Andrews, and I need to back in Coleford for my afternoon surgery at 1pm." And with that Edward started towards the shed leaving the two brothers little choice but to trail in after him.

Inside the shed was surprisingly neat and tidy given the general look of dilapidation outside in the yard. A couple of wooden chairs and a rather rickety looking stool were gathered together around a small pot-bellied stove. Tools, hats, and oilskins hung from hooks around the hut walls, and an old cracked washstand stood in the corner so that the men could wash away the worse of the dirt before eating the packed lunches that stood in a line on the windowsill next to a small bunch of wild flowers in an old jam jar. The glass in the small window was clean, and the floor had been recently swept. Someone had clearly taken a little time to try to keep the men's hut as pleasant as possible. In the middle of the hut stood an old battered table which had clearly seen better days. One leg had been completely replaced, and another had been splinted with what appeared to be an old axe handle, but the surface gleamed white as it had been recently, and thoroughly, scrubbed. On top of this lay a man's body.

    Doctor James went straight to the body, but it was obvious to him before he even began to touch the corpse that the man was past any help that he could offer. Lying flat on his back, the man stared with unseeing eyes at the huts ceiling. His features pale and waxy and his lips tinged with blue. Long scratches covered the man's face and forearms as if he had been running through brambles and his clothes were grubby and torn. One leg was clearly broken, bent at the knee at an unnatural angle, and his hands were swollen and bruised. Although the man appeared to be much the same age and was dressed similarly to the other two men, he seemed different to the two brothers. Edward instinctively felt that the brothers were inherently decent and hardworking. Although there was nothing physical that he could point to explain it, Edward couldn't help the feeling that here was a man that was best avoided; something about him just felt *wrong*. Perhaps it was the sullen look that his face wore even in death, or the heavy-set features already showing the signs of the habitual heavy drinker, or maybe even the knowledge that this man used to routinely beat his wife. But whatever the cause Edward couldn't help thinking that he was of no loss to his community. Shaking his head sadly to dispel his uncharitable thoughts, he reached over to the close the man's staring eyes and noticed for the first-time blood stains on the otherwise clean table. Tentatively he reached around behind the head, his strong fingers gently searching. There he found, as he expected, a patch of hair sticky with blood, and small dent in the skull. The skull bones moved and grated together as he probed with his long sensitive fingers.

Looking over that the two brothers who had silently followed him into the shed, he saw them both wincing with disgust as they watched the doctor examine the man's head and heard the skull bones grate together.

"How was it you said you found him?" asked Edward sharply. Edward was suspicious. While some of Pete's injuries might be explained by him falling badly, the broken leg, the cuts and bruises. It was unlikely he would have hurt the back of his head at the same time. He was suddenly acutely aware of how vulnerable he was. As he stood next to what he strongly suspected was a murdered man, he looked from brother to brother, wondering if either of them was the killer, and whether they would make him their next victim.

"T'was round the back of the shed, over towards the old workings. No idea what he was doing round there like though. We use that area to dump spoil and rubbish." Thomas mumbled, staring at the floor. "I'd just gone for a piss like, and there he was lying face down next to a pile of old props. Horrible it was. Suppose he must have been out..." Thomas searched for an explanation that would not mean he had to reveal Pete's poaching "...for a walk and tripped and fell. It's right overgrown round there, and he'd been drinking hard last night. Aye, Jack had to throw him out the bar again last night. He could be right nasty when he'd been drinking. He drank a lot did our Pete, God rest him."

"God rest him" echoed Samuel and led the way back out of the hut and into the weak winter sunlight. "Now where's that boy got to with the vicar and Agnes?"

Edward looked at the brothers. They were hiding something he thought. But they did seem genuinely perplexed by Pete's death. They're not the killers. Edward thought. But they might know who is.

Chapter Four

Wednesday 5th November, 1851.
Coleford, Forest of Dean.

Several days passed. Edward lent back in his chair in his small consulting room and let out a deep sigh. The clock in the hall chimed twelve, marking the end of that mornings surgery, and Edward was relieved he would be able to escape the confines of the rather dark, if grand, Georgian house to make some house calls to visit a few of his weaker patients. He was also looking forward to meeting with Sir Cyril to discuss their plan to set up a small charitable hospital. Edward had always found treating the poor, with their myriad of different illness and accidents, far more interesting and rewarding that he had treating some of his wealthier patients, many of who suffered from little more than boredom and overindulgence. The previous week he had been invited to dinner to with Sir Cyril to welcome him to the area. Knowing that many of the foresters often went without proper medical treatment as they were unable to afford the high doctor's fee, he had taken the chance to discuss with him at length the lack of health care for the parish poor. Together, they had set upon founding a Friendly Society, a new idea which was growing in popularity across the country. All they needed were some wealthy benefactors willing to help with the initial set up costs and another doctor or two to help share the medical load.

Standing up and stretching his back, Edward walked across the hall towards the dining room and the kitchen beyond already planning his vision for the new hospital. Deep in thought, the jangling of the front door bell made him jump. He turned to open it, sighing as he thought that there was always a patient who thought that surgery times didn't apply to them. Opening the front door, he was about to send whoever was there away with a flea in their ear and instructions to return the next day when he saw who it was. Jane Andrews stood on the top step looking furtively around. Intrigued as to why she was there - he had visited the previous day and she was healing well, physically at least - Edward welcomed her in to the house and led the way back into his surgery.

Directing her to a chair, Jane nervously shook her head.

"I shan't take your time up long Dr James. I know that its past hours, but this was the first time I could get away. Me Pa, he wouldn't want me to come see you like this, you understand?" she said looking at him pleadingly. Edward smiled reassuringly, while secretly pitying the young women, who having left home to marry (and Edward rather thought to escape her domineering father) had found herself tied to an abusive drunk. After years of abuse, now Jane was back where she started, with her father, who, while he clearly loved his only daughter, thought of her as a silly wayward girl – and treated her accordingly.

Jane took a deep breath to gather her courage, and then blurted out in a rush "It's just, well, Doctor, I'm pregnant, and I was wanting someone to help with the birth like. Normally folk use Agnes, but I don't like her much, and she, well, she ain't been about lately. Now what with me being over here in Coleford with Pa, I wondered if you knew anyone who could help?" The doctor smiled, noting how Jane had subconsciously moved her hand to her slightly swelling stomach, pressing her hand with her fingers splayed in the typical pose of an expectant mother.

"Well congratulations Mrs Andrews. I haven't had need to recommend a midwife as yet, but I can ask around one or two of my patients and see who women normally use if you like." Seeing the panic spread across Jane's face, Edward continued quickly "You can of course be assured of my complete discretion - I would never mention who the midwife was for. Although I would perhaps suggest that you tell your father sooner rather than later, or you may find that he works it out for himself. Have you confided in anybody yet?"

Jane shook her head. Slumping down on one of the doctors hard wooden chairs, she began to sob. Offering her a clean white handkerchief, Edward walked awkwardly around the room. He had never learnt the knack of how to deal with upset patients, and in particular crying women. While it always seemed that while his fellow medical students knew instinctively how to comfort upset patients, Edward could never think of the right words and his attempts at sympathy always sounded to him like empty platitudes. Equally, he could not cajole and bully patients into stopping crying as some of the more senior doctors had. Any attempts at a brusque bedside manner left Edward feeling rude and awkward and his patients even more distraught than before. So Edward had learnt that the only way he could help a crying patient was with patience, and to hope that they would eventually stop crying of their own accord.

While Jane cried, Edward looked around the consulting room. What in other houses might have been a small pretty morning room, the consulting room was dominated by a large, rather old-fashioned examination couch. Three hard, uncomfortable chairs and a small sideboard completed the furniture and left the room feeling cramped and overfull. The large windows which should have let in plenty of light were narrowed by heavy brocade curtains. In all the room felt dark and oppressive. Through an ornately carved door set into the back wall was Edward's study. Largely filled by an imposing wooden desk, the room felt dank and cave-like. The light almost completely blocked from the window by a pair of tall sycamore trees, so that Edward was obliged to light a lamp on even the brightest autumn day.

Edward had taken on the property following the sudden death of the previous doctor. Having only been in residence for a month, he had not yet had the time, or the inclination, to alter the property to suit his own taste and needs. Edward's predecessor, Doctor Thomas, had been the town's doctor for the best part of forty years, running his practice as was the usual way from his house. A confirmed bachelor, Doctor Thomas had had no immediate family to take an interest in his estate, and so Edward had purchased the house complete with its entire contents. Everything, from the tables and chairs, to the pots and pans in the kitchen and scullery, and even the bed linen had been included in the sale. The house was a grand Georgian villa, containing two other good-sized reception rooms all with high ceilings and large windows which should have filled the house with light. Instead, the house felt cold and dark, as forbidding as some of the older parts of the forest, its windows shaded by tall trees and covered with thick, heavy velvet curtains. The large rooms were all filled to bursting with furniture, ornaments, and heavy old books. Edward looked out of the rather grimy window – he would have to speak to his house keeper about having them cleaned – at the tall trees which dominated the back garden of the house. Where he would have liked to see a pleasant garden laid to lawn with a few scattered flower beds, the garden currently held little more than patches of scrappy, half dead grass, surrounding the tall sycamore trees, their branches reaching towards the windows casting ominous shadows across the rooms. "They'll have to go" muttered Edward to himself, wondering just how he would set about getting the two massive trees felled.

"Aye, those trees don't look right healthy; you should ask my cousin Samuel to come cut them down for you. He's right good with trees he is, and he'd be right glad to help you what with all you've done for me and Pete" Edward turned to Jane with surprise. So absorbed had he been in his plans for the house that he hadn't noticed that she had stopped crying. While her face was still tear-stained and her eyes puffy, she was calm once again.

"Thank-you for the recommendation. I must confess that I would not know where to start in finding a good tree surgeon. Now, shall we discuss your pregnancy? Would you like me to examine you?"

Jane backed nervously away, "No, no Doctor that's fine. If you could just find out for me who the local midwife is, I would be grateful. I don't want to take up no more of your time. I'll think about telling Pa the news like you said too. How, how much do I owe for the appointment?"

"If you are quite sure you don't wish me to examine you?" Jane nodded her head vigorously, visibly relaxing when she understood that Edward would not press her. "Then there will be no charge Mrs Andrews. Perhaps we could view this consultation as an exchange of recommendations? I shall drop you a note when I have heard of a reputable midwife. Will you still be staying with your father?"

Edward escorted Jane to the front door before heading once more for his lunch. Despite a fire burning cheerfully in the grate, the dining room felt dark and chilly. A large oak table, capable of seating a dozen diners in comfort filled the centre of the room, whilst against one wall stood a matching sideboard and wine cooler. Squashed in either side of the window and fireplace stood tall bookcases, each reaching from the floor to ceiling and both completely covered with redundant books, dusty ornaments and faded curiosities. Above the hearth hung a large oil painting of a severe-looking couple. The man was dressed in an outdated dark frock coat and top hat, while the women at his side was wearing a high-necked dress and tight white bonnet, of the kind that Edwards grandmother had occasionally worn to church. This was the only picture of people in the house, Doctor Thomas apparently having favoured paintings of dogs and horses. Edward assumed that the couple must have been Doctor Thomas' parents. If Edward was completely honest, the picture was rather forbidding, and he disliked the way in which the artist had painted the couple so that wherever you were in the room, they appeared to be watching you disapprovingly. Indeed, such was the effect of the portrait on Edward that he found himself muttering "Sorry!" to himself as he finally sat down to his lunch.

Another thing that needs to go he thought, as he lifted the cover that had been placed over his food by his housekeeper. Edward looked at his lunch and sighed. A pork chop fried until it was black, two hard boiled potatoes, and a few wisps of rather slug ravaged cabbage greeted him, all smothered in thick, congealed gravy, and by now stone cold. Miss Bates, Edward's housekeeper and cook, had previously been the housekeeper and cook for Dr Thomas, and had practically come with the house, furniture and effects. Indeed, when Edward had moved in, coming to the house from the railway station with little more than a trunk of clothes, his medical bag, and a few, as yet unpacked, boxes of his own books and curiosities, it had been Miss Bates who opened the door for him. She had greeted him severely, announced that he had missed tea, but that supper would be served at 7pm sharp, and then left him to explore the house with no further explanation of who she was, but a clear expectation that he would fit into her routine and things would continue as when she had worked for Dr Thomas. Edward was not yet sure whether or not this would be the case. However, it was becoming increasingly clear to him that he would need to assert himself as the new master soon otherwise he would never be able to make any of his intended changes to the house. Already there had been an unpleasant stand off when he had had to escort Miss Bates from the consulting room when she tried to enter to dust while he was seeing patients – apparently Doctor Thomas had never objected to her presence while he was seeing patients – but Edward did. He could see that she would not take kindly to the further changes that he was planning on making. Edward wondered how he could replace Miss Bates without overly upsetting her, and by extension alienating many of his potential patients in the close-knit forest community. Edward was still pondering his domestic worries as he collected his horse from the stables at a nearby inn and rode out along the forest tracks towards his meeting with Sir Cyril.

Chapter Five

Thursday, 6th November, 1851.
Stauton Meend.

Sir Cyril lived in a grand mansion, overlooking the common land at Stauton Meend. Originally a fortified mediaeval farm, the house had been expanded over the years by various members of the Houghton family as funds allowed. The resulting house was a rambling mixture of styles, alterations and extensions. This could have rendered the house an unedifying mess, but somehow it had instead created a striking home. Houghton Hall was surrounded by beautifully manicured lawns and flower beds. The landscaping of the grounds, the obvious great age of the house, and a high perimeter wall with large wrought iron gates, made it seem to Edward as if the house was at once part of, and yet separate from the surrounding area; both a part of forest, and yet somehow aloof from it as well. Much like the house's current owner, mused Edward as he rang the bell at the grand main entrance. While Edward liked Sir Cyril, and his progressive attitude towards the health and welfare of his workers and the wider community, Edward thought that Sir Cyril saw himself as something of a feudal overlord. Caring for his workers and tenants but expecting servile gratitude in return. Edward gave a wry smile, despite having only been in Coleford for a short period, he was already aware that the foresters were an independently minded and truculent group not given to overblown displays of gratitude at the best of times.

    Admitted by one of Sir Cyril's maids, Edward was led towards a grand parlour, where he found Sir Cyril and his wife Lady Annabel in discussion with another woman. The conversation broke off as soon as they saw Edward, however from the little of the conversation that Edward had overheard he gathered that the second lady was the children's nurse, and that there was some problem with the youngest member of the family. A baby girl, by the name of Victoria, and as yet only a few weeks old, Edward had been introduced to on his previous visit. Her parents pride in the little girl, the couple's only child, had been clear, and Edward had had the impression that the little girl was a much longed for, and long awaited, addition to the family. As Sir Cyril stood to greet Edward, the nursemaid turned and left quickly through a different door. Edward watched her rapidly departing back. Having met her on his previous visit, there was something about the nursemaid that made Edward feel deeply uncomfortable.

    Edward shook hands with Sir Cyril.

"Good afternoon Sir Cyril, Lady Annabel. I trust that you are both well, and Miss Victoria too?" As he asked after the health of the little girl, he noticed Sir Cyril stiffen slightly and Lady Haughton's eyes widen, as if both were surprised by the question, and unsure of the whether to answer or not. Lady Annabel glanced quickly at her husband, before bursting into tears. As Edward looked uncomfortably between the couple, unsure of how, or even what, reassurance he could give, Sir Cyril placed his hand comfortingly on his wife's shoulder. He sighed deeply.

"As you know Doctor, Victoria is our only child, and Annabel is understandably protective of her. The nurse was just telling us that Victoria has developed something of a cold, with a slight fever. I'm sure, I hope, that she will recover in a few days, but you know how mothers are over their babies. However, I would see it as a personal favour it if you would take a look at her. Make sure that a cold is all that ails her, for her mother's sake if nothing else." He said quietly, torn between genuine concern for his only child and exasperation that such a fuss was being made over what he regarded a minor, common place ailment.

"Of course, Sir Cyril, I would be delighted. Perhaps Lady Annabel you could show me the way to the child's nursery?"

The nursery at the top of the old house was a bright cheerful room, painted in a delicate pastel blue with gleaming white woodwork. A large fire blazed in the hearth, and the windows were all tight shut against the December chill. The baby lay in a small hand carved crib. Despite the sweltering heat she was tightly swaddled and wrapped in thick blankets. Edward tugged at his cravat to loosen it slightly, before turning to the child's nurse, and instructing her to open some windows in the hope of reducing some of the stifling heat. Reaching delicately into the finely made crib, he picked the baby up from where she was drowsing and placed her on the nursery table. Carefully he began peeling back the many layers of swaddling.

"Is that wise Doctor? We was always taught to keep the bairns warm" said the nurse abruptly, reaching forward as if to stop the doctor from removing the many layers that covered the baby.

"Warm, yes, but not stifled. And anyway, I need to examine Victoria, and I can't do that without first removing some of these clothes from her." He replied firmly, irritated to have been challenged by the nurse. Edward continued to remove the many layers of clothing before finally reaching a rather grimy dress and a soiled nappy that clearly had not been changed for some time. Edward turned to the nurse, and pointedly raised an eyebrow to show that he had noticed that the baby had not been changed for quite some time. It was this, as much as her cold that was making her fretful. Expecting the nurse to be somewhat embarrassed at this exposure of her failure to carry out some of her most basic duties, Edward was surprised that instead of shame, the nurse returned his gaze with belligerence. Finally, as the last layers of clothing were removed, Victoria, who had been fretfully whimpering throughout, began to scream loudly.

"Well there's nothing much wrong with her lungs! Now, just a quick listen to her chest" at the touch of the cold stethoscope on her chest Victoria let out a scream of pure outrage "There, there, nearly done now, nearly done" Edward murmured to the child reassuringly, before handing the baby over to her now anxious nurse to be cleaned and re-wrapped. He turned to Lady Annabel who had begun to cry again.

"Well my lady, I must say that Victoria is a credit to you. She is a fine lusty baby, although she does have a touch of a cold. Nothing to worry about! I would recommend that you don't swaddle her quite so tightly and allow the fire to die down a little. While she should be kept warm, my Professor always taught that too warm a house was as bad as too cold. And perhaps a little fresh air each day? A walk in her perambulator around the grounds of the house on a fine day like this would do her the world of good I am sure. Now Lady Annabel, if I leave you and Nurse to settle her, I shall return to Sir Cyril." And with a bow, Edward left the nursery, heading back down the wide sweeping staircase to Sir Cyril's magnificent study.

Chapter Six

Several hours, and much discussion later, Edward left the Houghton Hall pleased with the progress that had been made. Sir Cyril had agreed to put proposals to several of his friends and fellow landowners to found The Forest of Dean Recreative and Medical Aid Association as a friendly society where foresters could, for a small monthly subscription, access subsidised medical care. Sir Cyril was hoping that he could encourage some of his friends to become fellow benefactors and together build a small hospital with a dispensing clinic for minor maladies and a six-bed ward where more serious cases that required an inpatient stay could be treated. Edward was hoping that he would be able to convince some of his fellow physicians, and possibly a surgeon or two, to agree to provide medical treatment from the hospital in exchange for a small monthly stipend alongside their current private practices. Altogether, Edward was hopeful that soon they be able to draw up the societies articles, and that work would quickly begin building the new hospital.

Although it was still only early evening, darkness had already fallen, making it difficult for Edward to see his way along the Coleford Road. Allowing his horse to pick her way carefully along the rough track, Edward pondered that practising medicine in a sprawling country practice in the forest would be a very different prospect to working at St Thomas', the large London hospital in which he had worked after he completed his medical training at the nearby Webb Street School. Not for the first time, he felt a simmering hatred for the man who had caused the scandal that had made it impossible for him to continue to practice medicine in London and had forced him to leave his small, but comfortably furnished rooms near Bow Street, and move out to the sticks to take over the late Doctor Thomas' practice. He had previously been well respected in London. With a growing private practice which included minor nobles, he had felt accepted within the saloons and dining rooms of fashionable society. However, when the scandal broke his erstwhile friends had deserted him and his patients had left him in droves. His position at St Thomas' had become untenable, and it had been made clear to him that he could leave voluntarily before he suffered the ignominy of being dismissed. It was a great relief to him when he received a rare letter from his mother's distant cousin Frank Lucas, suggesting that he might like to take over the practice of the late Dr Thomas and offering to organise the sale with his executors. The sale had taken place so quickly that it had barely been three months between Edward receiving his cousin's letter and finding himself ringing the bell of his new house in Coleford surrounded by all his worldly possessions - not that they amounted to much he thought ruefully - no more than two trunks full of clothes, a large box of books, and his small, but well packed, medical bag.

Ambling along in the gathering gloom, he was fortunate that it was a clear night, and that the light of the full moon was sufficient for him to be able to see his way. However, in future he would either need to ensure that he had returned home to the town by dusk or remember to bring with him a lantern so that he could find his way. Riding carefully along the turnpike road, Edward mused that it had been a productive day and as his stomach began to growl he wondered whether he should risk offending Miss Bates by eating his dinner in one of the many local inns. He was just reaching the conclusion that however tempting a hot cooked meal at an inn might be, he should probably return home for his dinner, when he heard his name being called.

Smartly wheeling his horse, Edward was able to pick out the slight figure of Nesta hidden in amongst the trees in the deep gloom at the edge of the forest. In a pale green dress, brown overcoat, and tidy white bonnet, Nesta blended in well with the surrounding trees. She stood frozen to the spot, hugging a large wicker basket filled with an array of different mushrooms to her as if it could protect her from some awful demon. As Edward approached he could see how dishevelled Nesta was. The hem of her dress was torn, and her coat covered in mud where she had slipped in her headlong dash through the trees. Small scratches covered her face, while larger, deeper gashes to her hands and legs from forcing her way through the dense undergrowth. Her eyes were wide with fear. Edward swiftly dismounted from his horse. As he approached her, she dropped the basket she had been clinging to and stepped into his open arms. Leaning into his shoulder she began to sob desperately as shock finally overcame her. Instinctively, Edward wrapped his arms around Nesta as she was wracked with tears. Holding her close to him, Edward felt none of his normal awkwardness when confronted with a crying patient. Instead he was aware of a strange sense of contentment, and a desire to protect Nesta from whatever trouble had befallen her. Breathing in deeply, Edward caught Nesta's scent, a mixture of wood smoke and the rosemary that she used when washing her hair and found himself comparing it favourably to the expensive perfumes used by ladies that he had met at the fashionable London soirees he had attended as a young doctor. Abruptly Nesta stopped crying, stepping back away from him. She wiped her eyes on her coat sleeve and blurted out.

"I'm sorry Doctor, it's just, I'm so glad to see you. I need to raise the hue. You see she's dead, and I don't think it was natural like, and I don't right know what to do". Tears stung at Nesta's eyes and she was barely able to maintain her composure, such as it was. Shock at her gruesome discovery, embarrassment at having grabbed the doctor and cried on his shoulder (leaving a damp patch she was ashamed to note) and genuine sadness for woman that Nesta had known all her life, had left Nest a feeling uncharacteristically, if understandably, shaky.

Edward reached out and grabbed Nesta's hands, gripping her two small, work calloused hands tight in his larger, well gloved ones. Although he didn't understand completely Nesta garbled report, it was clear that she had found something in the woods.

"What is it Miss Phillips – who is dead Nesta? Where is she?"

Nesta took a deep breath to try to suppress the panic she could feel welling up inside her. "It's Agnes. I was collecting mushrooms from amongst the felled trees at the edge of the quarry, and I, I just found her there. She'd been covered with some brush. As I bent down to pick up a mushroom I saw her hand, well part of a hand, it was all chewed! I moved the branch, and there she was staring up through the twigs. So, I just grabbed my basket and ran." She looked up at the doctor. "What happens now? Do I have to go back there?" Edward was struck again by a sense of how young and vulnerable she was and felt again strong desire to protect her. He shook his head.

"No, not now." Edward looked into woods, noting that while the moon afforded them some light on the more open toll roads, amongst the trees it would be far too dark to see anything clearly. Any clues as to what had befallen Agnes would be missed, and the searchers would risk turning ankles -

and worse – as they stumbled through the trees and undergrowth. Far better to wait for morning, particularly since from Nesta's description of the state of the body, Agnes was well past any mortal help. Indeed, as early evening progressed towards night, the temperature was plummeting. Clear skies and a bitter easterly wind promised freezing temperatures and a thick frost. Nesta began to shake uncontrollably. Edward was acutely aware that she was in far greater need of his skills.

Nesta let out a small shriek, an equal mix of alarm and pleasure, as putting his hands around her slim waist Edward lifted her swiftly into the saddle of his patiently waiting horse. Taking the reins, he set off leading the horse and its passenger the half mile or so towards the small hamlet of Berry Hill. It wasn't long before they reached the first building, the King's Head, a small alehouse which served the hamlet and surrounding quarries and mines. Built of the local limestone about 20 years earlier, it stood slightly apart from its neighbours. Downstairs was a large room which served as the public bar, with lean-to kitchen at the back. Across a cobbled yard a separate smaller building was a small brewery, while upstairs was the accommodation for the landlord and his family. Angry shouts from several men could be heard ringing out across the dark, still evening. As they passed the alehouse, the front door banged open, and was slammed shut again. The sudden crash and appearance of a strange man almost right underneath his feet, made the normally placid horse begin to shy a little. It was only with extreme skill, and not a little effort, that Edward was able to keep his control of the prancing animal, and prevent it from rearing, probably depositing a now terrified Nesta onto the floor in the process.

"I think I'd like to get down now please Dr James" asked Nesta in a small voice.

As Edward turned to help her dismount the man stopped and turned. The candle light streaming through the glass of the alehouse windows shone onto his face. At once Nesta recognised the solid, dependable features of her uncle Samuel. She ran to him, and he wrapped his big strong arms tightly around her small frame. With a quick glance he took in her dishevelled appearance and obvious distress. He shot an accusatory glare at the doctor, before looking back down at his niece.

"Now, now lass. Wipe those tears. What's been happening" he said gently. Nesta looked up, her face once more tear stained.

"Oh, Uncle Samuel it was horrible, I've found her. I've found Agnes!"

Edward soon found himself ensconced in one of the large wooden settles at the Kings Head. He had been pressed with one of the landlady's fidget pies – a surprisingly tasty hand raised pie filled with potato, apple, and lamb – and a pint of the strong local ale. A cheerful fire burned merrily in the heath at odds with the sombre atmosphere in the tap room. Although Samuel had originally suggested that they should leave straight away to recover the body, Edward was pleased that good sense had prevailed. The temperature outside had continued to drop, and a thin skin of ice was already beginning to form on puddles. Walking through the woods and pushing through the undergrowth by candlelight would be incredibly difficult, if not downright dangerous. Trying to find a body that had been carefully concealed at the same time would be practically impossible. Thomas had argued that it would be better, and safer, to stay home and plan in the long hours of darkness. Then they could set off fresh in the day light. Besides, a voice from the back had pointed out, it was best not to go abroad into the woods late at night, for fear of meeting the Cŵn Annwn. This had appeared to have clinched the argument. At this, most of the men in the tight knit community had retired home to bed to be ready to set off to scour the woods at first light. Nesta had been spirited away to the care of her slightly hysterical mother, and more practical Aunt Rose. It was understood that Rose would gently probe until she had coaxed as much detail from her shocked niece as possible, ready to help guide the men to the body in the morning.

Soon only Samuel, Thomas and Rose's husband the landlord Jack remained, quietly sitting around the worn table. Taking a long drink from the dented pewter pint pot, Edward looked at his companions. Accustomed to working long hours in dangerous conditions in the mines and quarries, they were all hardened to accidents and fatalities that formed part of their everyday working lives. All seemed surprised and distressed by Nesta's description of finding Agnes' body. The three men sat in wary silence, probably waiting for him to finish his supper and leave Edward realised. Well, if they thought that he was going to leave now they had another think coming. Stretching his back, Edward looked carefully around the small group, wondering if one of them had a motive, beyond the foresters' natural wariness of outsiders, for trying to get him to leave. Was it possible that one, or more, of these three hard men had murdered Agnes and then concealed her body up in the woods, leaving it for the wild animals to eat? The three men, the brothers Thomas and Samuel, and Jack, the landlord of the inn stared back until finally, unable to sit with the strained silence any longer, Thomas asked.

"So, Doctor, do you think you could explain to us exactly where you were when you met my daughter? It'll help us know where to start looking tomorrow. Nesta roams all over when she's gathering mushrooms. She never takes too much notice of where she's going, so it's unlikely that she'll give us much to start with even with all her Ma and Rose's questioning."

Edward frowned and described in as much detail as he could how and where he had come across Nesta. "However," he said "given the state she was in she'd probably been running all over the place. I doubt that she headed to the turnpike in a straight line, so where I met her may not help us to find Agnes, but it will give us somewhere to start."

The three other men looked at each other in consternation "*Us* Doctor?" blurted out Samuel "but surely you're not planning on coming with us? We'll need to be away at first light and you don't want to be coming up here for the dawn. Besides it'll be tough going amongst the thickets, you won't be able to ride your horse."

"Gentlemen, I wouldn't dream of leaving you to the search on your own, and I assure you that I am more than capable of walking miles over rough terrain. Anyways, it might be worth you have an, um, *independent* witness as it were. For the coroner, you know." Edward smiled inwardly to himself, he knew he had successfully seeded a grain of doubt over what the response of the authorities to the death might be. He knew that they would now accept, if not exactly welcome, his company in the morning.

Thomas looked at Samuel and Jack. "He's right you know. After what happened to Pete, it might be as well to have somebody with us, just in case the bleeding coroner gets it into his head to ask any awkward questions. Someone who can answer them back might not do us or ours any harm"

"Aye, mayhap it won't do any harm. He were alright with Pete, and Uncle says he ain't charged owt for our Jane. I say let un come" agreed Samuel and turning to look at Edward "We'll meet back here at sun up, but I warn you, it'll be heavy going. You'll need something other than that fancy gear."

Edward inclined his head to show that he understood, both the time for meeting, and that he was being allowed to accompany them on sufferance only. Placing half a shilling on the table in payment of the beer and pie, he reached for his hat off the stand. "Until tomorrow gentlemen" he said touching his brim. With that he went out into the cold night.

Edward walked away from the front door of the inn towards where his horse had been tethered making as much noise as possible. Then turned and crept stealthily back as quietly as he could, crouching low to the ground to ensure that he remained out of sight of the windows. As he got closer he could hear the voices within.

"You sure he's alright though Tom?" asked a gruff voice which could only belong to the landlord Jack. A taciturn man, Edward had not heard him speak previously, preferring to communicate instead in a serious of scowls and grunts. Edward was gratified to hear Samuel support him "He were good with Jane, and he looked after your Nesta. Some folk would have left at the side of the road, not led her home on his horse. And he didnae kick up a stink over Pete neither. Besides, he's right, if that poxing coroner decides he's gonna cause trouble, it's best we have him with us. No toff is going to doubt the word of the Doctor, he's one of them in't he. We might be grateful to have him with us, that's all I'm saying." A grunted reply, followed by a loud yawn, alerted Edward to the possibly of discovery. It would not do for him to be caught eavesdropping on the locals! Returning to his horse, he rode off into the night, unaware that he had been watched from the shadows from that he left the alehouse. The watcher's eyes hardened as the doctor's figure disappeared into the darkness.

"We'll have to keep an eye on you, oh yes we shall" the watcher muttered to themselves.

Chapter Seven

Friday, 7th November, 1851.
Berry Hill

The sun was just beginning to rise as Edward arrived back at the village the next day feeling somewhat jaded. It had been a long and difficult ride home the night before. When he finally arrived back, it had been to a cold dark house. Miss Bates had demonstrated her approbation at his late return by allowing all the fires to die out, and by not lighting any of the lamps. Edward let himself in through the front door to a hallway which was almost as dark and cold as the forest tracks. Creeping into the kitchen, he found the range cold to the touch – there would be no hot drink for him to warm himself with and his uneaten dinner was reduced to a pile of scraps heaped into the waste pail covered with carrot peelings.

He found sleep elusive and it was with difficulty that he rose early, long before dawn, to complete hurried and basic ablutions. Shivering in the cold, he quickly dressed in his warmest clothes. Retrieving his horse from the stables he set out yawning back towards Berry Hill.

Riding into the small hamlet, Edward was surprised by the sense of busy industry and the number of people gathered around the King's Head. Twenty or so men and older boys milled around impatiently, several of them held a mixture of dogs some sat. Women stood either with their men folk, or with the large number of small children who ran excitedly between and around the adults. Tying his horse to a low rail, he walked over to join the group of men. Stopping mid-sentence, they fell silent as he approached. In the middle of the group stood Nesta with her aunt and parents. The two women were like chalk and cheese. Nesta's mother was tall and thin, with the hollowed cheeks of someone who has not been eating properly. Deep lines covered her face, making her look stern and forbidding, with the slightly pinched look of someone suffering from a soul-destroying pain. Her clothes were old, but clean and neatly mended, and her hair was pulled back in a tidy and functional bun. Her sister Rose was her complete opposite - shorter, with a round cheerful face full of smile lines. Although she was dressed similarly in dark dress, with a white apron she somehow looked slightly more dishevelled, with a few strands of hair escaping from her bun. The whole effect was to make her look friendlier, more approachable. Like a mother to whom you could tell all your woes. However, there was a hardness in her eyes. A woman that it would be best not to cross, Edward thought.

Doffing his hat, Edward gave a short bow "Good morning ladies, Mr Phillips, Miss Phillips. Are we ready to set off?"

Thomas looked Edward up and down, taking in his thick tweed jacket, practical leather knapsack, and stout, well worn boots. He was surprised that the doctor had come dressed so practically, having put him down previously as something of a dandy in his fashionable, well cut clothes. That the doctor also possessed stout, well used practical clothes boded well, suggesting that he might not be such a hindrance on what promised to be a difficult search in the woods, and showed a different side to him. This doctor, with his practical approach to a crisis, his tendency to waive the fees of poorer patients (his uncle William had reported that he'd charged only 6d to treat Jane's arm and for all the medicines that she needed), and his keen eye for a mystery intrigued Thomas, and he decided that he would like to get to know him better – that was of course assuming that Edward himself would be willing to spend time with a mere freeminer. Thomas gave the doctor a genuine smile,

"Morning Doctor James. Can I present my wife, Mary" he said indicating the taller, thinner woman. Edward nodded to Mary and turned as Thomas continued "And I believe you have met my sister-in-law Mrs Rose Jones. We're almost ready to set off, just need to convince this 'un" he nodded towards Nesta "that she can't come with us!"

"But why not Pa? I knows where she is. You'll be much quicker with me, and you know that I can cover ground just as fast as any lad. Besides, I ain't afraid! I found her didn't I? I owe it to Agnes, Pa. I owe it to her help bring her home, after I left her." Nesta looked at Edward beseechingly. "Tell them Doctor. Tell them that you need me".

Edward looked kindly at Nesta "Well Miss Phillips, I'm afraid I must agree with your father. I fear the body will be no sight for a young lady, however brave and stalwart." Seeing Nesta slump dejectedly, Edward reached out instinctively and touched her arm. "However, you are quite right that it would be easier to find the spot with you to help guide us." He turned to Thomas, raising an eyebrow meaningfully. "Perhaps a compromise? Could Nesta accompany us far enough to show us more that the general area in which Agnes lies, but return home before we begin to, um, *recover* the body? This way would give the greatest chance of finding Agnes quickly, but wouldn't expose Nesta to anymore unpleasantness."

Thomas frowned. He looked set to refuse, when Rose nodded. "Yes Thomas, that's a good idea. And I'll come too, to walk home with Nesta." And make sure she leaves was the unspoken injunction.

"Right that's settled then. Make sure you mind your Aunt Rose and come straight back once you've found Agnes. You can help me prepare things. There'll be much to do," said Mary briskly. Her voice was calm and melodic. She gave off a sense of quiet efficiency. Edward remembered being told on his first visit to the village that Thomas and Mary had recently had a still born child, and that Mary had been gripped by a deep melancholia following the loss of her child. That she was up and about, helping with the latest crisis to grip the community, showed that she was learning to live with the pain at least.

A shrill whistle rent the air, and Thomas waved his arm to attract attention.

"Right lads let's be off then! Remember to mind where you're putting your feet and keep a sharp look out for anything that shouldn't be there. Our Nesta is going to show us where she thinks she found Agnes, but we'll still need to keep a close eye out to find her. Come on then, let's be off!" With that, Thomas led the way up the hill, retracing the route that Edward and Nesta had taken the previous evening.

It was a cold, hard slog through the trees. At first they were able to follow a rough forest track way, but all too soon they had to turn off onto a path that was barely more than an animal track. The going became increasingly difficult as they had to force their way between low tree branches and thick brambles. Frost had settled on cobwebs, making pretty lacy patterns which hung down from trees, but their fragile beauty was soon destroyed as the party made their way along. This part of the forest was ancient woodland. A mixture of tall oak trees, beech and sweet chestnut spread their branches wide, reducing the weak winter sunlight that reached the forest floor. Despite this lack of sunlight, which could only be worse in summer with the trees in full leaf, the ground was covered with a thick spread of brambles, thistles and other scrub. Hidden amongst the brambles was a complex mess of rabbit burrows at the warren spread across the forest floor. Larger openings suggested the dens of foxes or badger setts. Walking with Edward, Samuel warned him not to stray too far for the risk of falling down old mine shafts. These remains of ancient coal and iron workings, their entrances long since forgotten provided a trap for the unwary, and it wasn't uncommon for deep pits to appear on the forest floor. All this made the land difficult to walk over, and it was necessary for the group to weave their way across the ground rather than walk in a straight line. Edward began to appreciate for the first time how difficult the terrain in this part of the forest was, and to understand the men's reluctance to start the search the previous evening, with only the faint flickering light of tallow candles to light the way. He also marvelled at Nesta's resilience, as she led the way through the trees, uncomplaining of scratches from brambles and thistles.

Suddenly the woods thinned slightly, and the group found themselves in a quiet clearing at the base of low limestone cliffs, the remains of an abandoned quarry. Here the trees were much younger, barely more than saplings. There was a greater array of wild plants carpeting the forest floor. Looking carefully around the clearing, Edward saw evidence of digging around certain plants. Kneeling for a closer look, he realised that they had been carefully dug up to the remove the root. Not recognising the plants immediately, he carefully picked some tucking them in his knapsack to identify later. Nesta stood in the middle of the clearing, her aunt protectively by her side, and pointed across towards where Edward stood.

"She were just over there, where those branches are" she said in a faltering voice, pointing to a low pile of brambles near the foot of a cliff.

Gingerly, Edward and the other men walked towards a rough pile of branches. As they got closer Edward detected a faint cloying smell, familiar to him from his time spent attending anatomy lectures, it was the sweet smell of a slowing decomposing corpse. Edward held up his hand.

"Stop everyone. Look closely at the ground. Look carefully for any clues as to who has done this, because this can't have been an accident"

"What makes you say that? We ain't even found a body yet! Anyways, if Agnes is here, it stands to reason that she fell and hurt herself. She was always pottering around the woods in the dark. God knows what she was up to, but, God bless her, how she never hurt hersen before is a mystery!" declared Samuel, and he defiantly walked forward towards the mixed heap of brambles and stones where Edward had stopped. Kicking out at the stones, Samuel dislodged something, and the whole pile began to slip and slide. Samuel huffed. He leant forward, then turned and ran off into the trees on the other side of the clearing. There he stood and vomited, retching until his stomach was empty, before subsiding on the floor, and leaning back against a tree.

Edward coolly watched him run off, before turning back to Samuel's gruesome discovery. Hidden beneath the pile of branches and scrub was the remains of middle aged woman. Edward noted dispassionately that she had been dead for some time - at least a week given the state of decomposition. While the branches might have served to hide her body from humans, they had done little to conceal her remains from the four-legged inhabitants of the woods; some of which had clearly viewed the corpse as a tasty snack.

"Well, is this Agnes?" he asked the group at large, all of whom were keeping well back.

Jack edged forward, gingerly heading towards the corpse. Taking a deep breath, more to save him from breathing the in the pungent smell than anything else, he looked down at the body. His face betrayed a mixture of horror, disgust, and compassion.

"Aye, that's Agnes, God bless her. Poor sod. God knows we didn't always see eye to eye, but no-one deserves to be left like that. The doctor's right. Someone did for her and hid her body. This ain't no accident, no matter how much some would like it to be!" Jack turned to stare hard at the figure of Samuel, who was still leaning back against the tree, and drinking from a flask that Rose had produced from the pocket of her apron. "But that's for later. Now we need to get her home. Where's that sheet got to?" With that the men sprang into action, one producing a thick canvas sheet from inside his knapsack. Carefully they lifted the body, gently easing the stiff fabric underneath her until they could lift her clear of the forest floor. Another sheet was lain reverently over her, covering the ravaged body from view. Edward was intrigued to note that the sheet, far from being a simple piece of cloth, was sewn together from several pieces of fabric so that when carried it was almost box like. Stout rope loops had been attached at each end and in the middle of the sides to aid carrying. Thomas saw Edward's interest, and gruffly explained that it was what they used to carry anyone who had been injured down on of the mines. Sadly, accidents were common underground, and the simple fabric stretcher made it easier for men to carry out anyone who had been injured, whether they had survived the accident or not.

The journey back through the woods was even worse than the trip up. Men took turns to carry the awkward, unwieldy stretcher, working together in grim silence. A tall thin woman in life, Agnes weighed heavily on them all as each began to consider the possible repercussions of Agnes' murder and the concealment of her body. Each member of the group was looking around surreptitiously, wondering who amongst their friends, neighbours, family had committed this terrible crime. Nesta, walking behind the men and observing them closely, realised that Agnes' murder could rip the tight-knit mining community apart. Already the men were looking at each other askance; in particular her father was looking oddly at her Uncle Samuel. If her father could question the honesty of his brother, her own god father, then he might question anyone. If the bonds of trust that held the community together were broken, then that could spell disaster when men relied on each other to keep them safe as they worked in dangerous conditions underground. Nesta knew that the only way to save the community that she loved would be to find the murderer quickly, before distrust could tear the village apart.

Chapter Eight

Such was the state of Agnes' body, that the coroner, having been alerted to the probability of an unexpected death by one of the village women, took one sniff and ordered that the inquest should be held with all haste, preferably, outside. So it was arranged. A large table was dragged out of the Kings Head and Agnes was placed on top, much to the alewife Rose's displeasure. The coroner then convened the inquest, calling upon all of the village men, and Edward to form the jury to establish the cause of death. The coroner, James Rudge, an aging doctor from Monmouth, called the proceedings to order. He was a large man, with a rather florid face. Whatever the weather, he always dressed the same in a thick three-piece tweed suit, with a mustard yellow cravat. A jovial man, he loved good food, and French wine. He was known for being kind to women and children, while not tolerating fools gladly. The men of the forest generally regarded him as being a fair man, if somewhat brusque, and a good coroner. As his clerk administered the oath to swear in the fourteen men that had been chosen to serve upon the jury, Dr Rudge leaned back in the grand basket backed chair from the King's Head and looked around the villagers. From the brief details that he had gathered, he knew that Agnes had been found, most probably murdered. Looking around the silent villagers who had assembled to watch the inquest, he knew that it was likely that one of them was the murderer, but he equally knew that there was scant chance that they would ever stand trial. The foresters were an introspective group, likely to close ranks in the face of the any outsiders who might come in to investigate. The distrust had only deepened following the Riots in 1831 when the government enclosed large areas of the forest removing ancient grazing and mining rights. Coupled with harsh winters, the foresters were unable to feed their families. Heavily armed soldiers had been called in to quiet the growing unrest. Dr Rudge remembered only too well the sense of anger and rage. The anger caused by the transportation of the foresters' leader to Australia had caused deep rifts that had yet to heal twenty years later. No, far more likely that the villagers would seek to find the culprit for themselves. Then no doubt he'd be called out again, this time to pass verdict on an accident that was no accident at all. Such was the way of things, he mused. The newly established police force was trying to take control of law in the forest, but it was an uphill struggle. A slight cough from his clerk warned the coroner that the last juror had been sworn in, and he needed to pay attention again.

Dr Rudge carefully listened as a villager solemnly swore that the body was that of Agnes Jenkins, a widow of Five Acres, near Berry Hill. Having formally identified the corpse, the coroner then called upon Nesta to give an account of how she first found the corpse.

Nesta tried not to let her nervousness show as she moved to stand before the coroner. She gave him a quick curtsey, then stood, nervously twisting a strand of hair that had escaped from under her mop cap. Dr Rudge smiled, he glanced quickly to make sure that his clerk, a thin weaselly man uncomfortably perched on a three ledged stool, was ready, and then cleared his throat.

"Now" he said to her in a kindly voice "I believe that you are the first finder?"

"Yes Sir" said Nesta in a nervous voice "I found her."

"Good. Now, you are Nesta Phillips, a maid of this parish?"

"Yes Sir"

"Please can you explain exactly how you came across the body?"

"Well, Sir. I had gone up towards the old quarry looking for mushrooms. It's a good spot up there, what with all the fallen trees and all. I normally manage to get a few. I was just looking around at an old pile of logs and stone, when something caught my eye. I didn't realise what it was at first, then I realised it was a hand. But it wasn't like a normal hand. It was all chewed up, like something had been worrying at it. Well Sir, I was proper a-feared. So I ran, and I ran. Eventually I reached the turnpike road, where the Doctor, that is Doctor James here, found me. He brought me back here and we raised the hue and cry. And that, well that's it Sir."

"Thank-you Miss Phillips." Dr Rudge smiled at Nesta and then turned back towards the jury "Now gentlemen, we've heard how the body came to be found now it's high time we examined the corpse." With that Dr Rudge levered his considerable bulk up out of the chair and waddled towards the body lying under a dirty sheet.

While most of the men hung back, keen to stay as far away from the decaying corpse as possible, Edward stepped forward. He carefully began an examination of the body, carefully describing his findings so that all the men of the jury, and the coroner's scribe could hear his report. It did not take long for Edward to discover the cause of death - a single stab wound to Agnes' chest. Gently probing the wound with a scalpel drawn from his medical bag, Edward decided that the stab wound had been inflicted with a long thin blade which had probably penetrated Agnes' heart. Death would have been instantaneous. The rest of the substantial damage to the corpse was probably the result of foxes and other scavengers seeking an easy meal he announced.

"Hmmm. I concur" announced Dr Rudge. "Does anyone have anything else to add?" He glared around, his question met with a chorus of denials. Silence followed. Some villagers seemed genuinely shocked by Agnes' death, others began to guilty shuffle their feet and would not meet his gaze. There's something going on here Dr Rudge mused. Something that I'm not being told but blow me if I know what it is. The coroner allowed the silence to stretch on for a few more awkward minutes, before finally announcing his verdict.

"I find that Agnes Jenkins, widow of this parish, has been Unlawfully Killed, by Person or Persons, Unknown." With that Dr Rudge formally closed the proceedings and dismissed the jury. Thankfully the men made their way into the Kings Head, all seeking a restorative pint of ale.

Soon it was only the two doctors and the coroner's clerk left. As Edward continued to look at the body, Doctor Rudge approached. "You seem to be taking quite an interest in this case, did you know the deceased?"

"No. I'd never met her, although of course I'd heard about her. She was the local midwife and seemed to be some kind of folk healer."

"Hmmm, well I suppose folk healer is one way to describe her," chuckled Dr Rudge, "others of course would term her a witch. But that said I'd not heard any particularly outrageous claims about her, so she must have been fairly respectable as far as these people go. Between you and me, I had heard whispers that as well as helping women give birth, she wasn't averse to helping those who did not want to be pregnant, if you catch my meaning. Not that there was any real evidence against her. We'd have had her up before the assizes double quick if we had. A tight-lipped group these foresters, and rather prone to taking the law into their own hands. Obviously, there is more going on here than anyone is letting on. But we'll never break the wall of silence that surrounds the goings on around here. Well good day to you, Doctor James. I must be off, I'm dining with Sir Cyril. Some proposal he wants to put to me. Well good day to you". The two men shook hands, and the coroner stumped away to his carriage. Tapping on the roof of the carriage with his ebony walking stick, the driver whipped up the horses, and they sped away towards Staunton Meend and Houghton Hall.

Edward stood and watched the carriage leaving, pondering the coroner's information about Agnes. While it wasn't surprising that as well as helping women to give birth, Agnes might also have been involved in helping women to end unwanted pregnancies, Edward wondered if this was true, and whether it had any bearing on the women's death. During Edward's training at the London Hospital Medical College, a charitable hospital which cared for poor patients primarily from the East End of London, he had encountered many cases of women of who had sought to end their pregnancies, either to avoid the social shame of being an unmarried mother, or because they simply could not afford to feed another child.

Edward had felt nothing but pity for the women who were desperate enough to resort to dangerous procedures often carried out by inept practitioners who left them with internal injuries, infection, or severe blood loss. Many of the women had not survived, and no doubt there were many more that had died without ever seeking medical aid. Staring down at the body, Edward wondered what had led to her death. Whether it was a case of her disturbing a poacher, as the villagers seemed to think, or whether her death was linked to her practice as a midwife, folk healer, and if the coroner was to be believed, abortionist. Sadly, he recovered her. He supposed that he would never know.

A gentle touch to his arm jolted Edward from his ruminations. Looking round he saw Nesta nervously waiting besides him. "I said your name several times, Doctor James, but you didn't seem to hear me. I'd like to talk to you about Agnes, if I may".

Edward frowned, "I'm not sure that your father and mother would approve of me discussing the murder with you." He said kindly.

"I don't care what they say." She said shaking her head emphatically "I found the body. I feel responsible for finding out what happened." Sensing that Edward was about to interrupt, to cut her off and tell her to leave Agnes' murder well alone, to leave it to the men to deal with. She continued at a rush. Her words merging and running into each other in her hurry to tell him her fears before he could stop her "I don't believe that it was just a case of a poacher in the wrong place, and I can tell you don't either. And nor do most folk truth be told. If we don't find the killer, they could strike again. Even if they don't, the suspicion will tear the village apart. You saw the way folk were looking at each other at the inquest. Everybody is on edge. Nobody knows who to trust. We all used to go to Agnes, who knows what secrets she knew. I think it was those secrets what got her killed. And I can't help but think that if I don't do summit, something terrible will happen." Nesta looked up at Edward beseechingly. "Please help me Doctor, please help me find whoever did for Agnes."

Looking into her clear blue eyes, Edward felt his resolve weaken. He knew that he was already too busy, with his practice, his hopes to found a charitable hospital, and becoming established in his new home. However, he had to admit, he was intrigued by Agnes' death, and more than a little worried that it might somehow be connected to the death of Pete earlier that same week. The local authorities, such as they were, didn't seem to be taking any interest. Pete's death had been put down as an accident befalling a man known to be a poacher and a drunk. Jack had testified that he'd had to throw Pete out of the alehouse again on the night he'd died. He was a belligerent drunk and having been refused another drink had stomped off into the night announcing to everyone he was off rabbiting. This had led the coroner to conclude that Pete had probably tripped over in the dark and hit his head. The combination of the alcohol and the head wound meant that he had failed to get back up and he had simply frozen to death on what had been one of the first bitterly cold nights of the winter.

Agnes' death was more complex, but Agnes was also known to wander the woods on her own after dark. People were saying that she must have come across a poacher, who, keen to protect themselves from discovery and prosecution, which could lead to imprisonment, transportation, or possibly even hanging, had decided to silence her permanently, stabbing her to death and concealing her body in the hope of removing all evidence of their crime. It would be nigh on impossible for the local constabulary, such as they were, to identify the perpetrator, who was commonly held not to be local and to have long since vanished.

But, all the same, Nesta was right. There was something odd about Agnes' murder. Something didn't sit right with the official version of her death. People trusted Agnes, they went to her with their problems and she must have known a great many secrets. Nobody had suggested that Agnes was a gossip, so why worry that she might go to the authorities with stories of poaching, which was a pretty common pastime in the forest anyway? Something about the whole story didn't ring true. Edward looked down at Nesta and saw the determination in her face. He knew that no matter how much her parents forbade her to get involved, she would worm away at the case until she found the truth. If the murderer had already killed to conceal one crime, it raised the disturbing possibility that they would kill again without compunction - particularly if someone came close to exposing them. In that moment Edward knew that he could not allow Nesta to expose herself to such dangers alone. He would have to help her investigate. Nesta had led a fairly sheltered life, protected by her mother and father. He didn't think she would be much of a match for a ruthless cold-blooded killer.

Chapter Nine

Having agreed to help Nesta investigate Agnes' murder, Edward had no idea where to start. Just how did you go about tracking down a killer? He decided that for now the best he could do would be to join the rest of the jury in the packed bar of the Inn. There he would hear all the gossip; hopefully the sense of relief that the inquest was over, and the exceptionally good ale brewed by Rose would loosen the men's tongues. He could sit quietly with a pint and see if any ideas presented themselves to him. As Nesta made to follow him, he sent her home instead. Telling her go and sit with her mother and aunt. As their conversation was likely focus on Agnes, sitting quietly at the edge of the kitchen Nesta might learn something helpful from them.

Nesta safely dispatched, he pushed open the heavy oak door to the alehouse. A warm fug hit him. Despite it being a crisp, cold late November morning, inside the inn was stifling hot. Many of the men within were smoking short clay pipes, and the rich scent of tobacco was mingling somewhat unpleasantly with the smell of unwashed body, mildewed clothing and damp dog. As well as the fourteen members of the jury, crowded inside were other men from the hamlet and outlying settlements, along with various dogs, and several young boys who should probably have been at their lessons at the small school held in the chapel at Christchurch. The discovery of Agnes' body seemed to have caused all normal work to stop as the men gathered together to discuss the inquests findings, and inevitably, who they thought the culprit was.

Sliding onto the edge of a bench, Edward joined a table with Thomas, Samuel, and Jack. While some of the other men turned to stare at him - the previous doctor having rarely set foot in the village, let alone joined them for a drink - his presence, if not welcomed, was accepted.

Jack stood, calling over to the bar for a pot boy.

"Bring us some more beer lad, and a pot for the doctor as well." He nodded to Edward "that was right thirsty work." Edward smiled. Not only was that one of the longest speeches he'd ever heard the landlord make, but he sensed that Jack was making his approval known to the other men. He was beginning to be accepted into the small community. Edward was surprised to find, pleased him enormously. First Nesta, then Jack, Edward thought. The foresters were starting to get under his skin.

Edward raised his pewter tankard to the other men in a silent salute, and took a long drink of the sweet, nutty ale.

"Thank-you Jack. God, I needed this! I've always hated inquests. Particularly when they leave so much in doubt. Dr Rudge seemed to suggest that there would be no further investigation into Agnes' death. Are there no police here abouts?" he asked.

The men looked at each other. "Well there's a police house back in Coleford" said Jack slowly.

"And one down at the old gaol at Littledean, but they don't bother round here much. Besides, there have been a few travelling tinkers about. Most likely one of them did for Agnes. They'll be long gone. It's not like it would be one of us what done it. We looks out for our own" continued Thomas.

Samuel was staring sorrowfully into his own pint pot, as if the answer to all life's questions could be found in its depths. At Thomas' words, Samuel looked up, and smiled gratefully at his elder brother, before returning to his silent contemplation. Catching Samuel's smile, Thomas looked worriedly at his brother. Samuel had always been his talkative little brother, friendly and optimistic; he always had a good word and a happy smile for everybody. The two brothers were close. They had to be working together in their small pit. The dark and dangerous conditions meant that they had to rely upon and trust each other completely. However, recently Samuel had become increasingly downcast and introspective.

Something was clearly worrying him, something that he was keeping to himself and had so far failed to share with his older brother. Thomas was determined that as soon as he got a chance, probably the next day sharing their snap, he'd get out of Sam whatever was bothering him. He might be able to hide his secrets from the rest of the hamlet, but he would be unable to keep them from his big brother for long. Thomas did not notice that someone else was watching him closely. Edward narrowed his eyes. His old mentor had hammered home to him the importance of reading body language. Knowing when a patient was holding something back, either from fear or embarrassment, or conversely, when a patient was exaggerating their symptoms was vitality important when reaching a diagnosis. More than one patient had tried to hide the real nature of their condition from Edward, and he was now able to tell instinctively when there was something wrong, and he was determined to find out what.

When Jack firmly asserted that the murderer would not be someone local, to widespread grunts of approval, Edward knew that it would be pointless to argue with them. A strong sense of family loyalty bonded the men together, and they would not break ranks to discuss the case with an outsider any further. Any grudging respect that he had earned that day would be quickly lost if he tried to press the case, so Edward decided it was time to return home to Coleford. He had placed a note on the door before he left that morning explaining that the surgery would be closed while he attended to pressing business elsewhere, but he was keen to return home and check that there had not been any urgent summonses. If no patients required his immediate attention, he would then tackle Ms Bates. Since he took up residence in October he had fitted in with Miss Bates timetable, eating meals at the times she decreed, and having the house cleaned, or rather not, as she saw fit. Now it was time for him to assert his authority as master over the household, and to issue his instructions as to how he wanted the household to be run. He knew that the longer he left it, the harder it would be to impose his will. It was not a problem he could avoid any longer.

   As he collected his horse from the rail outside, Edward decided that he would check in with Nesta. He walked his horse down the road to where Nesta's cottage stood, one of a small row backing into the hillside. Making his way through the shared yard towards the kitchen door – he had learnt enough of the local customs to know that only a stranger would approach the more formal and seldom used front door – he passed the cottage that belonged to Jane and Pete Andrews. As he knew that Jane was currently staying with her father after Pete's death, he was surprised to see signs of occupation. A half full bucket of soapy water stood by the kitchen door, which swung open at his gentle touch. Inside, a jug of fresh milk stood on the dresser, and the kitchen retained a slight heat, as if a fire had been lit in the grate that morning, although it had since been allowed to die out. Wondering whether Jane had returned, he quietly shut the door, and moved back to the yard outside. A strong hand dropped onto his shoulder, making him jump.

"Here, what you up to? Why are you poking around where you've no call to be?" asked a gentle, but insistent voice. Shaking off the woman's firm grip, Edward turned to face Rose, Nesta's aunt, and the wife of the inn keeper Jack. For a second Edward wondered whether to lie and say that he had got the wrong house, but one look at Rose's face told him that that would be a mistake. Instead he decided to tell her the truth.

"I was coming up to see Nesta. I wanted to make sure that she's recovering from the shock she had yesterday before I return to Coleford. I noticed that the Andrew's cottage seemed to be lived in, and I looked inside to check that squatters hadn't moved in. Mrs Andrews is my patient, and I know that she is still staying at her father's house."

Rose looked hard at Edward to judge the truth of his story.

"Humph, we've been keeping an eye on it for her don't you worry. People round here look out for each other, and we wanted to make sure it'd be all ready for her and the bairn to come back to. She sent word she might come back today, so I got one of the girls to give it a good scrub out." She looked him up and down taking in the well-cut clothes that showed his lean figure. "I don't suppose that husband of mine thought to feed you did he. Come on, Mary has a pan of cawl on the stove. We'll set you on your way with a bowlful inside you.

It'll be better than anything you'll get from that Doris Bates." And with that she set off towards Nesta's house, opening the door and shooing him in.

Soon Edward found himself sitting in the best chair at the table in the Phillips's cosy kitchen. A bowl of Mary's cawl in front of him. Gingerly he tried moving his spoon around in the thick brown liquid, stirring up wisps of steam. Sniffing admiringly, he cautiously tried the boiling hot stew. It was delicious. Filled with root vegetables, pearl barley, and tender lumps of an unidentified meat all cooked together in thick, rich gravy, it was like ambrosia to him. Quickly he finished his bowl, and then used a crust of warm bread to mop up the last of the juices.

Leaning back in the chair, he sighed appreciatively. "Thank you, Mrs Phillips. That was the best meal I've had since I left London."

Mary laughed, pleased with the compliment. "Well, it's true, Doris was never famed for her cooking. Right put out she was that you've not hired a cook. She's been complaining all over Coleford that you've got her working all hours."

Edward went red and stuttered embarrassed "Miss Bates has been talking about me? Oh dear. I had no idea that I was supposed to hire a cook as well. I just thought that since it's just me that I only needed a housekeeper. I've never really had my own domestic staff before, previously my landlady dealt with all that for me. I don't suppose you'd like to come and cook for me, would you?" He added hopefully, flashing Mary his best cheeky grin "I could get used to your cooking!"

Rose chuckled to herself, while Mary laughed again, a genuine chuckle of pleasure. The laughter chased away the pinched look of pain, and Edward could see traces of the happy, friendly woman she had once been.

"Well no doctor, I can't be chasing off to Coleford every day to cook for you. I'd be neglecting Tom and bairns, and I've done that for too long already" She looked down at the table, her face tightened with pain once more, the cheerful, bubbly woman vanishing in an instant. Mary closed her eyes to stop the tears that had been all to ready to come over the past month. The loss of her daughter was a raw wound inside of her. It mixed and coupled with the guilt that she had been neglecting both her children and husband, and that Nesta had had to stop attending school to step in to fill her place. Rose placed a hand reassuringly on her arm. Nesta, who had been sitting silently at the table, reached forward and squeezed her hand tightly, trying to reassure her mother that whatever work had come her way, she understood, and had been glad to help. Mary turned to look at her eldest daughter and smiled sadly. Looking at Nesta, she thought that although she often saw her daughter, she hadn't *looked* at her properly for long time. In her mind, Nesta was still a little girl, her hair loose, running around the woods. Coming home, full of laughter and covered in mud to tell her of her latest adventures. Sat in her familiar place at the end of the table, Nesta had spent years quietly watching her, learning the hundreds of daily tasks that Mary completed to keep the household running effectively. The grubby, adventurous child was gone, replaced by a capable young woman, on the cusp of being fully grown. She had shown over the past month that she was not afraid of hard work and was accomplished in managing the day to day running of a household. Mary's heart ached as she realised that soon Nesta would be leaving home. Perhaps, as many other young women in the forest, to go to take up domestic service in a big household far away in Gloucester, Bristol, or even London. Mary knew that many of those youngsters did not return home, staying and making lives for themselves in their new homes. Their only contact with their families' all too infrequent letters. Having recently lost one daughter, Mary was not ready to lose another. But perhaps, she thought, she didn't need to. Maybe there was a way that she could keep Nesta close, for a while at least. Mary smiled broadly.

"Well, now Doctor, I might not be able to come and keep house for you, but perhaps I knowst another who can. How about our Nesta comes to work for you? She's a good cook, and a hard worker, and would make a fine cook - housemaid."

Nesta's eyes lit up. The idea of working in the Doctor's house, of leaving home to go and work away, even if Coleford was only a few miles walk, was exciting. But then her heart fell. Although her mother seemed to be returning to her old self, she still didn't seem right. Nesta had taken on so much of the household work while her mother had been grieving and she knew, and was proud, that her father relied on her. She couldn't leave until her mother was ready, but then... to go and work for the doctor in Coleford, this was too good an opportunity to miss.

"Oh Ma, do you mean it?" she asked worriedly. "Are you sure you and Pa don't need me here?"

Mary smiled, both at Nesta's excitement and her concern. She put her own hand over Nesta's and looked into her eyes, willing her to understand.

"You've been a great help Nesta, and I don't know what I would have done without you, but you're all grown-up now. You've shown that this past month. It's time you started to look to your future, and, if Doctor James will take you, at least this way you'd be close enough to visit sometimes. Not like if you'd gone off to London like poor Agnes' lass."

"Besides lass, I'll look after your Ma, you know that" said Rose "but it occurs to me that really we should ask the doctor if he's willing to take you on. He might not want you, young and untrained that you are."

All three turned to look at Edward. "Hmmm, well Mrs Phillips if you taught her, I'm sure Miss Phillips will do admirably as my cook. However, I think I should consult with Miss Bates on the matter. After all it is her that you'll be working with, and it'll be up to her to teach you the skills of a domestic maid." Nesta's face fell; sure that Miss Bates would refuse to have her. She would most likely want to choose a different maid, perhaps someone that she knew, or the daughter of someone she owed a favour too. Edward saw Nesta's face fall, and continued "Perhaps, if you'd be willing, we could undertake a trial? Maybe a fortnight, starting on Monday if that would be acceptable to you? And, of course, to you Mrs Phillips."

Rose snorted. "I can tell you now what that Doris will say, and it won't be owt good. She's been telling all that'll listen that the job will be going to her niece. And while I don't want to speak out of place, I'd sooner employ a jail bird from Lydbook, as that's what you'd be doing right enough. Nasty piece of work, that Anniabeh, for all her fancy name. Why the stories that old Charlie Drinkwater could tell..." she said shaking her head sadly.

Edward realised there and then that he could not leave the problem of his housekeeper any longer. Although Edward was even tempered by nature, he was annoyed that his housekeeper had presumed to discuss the running of his household with outsiders. Conscious that his patients expected, and deserved, complete discretion, Edward resolved not to allow Doris Bates anywhere near his surgery, and to keep all medical records safely under lock and key. He knew that he needed to establish once and for all that it was his house, and it would be run as he directed, whether Doris Bates liked it or not.

Rose watched Edward carefully. Her dark eyes missed nothing. She could see the annoyance on his face and knew then that Doris' days holding sway over the doctor's household were numbered. A smile played at the edge of her lips. With luck, Nesta would be kept away from the small hamlet and thus unable to continue her questioning of Agnes' death. Nesta had already begun to clumsily question Mary and her about the Agnes, trying to find out more about the services that Agnes offered beyond the basic medicines and midwifery that Nesta knew her for. While Nesta's questions had done little harm, she would find out nothing from her and Mary, as both women knew well how to keep their own council, there was a risk that if Nesta persisted she might find out more than she should. Someone in the hamlet would talk. Or, even worse, she might ask questions of the wrong person. It would be far better to have Nesta safely out of the way.

Chapter Ten

Sunday, 9th November, 1851
Coleford.

Edward poured himself a large brandy, and sat down heavily in what was fast becoming his favourite armchair. Normally he found Sundays to be most restful. However, that evening he was exhausted. The chair, a fine brown leather wing-back, represented just one of the days many trials. Edward had spent some time carefully choosing its position to both catch the last of the evening sun and also allow the occupant to watch people coming and going around the busy market place. Having moved the chair once, he had left the room only to find that it had been moved back to its original position in a rather dark corner of the drawing room by Miss Bates. An argument had ensued, which had resulted in Miss Bates storming off to the kitchen and slamming the door behind her so hard that it had rattled the plates on the dresser.

Gently swirling the amber liquid around in his crystal glass, Edward reviewed the last few days in his mind.

Returning from Berry Hill early on Friday afternoon, Edward had immediately sought out his housekeeper. He had insisted that she sit down with him at the kitchen table to discuss the running of the household. The conversation had been fraught but cordial, and some hard bargaining had ensued. Edward had agreed to some of her demands, most notably that he took on a domestic maid, to help with the cooking, cleaning and to act as a general dogsbody. Miss Bates had been delighted; sure that she had won the tussle of wills. Only to then be disappointed when he had insisted that he would appoint the maid, rather than her. Edward remembered with some amusement watching the emotions chase across his housekeeper's expressive face - from victory to uncertainty, then furtive, as her confidence grew that she would be able to manipulate Edward in the end. When he announced that he had already appointed someone, the colour had drained from Doris' face and she looked set to storm out in a dramatic gesture aimed to make him reconsider. One look at the resolution in Edward's eyes had shown her the futility of that approach. This was an argument that she would not win. Grudgingly she had accepted that Nesta would take up the post on a trial basis starting the following Monday. However, the sly look on her face warned Edward that he would have to be on his guard to make sure that Nesta was given a fair chance.

    Few patients had visited on Saturday morning, and Edward had spent the time sat in his study, planning his reorganisation of the house. Full of restless energy, Edward meticulously sketched out how he could rearrange the furniture to best suit his needs. Chairs were positioned to catch the best of the light, while occasional tables were consigned to the attic to gather dust. Ornaments and trinkets were ruthlessly culled, consigned to boxes to be disposed of. Whole shelves of old medical texts were removed, and replaced with Edwards own, newer editions. Sorting the bookcases revealed that Doctor Thomas had been something of a bibliophile with wide and varied taste. Books on flora and fauna were mixed together with theological texts – many of them relating to non-conformism – and sat alongside the latest novels and railway literature. Well-thumbed copies of Ivanhoe, and Frankenstein, Wuthering Heights and Jane Eyre, were placed next to the latest scientific works by Robert Chambers and Phillip Henry Gosse. Edward's eye was drawn to a particularly battered copy of Elizabeth Barrett Browning's Poems; clearly it had been a favourite of Doctor Thomas. The books were kept on five large bookcases which all but covered one wall of the dining room. Sorting through them, Edward began to feel that he was getting to know Doctor Thomas a little. Although Edward did not want to keep all of the books - he intended to remove some of the floor to ceiling bookcases to help stop the dining room feeling so crowded - he was loath to throw them away, understanding that they had been prized above all else by Doctor Thomas, getting rid of them felt like some kind of sacrilege. Edward decided he would box them up. The books could sit upstairs in the attic until he decided what to do with them.

The clock in the hallway chimed 9 o'clock. The drawing room was warm and cosy. A cheerful fire burning and the oil lamp on the table next to Edward was turned low, giving off a mellow, yellow glow. As he leant back in the armchair, Edward began to doze, his head nodding to one side. It had been a long, busy week. The retrieval of Agnes' body, the inquest, his discussion with Miss Bates, and his attempt at sorting out the house, had worn him out. Edward leant back in the chair and slept.

He woke, stiff and aching at the discordant jangling of the door bell. Pulling himself to his feet, he rubbed his face his hand rasping on the bristly stubble. Feeling rather lacklustre – although he had slept all night, he had not slept well. Disturbing images of Agnes' body had flittered in and out of his dreams, and something else was niggling at him. Something important he had missed. Shaking his head to dispel the feeling that he was missing something important, he headed towards the front door. A glance at the clock showed that it was only seven o'clock- unless there was some kind of emergency he would not normally expect patients to arrive until at least nine. Hurrying to open the door, he found Nesta standing on the top step. A small bag by her feet. Outside in the street sat her great uncle on top of his cart, which was piled high with sacks of coal. Despite the early hour, he had already made the return trip to the mine and had given Nesta a ride into town on his return. Raising his whip in silent greeting of the doctor, and as a goodbye to Nesta, he shook the horses reins and drove off, heading down the street to his coal yard.

    Edward stepped back and indicated that Nesta should precede him down the hallway. As she did so, Nesta looked about her in wonder, overawed by the wide hallway, high ceilings and sweeping staircase which were so very different to her parents' cottage. She couldn't help comparing the small windowed, low ceiled cottages she was used to the doctor's house. It felt like a palace in comparison. Her parents' furniture was comfortable and practical; here everything was decorated and carved. Everywhere she looked were the trappings of wealth, from the brightly coloured glazed tiles on the floor, to the wall mounted oil lamps and large, ornately carved mirror. But as she looked more closely she saw that the rugs were faded, and the brass of the oil lamps tarnished. This house needs some love and attention, she thought. Edward showed Nesta his consulting room and study, and the drawing room and dining room on his left. At the end of the hallway, a door led into the kitchen. It was good-sized, with a modern range cooker built into the fireplace on one side. A pine dresser stood against one wall, covered in plates and serving dishes. Bunches of herbs hung drying from the ceiling and in the corner a smaller door led through to a small pantry and with a damp cellar below. A large china sink was set below the window, which filled the kitchen with weak November sunlight. Set in the middle of the kitchen was a large scrubbed table. Two small stools were tucked underneath the table edge, while at one end stood a large high-backed oak basket chair. Filled with soft cushions and placed to catch both the best of the sunlight, and the warmth of the range, it was filled with the bulky body of the housekeeper. Miss Bates looked disapprovingly at Edward, taking in his dishevelled appearance and the obvious fact that he had slept in his clothes, and harrumphed. Turning her gaze to the small, slight figure of Nesta behind him, she smiled to herself. This little slip of a girl would prove no match for her. Young and easily cowed, Doris would have her dismissed within a week. She didn't look capable of the hard-physical work that she had planned for her, and a few well placed comments would have her running home to her mother. Aware of the scrutiny, Nesta bobbed in a small curtsey.

"Good morning Ma'am. I'm Nesta." She said timidly. Unsure of how she would cope away from home for the first time, Nesta had sought advice from both her mother and her aunt. Aunt Rose in particular, who had been away on service herself in her youth, had given her plenty of good advice, especially in how to handle the housekeeper. Doris gave Nesta a calculating look.

"Good morning Doctor James. Thank-you for showing Nesta in Sir, I will instruct her from here. Not least in that the front door is for visitors and patients only. Not under-maids!" Doris said sternly, turning to Nesta, Edward felt like he had been dismissed. "I am Doris Bates, you may call me Miss Bates. I see you have your things. I'll show you where to put them.

Then you can carry a jug of hot water upstairs for the master. No doubt he will wish to wash and change before his first patients arrive. You will also need to prepare his breakfast." She pulled herself to her feet. Indicating that Edward should precede them out of the kitchen, Doris showed Nesta out of the kitchen and upstairs. The bedrooms on the first floor of the house were all large, the grandest being Edward's room at the front of the house. Another slightly smaller room stood to one side. At the back of the house was a pair of interconnecting rooms, probably designed as a nursery with a small adjoining room for a nursemaid Nesta thought. Another, less grand staircase was half hidden in a dark corner behind a plain wooden door. The treads of this staircase were of bare wood and led steeply up to the attic. Here tucked amongst the eves were another two bedrooms, as well as the entrance to the attic storage space now filled to bursting with furniture, books and ornaments.

Doris pointed to the door which led to the bedroom at the front of the house. "That there's my room. Mind you don't go in there. This is your room here" she said flinging open a door. Inside was a small room with a thin bed, an upright wooden chair, a battered chest of drawers and a small empty fireplace. Being at the top of the house, the room was cold. A small window covered in cobwebs and incrusted with dirt let in little light. Nesta looked around the bare room which would be her home and felt a pang of sadness as she compared it to the homely, if cramped room she had shared with her parents and siblings. That room had been full of home comforts, rag rugs on the floor, and thick patchwork quilts on the bed. In summer a bunch of freshly picked wild flowers had always sat in a small vase on the window sill. It was a room which exuded happiness, while this room was dark, cold and gloomy. Everything was covered in a thick layer of dust which rose and swirled as she placed her small bundle of clothes down on the narrow bed, making her sneeze. Nesta carefully removed a freshly starched white apron from her bag. Still tying the apron, she turned and followed Doris back downstairs.

Nesta worked hard, fetching and carrying, scrubbing and sweeping, all the time watched by the beady, critical eye of Miss Bates. No sooner had she finished cooking and washing up the breakfast things than Doris was calling for Nesta to come and help her clean the bedrooms. Having finally finished blacking the hearths in the upstairs bedrooms Nesta made her way back downstairs to the kitchen. She was about to sit down, when Miss Bates bustled back in from the yard, her coat already on.

"Right, now you've got upstairs finished, you can make a start on luncheon. There're some vegetables in the pantry, and some pie leftover from yesterdays supper he can have. I'm going to the butchers to see if he's got owt for dinner. Make sure you keep an ear out for the bell" and with that injunction, Miss Bates adjusted her hat, picked up a large wicker basket, and was gone.

Nesta let out a sigh of relief and sat down heavily on a stool. Reaching out to feel the teapot she was relieved to find that it was still warm and gratefully poured herself a cup. Taking a sip, she found that the tea was lukewarm and well stewed. Reluctantly she pulled herself to her feet. A shake of the kettle revealed it was almost empty. She looked around for a jug of water to fill it from. Realising with a sigh that this too was empty, Nesta slipped outside to the pump, filling both the jug and kettle to the brim. She returned to the kitchen, shoving the backdoor closed with one foot, her hands full. Setting the kettle on to boil, she turned towards the pantry, intending to make a start on preparing the vegetables for luncheon. She started and let out a small cry of surprise as she noticed the figure ensconced in Miss Bates throne. Putting one hand on the table to steady herself, and the other to her chest, she leant forward, and took several deep breaths, shaking her head slowly. Edward leapt up from where he had been silently sitting in the chair and crouched down to look Nesta in the face.

"I'm sorry I startled you Miss Phillips. Here, sit down, let me fetch you a drink" he said contritely.

Nesta shook her head, "Oh no sir, I can't have you fetching me a drink. Whatever would Miss Bates say to that? Here, that kettle'll be boiling in a moment. Where do you keep the tea caddy?" Edward looked around the kitchen, a room he seldom ventured into, unsure where anything was kept. Together, he and Nesta searched through a line of tins and jars on the dresser. Failing to find any tea there, they moved on to searching in the pantry, bumping into each other as they both tried to move around in the confined space. Moving a packet aside, Nesta knocked a large earthenware jar of rolled oats, which fell to the floor with a crash. As Edward turned to help her clear up the mess – thankfully the jar had survived intact - he noticed a small packet, little more than a twisted scrap of paper. Absentmindedly he picked it up, and put it in his pocket, continuing to help Nesta scrape up the oats. Putting the jar back on the shelf, Nesta finally located the tea, hidden right at the back on a high shelf. Taking it through to the kitchen, Nesta made a fresh pot of tea.

"Shall I bring you a cup through to your surgery, or would you prefer to take tea in the Parlour?" asked Nesta.

Edward shook his head "I'd rather take tea here with you if you don't mind. I wondered if you would tell me about Berry Hill. If we're going to start a new hospital and friendly society I need to know more about how people live around here. It's all very different to London."

"Do you miss it? London, I mean. I can't imagine London. Uncle Jack went once. He said it was a wonder, all those people living together. So busy - people everywhere bustling about. And so grand! I'd like to see London one day." Nesta answered wistfully, thinking how much she would love to travel and see new sights. She had been born in her parents' cottage in Berry Hill, and there she had lived until today when she had come to live in Coleford. The Forest of Dean was the extent of her world, and although she had ranged widely in the forest, Nesta had never ventured far from its borders. In fact, the furthest she had ever travelled was when she had gone with her Great Uncle William to deliver coal to the docks at Lydney. Growing up in the forest, Nesta was used to quiet woodlands, empty commons, bleak pasture lands and narrow track ways. Although the great turnpike roads of the Forest of Dean Turnpike Company crossed the forest, taking travellers quickly in their coaches from Monmouth, to Gloucester and beyond, Nesta was far more used to the ancient, winding track ways of the forest. Which, while they were not suitable for a coach to race along, were more than adequate for a girl on foot. And they were free. The idea of streets full of the wealthy parading along or riding in carriages, past grand houses and royal parks full of exotic creatures both thrilled and frightened her. For as well as the tales of the great and the good of the land, she had heard tales of the other side of life in the great cities, of families squeezed into a single room in a shared house, of cruelty, murder, and death from disease.

Not that the forest was exempt from such crimes she thought sadly. Although she had been told by her father, mother, aunt and uncle that Agnes must had disturbed some passing vagrant poaching and had been murdered to ensure her silence, Nesta did not believe them. Not many strangers passed through the woods in November, when heavy rains could turn even the well-maintained turnpike roads into quagmires, and cold winds would freeze you to your very marrow. In November, the travelling peddlers were more likely to stay close to towns where they could earn a few pennies selling their wares or singing Christmas carols, it was not a time of year that they normally visited the forest. The first itinerants generally appeared as the bluebells began to flower, when the worst of the cold weather was over. Then they would quietly spread through the woods, offering their labour to farmers and miners, looking for herbs to make potions, and setting up camp as charcoal burners. Nesta had spent several summers chatting to the charcoal burners and their women; she knew that they followed a set pattern and that it was unlikely that any would be roaming the woods in the winter. Besides, the travellers were generally a gentle folk, and they knew Agnes, they knew that she would never betray a poacher to the Verderers, after all how could she when she would have to explain what she was doing there herself! No, Nesta mused, it was unlikely to be an itinerant that killed Agnes, but who else could it be? Most strangers travelling through the forest kept to the turnpike roads for fear of becoming lost amongst the trees. Indeed, as it was some distance from any of the major routes through the forest it was most unlikely that a passing traveller would accidently find themselves in the old disused quarry in the dark.

"No" Nesta mused "it must have been someone who knew the woods. No-one else would find their way up there. Certainly not in the dark." She looked up to see Edward staring at her intently and realised that she had spoken aloud. Nesta felt her face flush under as he continued to watch her, staring as if he was trying to see into her very soul. Eventually, Edward ended his scrutiny of Nesta, leaned back and sighed.

"You know Miss Phillips, I fear you are right. Agnes must have been killed by someone who knew those woodland paths intimately. We had to go too far, by a circuitous route to reach that old quarry. It's not somewhere you go by accident. You'd need a purpose to be up there. Which does beg the question what you yourself were doing up in the woods as dusk fell? Why were you there Miss Phillips, and please don't tell me you were gathering mushrooms. There are many more places you can gather them much closer to home. And anyway, gathering mushrooms in the half-light when you're not able to make a proper identification would be a most foolish thing to do. And you do not strike me as a foolish young lady!"

Nesta felt her colour rising again. She began to sob. She liked the doctor well enough, and there was something about him that made her want to trust him, to pour out all her secrets to him. But she wasn't sure that she could trust him, not with this. She had kept her secret even from her beloved father. She hadn't even told her Aunt Rose, who she normally told everything too. Aunt Rose was good with secrets, and clever.

While Nesta cried Edward sat still sipping his tea. He knew that Nesta needed to cry, to let out whatever it was that was worrying her. Then once she had decided to share her problem with him, and Edward was confident that she would, he would help her. Abruptly Nesta wiped away her tears and looked up at Edward as he sat calmly watching her. In that moment she knew that she could tell him anything, and that he would do his best for her. And anyway, she thought, he is a doctor, perhaps he would be able assist.

Nesta took a deep breath "I was looking for Agnes. That's why I was up there. You see, I'd been slipping Ma St John's Wort in her tea because she seemed so sad. I thought it might help her past her melancholy. But we'd only had a little, and it don't flower at this time of year, so I was looking for Agnes to see if she had anymore. I know she keeps all sorts up in her cottage, and it's over that way. She lives up in an encroachment at Five Acres. Her cottage is just behind the quarry..."

Edward nodded. "St John's Wort? Hmmm. Well yes, that might help, I suppose, and it explains why you were up there. Did you reach Agnes' cottage?"

"Well no, I saw someone had been digging as I went through the quarry, and I bent down to look at what they'd be digging up. That's how I saw Agnes' hand. Sticking out like that, the flesh half gone from the bones. I knew straight away that she were dead. It was horrible. That and the branches all crackling, and there were a fearful rustling in the undergrowth. I know it sounds daft, but, somehow, I felt like something was watching me. Something evil. I had to get away. So I just ran."

Nesta shuddered, and Edward reached out instinctively and clasped Nesta's hands in his own.

"You had a terrible shock, Nesta. Finding a body like that, well it would play tricks on anybody's mind. Anybody would have run. It's alright to have been scared. However, if you're right, and I think you are, and it wasn't a passing itinerant who killed Agnes, it must have been someone else. Somebody killed her for a reason. We need to find out more about her, to see if there's any clues there as to who might have attacked her. Will you help me?" Edward said softly, looking straight at Nesta. Nesta looked back at Edward and realised that for the first time since she had found Agnes' body, she was not afraid. The warm touch of his soft hands – so unlike the calloused, work-hardened hands, of her father and uncles – and the gentle expression on his face reassured her. Staring back into his dark brown eyes, Nesta saw his quick intelligence, and a determination to solve the mystery of who had killed Agnes that matched her own.

She smiled at him, "Yes, Dr Edwards, I'll help you. What do you want me to do?"

The sudden creak of the back door as it opened made them both start, and they sprung apart. Edward jumped to his feet, while Nesta sat up straighter on her stool. Both looked guilty. Doris Bates looked from one to the other, and thought to herself: so, this is how the land lies it is. Under-maid indeed!

Placing her heavy basket down on the table with a thump, Miss Bates began to unpack.

"Well my, this is cosy. Is there anything you need Doctor?" She said icily. "Nesta have you made a start at lunch yet, and have you cleaned and dusted the front rooms?" Nesta shook her head, staring at the table glumly. She had quite forgotten the long list of jobs that Miss Bates had left her to do, and now felt worried. She knew that if she failed to meet her exacting standards, whether they were fairly set or not, she would be dismissed and have to return to her parent's house in ignominy.

Doris smiled her shark-like smile. "Well then, Nesta. You had best get on with the cleaning. I don't know how you were brought up, but in my household, you complete all the chores before you sit around with a cup of tea. Tea from my stores no doubt!" Nesta sunk lower on the stool, and Doris looked set to berate Nesta further, when Edward cleared his throat.

"Excuse me Miss Bates. I'd asked Nesta to join me in a cup of tea. I wanted to know how she was settling in and check that she understood her duties. If she hasn't completed her chore's then that is my fault entirely. I do apologise. The tea was of course from the caddy in the pantry." Edward gave Doris a long, cold look, "*My* pantry, Miss Bates, and *my* household. Are we clear?"

Doris looked first outraged, then indignant. Instructing that pip-squeak of a maid in her 'duties' indeed, as if Doris couldn't do that perfectly well herself. He might be the master, but everyone knew who really ran a household, and it wasn't the master. Doris could see that would have to quickly disabuse Edward of that notion. Indeed, she'd thought that she'd had him in his place before, but now he'd come in, and thought that not only could he dictate the arrangement of the rooms, and the way in which they were cleaned, but that he could also appoint staff, and instruct them in their duties himself. She looked between the Doctor and Nesta with disgust, assuming that the doctor had appointed Nesta to be not just a maid, but also his mistress.

Nesta withered under Miss Bates' basilisk glare. She had no idea what she had done to elicit such disgust. After all, she had only been sitting at the kitchen table drinking tea. As Nesta recoiled, seeming to shrink down into herself, Miss Bates smirked. Sure she would be able to use the doctor's relationship with Nesta to manipulate him. Edward saw her look of cruel satisfaction and began to laugh. A terrible cold laugh, born of derision rather than amusement, he looked straight at Doris, who recoiled, uncomfortable under his piercing gaze.

"I can see Miss Bates what conclusion you have jumped to, and I will tell you now that you are wrong. I am displeased that you would view me as such a cad, and that you would cast Miss Phillips as being of such low morals. That your immediate assumption on finding us innocently conversing in the kitchen was so uncharitable is more indicative of your own low morals, than our own." With that Edward turned and stalked from the kitchen. Walking to his study, Edward firmly shut the door behind him. Unable to maintain his outraged facade any longer, he sank into his chair and began to chuckle quietly to himself. The look of indignant, horror on Miss Bates face had been a sight to behold, and he had been amused to see that her first thoughts were that there was some kind of sexual relationship between himself and Nesta. Miss Bates was now firmly on the back-foot and had lost any kind of moral high ground that she might once have held. Edward thought that she might now be rather more agreeable in her household management. He turned contentedly to the work on his desk and filling his pen from the inkwell prepared to write. His contented smile faded as he realised that if Miss Bates thought there was a sexual relationship between him and Nesta, so might others. "Damn and blast!" Ink splattered onto the paper in front of him, and he balled the paper up and threw it towards the fire. He could not afford any further scandal, not after he'd had to leave London. Smiling wryly as his shot went wide of the mark and hit the wall, Edward got up to retrieve the paper. Placing it carefully onto the fire, he starred into the flames, remembering. The clock struck the hour, and then the quarter and still he stood staring into the flames, reliving past exploits. Finally, as the clock struck half past, he shook himself from his revelry, mentally closing the door on the bittersweet memories of his time in London. Returning guiltily to his desk, he analysed his feelings. Not only could he not afford a scandal, but neither could Nesta. If anyone suspected any kind of sexual impropriety between them it would ruin her good name, and she would be shamed, a fallen woman. He could not, would not allow that to happen to her.

Chapter Eleven

Wednesday, 12th November, 1851

Nesta carefully placed the heavy tray on the side table, and knocked gently on the study door. Hearing a distracted "come-in", she carried the tray inside placing it down on a side board amongst the doctor's various medical apparatus. She poured a cup of tea, added the milk and carried it over to where the doctor was sat at his desk reviewing medical notes. Looking for a space on the messy desk – it was covered with a number of papers, books, and what look suspiciously like a used urine inspection flask – she eventually found a space to set down the cup and a biscuit.

"Thank-you Nesta" muttered Edward, engrossed in his reading. He was just reaching out absentmindedly to take the tea cup when he realised that Nesta was still standing by his desk waiting to speak to him. He cleared his throat and looked up. Over the last two days that Nesta had been working in his house, he had been to great lengths to ensure that he was never alone with her again. Making sure that Miss Bates was always present, or if that was not possible, that the door was left open, and their contact kept as brief as possible. Doris Bates' suggestion that there might be an ulterior motive for Nesta's presence, however unfounded, had alerted him to the risk of scandal, something that he was very keen to avoid for both their sakes. Uncomfortably he cleared his throat again. "How can I help you Nesta?" he asked.

"Well, Sir, begging your pardon Sir, Uncle William popped by this morning with the coal delivery. While he were here he told me that Agnes' funeral is to be held tomorrow up at Christchurch, and I was wondering if you'd let me have the morning off so I could go. I asked Miss Bates, but she said I'd need to ask you, coz you're the master. Please Sir, I'd be back to cook dinner, and I'd work extra hard to make sure all my work is done." She asked him anxiously. Nesta was now a little afraid of the Doctor. She didn't understand why he had changed from being kind and friendly, to distant and aloof. It was as if he could no longer bear to be in her company. Nesta had wracked her brains as she lay awake in bed trying to work out what she could have said or done to precipitate the drastic change, but she couldn't think of anything. One minute they had been friendlily chatting over a cup of tea, the next Miss Bates had stomped in thrown around some wild accusations as she was prone to, and then the Doctor had got all angry and stormed out. She wished that her Aunt Rose was here for her to talk to. She would know what the trouble was, and she would be able to help Nesta to fix whatever it was she had done wrong.

Edward looked up at Nesta and saw the dark circles of tiredness under her own cornflower blue eyes, and the lines of worry etched her forehead. The cheerful, carefree attitude that he had so admired when he first met her was gone. His mind raced. Obviously, she was deeply concerned about something, and from the way she was looking at him, he began to suspect that it might involve him. Clearly, she was fearful of asking him for time to attend Agnes' funeral. That or she was concerned to be alone in the room with him. Was she regretting coming to work for him? She seemed so nervous to be near him. Surely, she couldn't be scared of him? She'd been so relaxed with him before. Unless she had heard about the scandal in London. Could it have followed him here? Please God no! He had thought, hoped, that by moving away from London, and from everyone who had known of his disgrace he could make a fresh start here in this country backwater. He had hoped to escape from the gossip and distrust which had dogged his last few months in London, forced his resignation from St Thomas'. Edward's heart froze at the thought that the story of his disgrace had reached Coleford. By heading to such a remote area, his destination known only to his mother and a very few close associates in London, he had hoped that he would be able to escape his humiliation. Even if the once glittering future was now closed to him, he might at least be able to carve out a respectable existence here instead. That even that modest dream should be taken from him was too cruel a fate for him to consider.

Edward leant back in his chair, closed his eyes and sighed. Nesta felt her heart sink down to the pit of her stomach. At that moment she was sure that she was about to be dismissed. It wasn't fair! She'd tried so hard to match up to the high, and frankly impossible, standards of Miss Bates, and now clearly the doctor had turned against her too. She would be sent home in disgrace, and all her friends and neighbours would know that she had failed as a house maid. That it was common knowledge that Miss Bates had been against her from the start wouldn't stop them from concluding that there must be something wrong with her – that she must be idle or slatternly in some way. Unbidden tears came to her eyes and ran silently down her face. Picking up her tray, she bobbed a quick curtsey and turned to leave.

"I'm sorry to have bothered you with this Sir" she mumbled as she walked towards the door. Despite her best attempts to disguise her upset, her voice was thick with emotion. Edward sat up straight in his chair.

"What is it Nesta, why are you crying? Of course, you can attend the funeral tomorrow" his voice full concern for her. Standing up, Edward walked over to Nesta, and taking her by the elbow guided her to his chair.

"I'm sorry Sir. What must you think of me crying like this on top of everything? I'm sorry that I haven't been able to match up to your standards." Nesta's voice trailed away as she again contemplated the shame of having return to her parent's home tears running freely down her face. Her arms wrapped around the circular tray as she held it to her chest like a small child clutching a doll. She had been so excited to leave home, and so pleased that she was going to work for the doctor that she admired so much.

Edward crouched down next to Nesta. Gently he eased the tray out of her iron grip and took her small work calloused hands in his larger soft ones. Speaking softly, his voice low he looked into her eyes and asked "What are you talking about Nesta? I've been very pleased with your work. Your cooking is excellent, and the house is already cleaner. Has Miss Bates been saying something to you?"

"It's just you've seemed so distant, like you couldn't bear to be in my presence. I thought I must have offended you somehow."

"Oh Nesta! You've not done anything to upset me, on the contrary in fact. It's just that well, Miss Bates suggested that I might have an" Edward paused, wracking his brains to think of a way to express the problem without insulting Nesta, "an *inappropriate* reason to employ you. That I was looking for more than just a housemaid, if you know what I mean, and I wanted to protect your, um, our, good names." Edward finished somewhat sheepishly. Nesta sat staring at Edward, a look of sweet confusion on her face. Several moments passed, and Edward began to squirm feeling increasing uncomfortable. Suddenly, as understanding dawned, she began to snigger and then giggle.

"You mean Miss Bates thinks that I'm here to be your molly! Why didn't you just say?" Nesta said between chuckles "Don't you worry about Miss Bates. I'll tell Aunt Rose, and she'll soon put that 'un right. What did she do? Threaten to tell Parson? Bloody hypocrite! Beggin' your pardon Sir!"

Seeing Edward's serious expression, Nesta suddenly stopped chuckling, and put her hand to her mouth in horror that she might have offended the doctor. "I'm sorry sir. I hope I haven't offended you. It's just everybody knows about the way her and Doctor Thomas carried on. And how she's right put out that he didn't leave her owt in his will. She'd been telling everyone that she'd been left a packet in his will for her good service and expected not to have to work no more you see. Then when the will was read, well, her face were a picture so it's said. Then you came, and you've brought me here to help out rather than Miss Bates' niece. Well, no-one will mind anything she says. They all know it'll just be spite. And as much as folk like to gossip, anyone who does mind her, well Aunt Rose won't stand for it. She'll soon put them right!"

Edward's mouth twitched slightly at the corners, amused by Nesta's conviction that people would see past the spiteful comments of others to the real truth. It was refreshing to see her simple faith in people in stark contrast to the cynicism he was used to from his former London colleagues. Remembering how his friends used to mock him for what they described as his naivety, he smiled wryly. He used to argue with them that people would see the truth, would know better than to believe malicious rumours, until he learnt the hard way that actually they wouldn't. His face hardened into a scowl, as he thought how his patients, his colleagues, people who he had considered to be his friends had turned against him, all because of a malicious tale from a disgruntled patient.

Seeing Edward's dark look, Nesta instinctively reached out to him, touching his arm. "It's alright Sir. Honestly, people might like to gossip here, but everyone knows what stories are true and which aren't. Besides, you'll have Aunt Rose on your side. Would you argue with my Aunt Rose if she told you summit weren't so?"

Edward smiled back. "You know I do believe you're right. I wouldn't care to argue with your Aunt Rose." He answered slowly and realised that it was true. There was something in Rose's manner that brooked no argument. Even the way that she had managed him, arranging for Nesta to come and work for him. He hadn't even been looking for a maid, and she'd not only told him he needed one, but convinced him to take on Nesta. And he had to admit that so far, she was being proved right. He had never been so well fed, or so well looked after, as he had been in the last few days. It was then that Edward realised that he did not care what other mean-minded people thought. He was happy in his new role as the local physician, it was looking likely that his and Sir Cyril's plans to set up a small charitable hospital would soon come to fruition, and he was starting to be accepted by the forresters. While there might not be the same opportunities for a glittering career physicking the high and mighty as there were in London, here he had a chance to make a real difference in the small, somewhat isolated, community. To his surprise, he was content.

Edward flipped open his diary. "Right, I have no appointments booked for tomorrow morning, so I'll tell you what - we'll both go to the funeral. Your Uncle has a trap for hire -we'll take that. Then, after the funeral I can have a word with Samuel about cutting down some trees in the garden – Mrs Andrews recommended him to me. We could pop by Agnes' cottage if we have time, to see if we can find out anything about her... Her..." Edward stalled trying to find a delicate way of describing Agnes' demise.

"To see if we can find out who killed her you mean" Nesta said forcefully. While she liked and respected the doctor, Nesta was starting to find his clumsy attempts to protect her sensibilities irritating. She was sixteen after all, practically an adult, and more than capable of looking after herself.

Chapter Twelve

Thursday, 13th November, 1851.

The following day, Edward rose early and dressed carefully. Peering through a gap in the curtains, Edward stood for a moment, watching the market town begin to stir itself to life. Although the sun was only just starting to rise on the horizon, there were already several carts moving around beginning their deliveries. Thick clouds hung low, obscuring the nearby hills from view. It looked likely to be a cold dank day. Edward was both pleased and surprised to find that Nesta had already left a fresh ewer of hot water by his door, ready for him to wash and shave at the small washstand in his bedroom. Then looked at the clothes hanging in his wardrobe. Normally he would wear his Sunday best to a funeral, but he would also be walking through the woods to Agnes' cottage, and he couldn't afford to have his best clothes ruined. After all, he had yet to locate a descent tailor and didn't want to have to make the long journey to Gloucester, or even Bristol looking for replacements. Eventually he settled on a dark waistcoat, and his second-best trousers, and frock coat.

Selecting a suitably sober cravat he checked his appearance in the long mirror. Presentable - in case he met anyone he needed to impress, but practical enough over rough paths he thought. Taking the stairs two at a time, he hurried downstairs in the hope of a hot drink before they set off. Walking into the kitchen, he found Nesta smartly dressed, with a large pinafore protecting her Sunday best from being splattered with fat as she carefully fried kippers for his breakfast. A tray was already set with breakfast things on the table, and the kettle was singing happily on the stove ready to make coffee. Edward stood in the doorway, taking in the cheerful domestic scene, and smiled.

"Good morning Nesta. I see you've got everything well in hand" he said as he took a seat at the large well scrubbed kitchen table.

"Good morning Doctor. Bertie has just been in from the yard. He's just putting Betsy into the traces, she'll be all ready for us once you've finished your breakfast. Uncle William says do you want to borrow Bertie to drive the trap, or will you be driving yourself?" Nesta asked as she bustled about the kitchen making the coffee, and slicing bread to have with the kippers.

"I'll drive I think. There isn't much space in that old trap. Any more than two would be a squeeze. Besides, won't your Uncle William miss Bertie when he's doing his deliveries?" Edward said taking a coffee cup off his tray and poured himself a coffee from the pot. He sat, elbows on the table, leaning on one arm in a way that would most certainly have caused his mother to squeal with outrage, completely relaxed savouring the smell of freshly brewed coffee and kippers. Nesta looked at him, pleased to see him at ease. Seeing that he clearly had no intention of eating his breakfast alone in the cold dining room, Nesta served him his breakfast at the table, and sat down herself with a thick slab of bread and a cup of milk. Edward looked over to her as she ate.

"Are you not going to have any of these kippers Nesta? They're delicious, just what you need on a cold morning." he asked

"No thank you Doctor. I'm happy with bread and milk. It's what we always had at home." Replied Nesta, thinking to herself that that was all that her parents could afford. After all, they were lucky that there was normally bread and milk, her Pa making a small profit from the mine. She knew that other families were not so lucky. Her Ma having many tales of growing up impoverished in a tiny encroachment cottage built on crown land into the forest itself.   Nesta knew that she was fortunate to have such parents. She had been brought up in a cottage that was normally warm, and there was always some food to eat. Her clothes, while patched and handed down, were warm enough for the weather, and she had had the chance to attend the local school and learn to read and write. She knew that many in the forest were not so lucky. They lived hard lives, living hand to mouth in small, cold cottages, working hard to eke out a meagre existence from the forest selling charcoal and labouring long hours down the big pits or at the foundry. Looking at the Doctor tucking in to his breakfast, Nesta wondered at how different their upbringings had been. Her in her parents' small cottage, him in what? A large house in London with lots of servants, always warm with plenty of food to eat, new clothes, never having to help out sorting coal at the mine, and an education that extended far beyond the basic lessons in reading and writing that she had had at the small school at Christ Church that she attended when her parents could find the fees. Nesta realised that she knew very little about the Doctor's background, only that he had studied medicine in London, and had worked at one of the big charitable hospitals. Beyond that Nesta knew nothing of him, of his family, his home, or why he had come to leave. But, she thought sipping her milk, she would. She sensed that there was some story behind his move, a hidden sadness and a deep-set reserve which seemed to make him wary of people and their motives. Much as he might want to hide his reasons for coming to Coleford, Nesta was determined that she would find out the full story one day.

  Finishing their breakfast, Nesta quickly tided the kitchen, before fetching her coat and bonnet from the stand. Removing her pinafore, Nesta carefully smoothed down her dress with her hands, checking as she did so that no fat had splashed her. Putting on her coat, an old one of her aunts which had been turned up at the hem and bonnet she turned as the back door opened. In ran Fredrick, out of breath and panting with the cold.

"The traps already for you Nesta!" He said, and then gazing around the kitchen in wonder. "Cor Nesta. Do you really live here? Look at the size of this place! You could feed an army from in here."

Edward strode into the kitchen well wrapped against the cold in a voluminous riding coat. "The trap is ready? Excellent! Come on Nesta. Time we were off." He said as he turned and led the way out the front door to the waiting horse and trap. Fredrick trailed behind, his small eyes darting around taking in every detail of the hall with its neat brightly coloured tiled floor and highly polished mirrors. Dark doors on either side closed off rooms that Fredrick longed to explore, while the stately staircase with its polished and carved wooden banisters tantalizingly led the way upstairs. Seeing Frederick lingering in the hallway engrossed as he watched the pendulum move inside the case of a grandfather clock, Nesta tried in vain to hurry him out. Edward turned.

"Come along Fredrick. There's no time to gawp!" he announced. Frederick hung his head in shame at the reprimand and scurried out quickly. Head down, he rushed past Edward with his shoulders hunched, hoping to avoid the blow he was sure was coming. Edward watched Fredrick closely, recognising the signs of a habitually beaten child. Unsure what, if anything he could do to help the small boy, he mentally filed it away as a problem for another day. Courteously he handed Nesta into the trap, and then sprang up into the driving seat. Taking the reins with the confidence of someone who is familiar with horses, he looked down at the small chastised figure. "Come back another day, and Nesta can show you around." He said kindly, before gently shaking the reins, and heading off up the road towards Christchurch.

It was an easy drive up the turnpike from Coleford to Christchurch. The Mitcheldean Road was a relatively new edition to the network of turnpikes, being built only ten years earlier. It was well maintained and as they jogged along in the horse and trap in the weak November sunshine, Edward was able to relax and admire his surroundings. Nesta was uncharacteristically quiet sitting huddled into her rather thin coat. As she began to shiver, Edward passed her a blanket. Accepting it gratefully, she tucked the thick blanket around her, grateful for its warmth. As they jogged along, she stared out into the trees feeling strangely apart from the doctor. The memory of the night she had found Agnes' body played over and over again in her mind. Staring into the trees she remembered her horror at finding the body. It had been late afternoon she remembered, the sun had already begun to set so that the forest had been overtaken by a peculiar half-light before full dark fell. Already apprehensive about asking Agnes for some St John's Wort for her mother, she was full of conflicting emotions, unsure whether she should be giving her the medicine without her knowledge, and yet desperate to help her in any way she could. Suddenly it had seemed much darker in the forest than usual. The trees more menacing. Nesta had picked up her pace, scurrying faster and faster, threading her way along the narrow, overgrown path. She had been relieved when she found herself in the old quarry where the trees were slightly thinner and the light a little better. But it was there, just when she was beginning to feel a little safer, that she had found her. Well, if she was perfectly honest with herself, she had almost tripped over her. Walking through the glade, she had failed to notice a rotten branch that had slipped down from a rough stack of wood. She had caught her ankle hard and slipped and fell landing heavily on the forest floor. As she tripped, the branch had dislodged some more of the unstable wood pile. Sitting on the floor amongst the fallen leaves and other detritus, she had she bent down to examine her ankle, sure that she would have a fine bruise at the very least. It was then that she had noticed Agnes' hand. It was a thing of horror. She had sat staring at it for what felt like an eternity, unable to grasp that the piece of ragged flesh, black, battered and gnawed, with several fingers missing, was in fact a human hand. It was only then that she had screamed. Suddenly she had began to feel claustrophobic, as though the very trees were crowding in on her. Menacing her. Strange rustling noises came from the undergrowth, and she felt as though she was being watched. Overwhelmed by a sense of dread, that some malevolent presence was hiding, watching her she had picked herself up of the floor. And run. She ran and ran, running for the road as if all the hounds of the Cŵn Annwn were chasing after her. Running as if her life depended on it. Running to put as much distance as she could between her and that place of horror. Nesta shot a sideways glance at the doctor. She remembered how grateful she had been to see him and how he had looked after her. Edward reached out and squeezed her hand quickly, reassuring her that he was still there, and would continue to look after her.

Chapter Thirteen

Christchurch, Forest of Dean.

A gnes' funeral was a dismal affair. Only finished in 1840, the church was in the modern gothic style, with tall thin windows. Originally built as a small school-chapel in 1812, the church was the first to be built within the forest and had expanded rapidly along with its congregation so that the small chapel had more than doubled in size. In November the church was always freezing. Little sunlight reached its dark recesses, and the church felt slightly damp. The few mourners shuffled and moved trying to keep warm, still wrapped in their thick outdoor clothes against the bone-chilling cold. The slightest sound echoed around the near-empty building. Everyone hoped the service would be over as quickly as possible so that they could make their way back outside to the daylight. It was not helped that the curate had a stinking cold, and the service was delivered amongst much coughing and spluttering.

Thankfully the service was brief, and it was with much relief that they were able to head out to gather around the grave set in a small, unpopular area of the graveyard. Following the internment, Nesta and Edward trudged slowly away from the graveside with the rest of the small congregation. Few people had come. The villagers needed to go to work in the mines and quarries. If they didn't work, they didn't earn, and if they didn't earn any money, there would be no food at the end of the week. Consequently, the congregation consisted of Nesta and Edward, a few of the women from the surrounding villages with young children – all of whom had been delivered by Agnes, Nesta's Aunt Rose, Sir Cyril's steward as the representative of the squire, and a couple of the village oldsters – men and women who were too old and infirm to carry out hard physical labour, but not yet so old that they were confined to their beds. Looking around, seeing the mourners chatting in the pale sunlight was a depressing sight Edward thought. A lifetime living and working in the community, and only a handful of people had come to mark Agnes' passing.

Walking out of the graveyard with the curate and Sir Cyril's steward, Alfred, Edward commented on the poor turnout, and was puzzled as both men pulled faces.

"I'm sorry, am I missing something? I thought that Agnes was well visited by everyone hereabouts. I'd thought more of them would want to come and pay their respects" he said, looking between the two men. The curate grimaced, and turned to Alfred who shrugged his shoulders, as if to say, we'd best tell him.

"People visited Agnes with their troubles, you're right. I don't want to speak ill of the dead, but that didn't mean she was well liked around here. You see she could be dismissive of people's problems and was often unkind. But what choice do the poor have if they need help? When they were desperate the choice was Agnes, or nothing." Said the curate sadly, blowing his impressively dripping nose into a large, and grubby handkerchief. "Yes, without meaning to gossip you understand, she was not above a bit of blackmail. You know the sort of things, young girl goes to her in trouble and Agnes helps, but there's a price to pay. And not just in cash."

Alfred gave the curate a sharp look. "That's enough now reverend. For all her faults and I won't deny that she had 'em, she's gone now. And gossiping about her won't help none. Let her rest in peace."

The curate, flustered at the rebuke, however mildly phrased, agreed readily. Together they made their excuses and hurried away, leaving Edward with a sense that they rather hoped that now Agnes was dead, whatever secrets she'd held would go to the grave with her. Idly Edward wondered what hold Agnes had had over the steward. He had seemed positively furtive at the mention of Agnes' blackmailing activities. As Edward stood in the sunlight, watching the mourners exchange gossip, leaving together in pairs and threes to head to back slowly to their homes, Edward felt acutely alone. The forest community was introspective. While he had been accepted, somewhat warily, by a few of the men, he knew that he was, and would remain an outsider. When a man from Gloucester or Monmouth was regarded uneasily as not being local, Edward was held in deep suspicion. His speech, manners, even his dress marked him out as different. Edward favoured the modern style of dress of a London gentleman. He wore well-cut waistcoats, close-fitting tailored jackets and bright silk cravats. In comparison the foresters in their rough homespun clothes dyed in the muted colours of the forest, he looked like a brightly coloured canary. The rich forest accent and curious dialect, a mixture of English, Welsh, and some words unique to the forest that had barely changed for hundreds of years jarred with the clear vowels of Edward's well educated, upper class accent. His voice was much more in keeping with the glittering drawing rooms of London society, than the tap rooms and kitchens of the forest. Watching Nesta chatting freely and happily with acquaintances from the surrounding hamlets, Edward felt increasingly alone and isolated. As if aware of the scrutiny, Nesta turned to look at Edward, a smile lighting her face. She bid farewell to her friends and walked over to rejoin Edward.

"Are you ready to leave Sir? If you're still thinking of taking a look at Agnes' place, we best leave soon, or we won't be back in time for your afternoon surgery." She said. Together they walked back to the horse and trap. With Edward driving,

Nesta began to give directions down the small country byways towards where Agnes isolated encroachment cottage stood. It was not long before Edward felt helplessly lost. The narrow track ways winding through the trees all looked remarkably similar to him. The old sunken tracks had been used for centuries twisted and turned, sometimes avoiding large rocks, sometimes avoiding marshy areas, and all looking much like one another. But Nesta directed Edward unerringly through the pathways that she had been wandering since she was a small girl. Eventually, she told Edward to pull over, and gathering her skirts in one hand, Nesta jumped elegantly down from the trap.

"We'll have to walk from here Sir" she said. "It's just a short ways up here" and she set off up a narrow, well worn track into the trees. Following behind, Edward scrambled to catch up, his smart leather soled shoes slipping on the wet grass underfoot. Eventually he caught Nesta as she emerged into a small clearing. Here the trees had been roughly hacked back, and to one side stood a small cottage. The encroachment cottage, built illegally on crown land, was roughly built from a mixture of wood, stones and mud. It looked like a witch's cottage from one of the Grimm brothers' fairy tales. The walls consisted of crudely made wooden uprights with long thin branches woven between them. Cracks were sealed with a mixture of straw, mud, and small stones, and the roof was covered in turfs in an attempt to make the whole structure weather tight. A rudimentary chimney was constructed into one wall, while a single unglazed window let in a little light. Carefully opening the rough wooden door, there was no lock, Edward went into the cottage, ducking to avoid the low lintel. Inside the cottage was freezing. A single room occupied the whole of the ground floor with a steep ladder staircase in one corner leading upstairs to the single bedroom. The low ceiling hung with bunches of drying herbs, rough slightly curving walls, and an all-pervading sense of damp and decay made the room seem positively cave-like. Gathered around the fireplace appeared to be Agnes' kitchen. One wall was filled with a dresser, displaying a few chipped plates and battered pans, along with various jars of dried herbs, grains and pulses. A wobbly table stood in the middle of the room, and a large basket chair, covered with cushions sat to one side of the fireplace. The whole cottage reeked of extreme poverty, and a miserable existence scraped out with little time or money for luxuries. Edward looked carefully around downstairs, fingering the dried herbs and opening the various bottles and jars and sniffing their contents. He was completely absorbed. Although he had visited the rookeries of London, areas that were no stranger to extreme poverty, he had never experienced anything quite like this cottage. To him, it seemed like the houses he had read about from the dark ages. That people should still live in such houses in the nineteenth century came as a complete surprise to him.

A shout from upstairs startled Edward from his inventory. While he had been engrossed searching through

Agnes's supply of potions, Nesta had slipped unnoticed up the ladder to the small sleeping area upstairs. What she had found had caused her a great deal of surprise. The upstairs chamber could not be more different to the one downstairs. While the walls downstairs were rough and drafty, the furniture battered, the floor simple beaten earth, upstairs was positively luxurious. Thick quilts and soft blankets covered the large bed. Pretty china ornaments covered every available surface. The upstairs window, while still unglazed, could be covered with a well-made, closely fitting wooden shutter, and the floor boards were covered with an array of rugs. More carpets and tapestries hung against the walls to keep out drafts. A small, well-made chest stood beside the finely wrought iron bedstead. Carefully removing an obviously high-quality lamp, Nesta lifted the lid and peaked inside. It was her shock at the contents of the chest that had led to her shout in surprise.

    The chest was full of money. A large bag of coins was open on the surface. Underneath were bags of sack cloth containing strange lumpy shapes. Peeking inside one bag, Nesta found a large brass platter, beautifully cast, but sadly tarnished. It reminded Nesta of one that belonged to a friend of her mother's and held pride of place on her dresser. As a young child, Nesta had always loved visiting her house, the platter always made her think that she had captured the sun, it shone so brightly. Continuing to rummage she wondered how Agnes could have come by so much money. It certainly could not have been honestly, as she could make little enough from her simple herbal remedies and basic treatments. So where had it come from? Hearing the floor boards creak behind her, she moved aside from the chest so that Edward could see what she had discovered. She watched the emotions chase across his face, from concern, to surprise, and finally puzzlement, and it was a puzzle. No-one ever had that much money, especially not in the precarious and illegal encroachments which could be demolished at any time. Nobody lived in the encroachments by choice. People lived there because they were desperate, but clearly Agnes had had a choice. She could have afforded any of the cottages of Berry Hill, or even a house in Coleford if she had wanted, yet she had chosen to live out here, in a ramshackle cottage on wasteland at the edge of the woods. Despite all the luxurious little touches, it remained a dismal place. Wind whistled in the trees, branches creaked, and various wild animals caused odd rustling and shrieking noises as they went about their business. It was a lonely, eerie place, somewhere that Nesta, so used to hustle and bustle of her family home, and now the quiet efficiency of the doctor's house, would never choose to live. Out here alone in the woods, anything could happen. All manner of creatures roamed the woods, and not all of them were friendly Nesta thought giving an involuntary shiver.

As if on cue the door downstairs creaked open. Nesta stifled a gasp and turned to Edward. He pressed his finger to his lips and tipped his head as he listened intently. It sounded as if someone was carefully and systematically searching the lower room. Knowing that it wouldn't take them long to fully explore the downstairs given how little was down there, Edward looked around to see if he could find somewhere for them to hide. Too late! The ladder moved slightly as it took the weight of a heavy adult. Edward held his breath as first the top of a man's hat became visible, followed by the rest of Alfred, Sir Cyril's steward. Unsure who was the most surprised they stared at each other for several long moments, before Alfred finally finished his climb. He stood at the top of the ladder looking down at them crouched besides the open chest, his view of its contents obscured by their bodies.

"Now then, Miss Phillips, Doctor, what've we got here then?" he said, full of suspicion. Alfred was well past middle age. A tall strong intelligent man, he had begun to work for Sir Cyril's father as a youth. Overtime, he worked his way up from being a general hand labouring on the home farm to managing Sir Cyril's estate as his right-hand man. Like many of the foresters he was taciturn, and wary of strangers, but he was also fair, judging a man by his own actions and what he saw of them with his own eyes, rather than listening to gossip. Fiercely defensive of his master's tenants, whom Alfred treated as part of a large, if often wayward, family. He had known Nesta since she was born. If she had got herself into trouble, he was determined to get her back out of it, and woe betide anyone who thought to harm her.

Alfred had heard much about the new doctor from Sir Cyril and his tenants. Everyone had spoken of him with praise, but Alfred intended to reserve judgement. A shrewd judge of character, he would watch and wait, and only then would he decide whether or not he was to be trusted. Finding the doctor in the bedroom of the deserted cottage with Thomas' eldest certainly wasn't something he had expected. Looking around carefully, Alfred examined the luxurious apartment. As he did so, he recognised various items that had formally graced the homes of other foresters. Clearly Agnes had not been content merely blackmailing people for money, she had also taken their most prized possessions from them, he thought grimly. Alfred narrowed his eyes, returning the items to their rightful homes was a problem for later. For now, he was more concerned as to what had brought the handsome new doctor and his pretty young maid to the bedroom of a deserted cottage.

  Alfred stood quietly watching the doctor. His work as steward dealing with petty infractions had taught him that if he patiently waited, people would often talk to fill the silence and give away more information than they had intended. It was often the case that if Alfred stood and quietly waited, tenants would confess to their indiscretions. Afterwards, many commented that there was no point in lying to Alfred, because he already knew the truth. For a moment Edward thought about spinning Alfred some yarn, wondering if he could lie his way out of the awkward situation. However, seeing the look of belligerence on Alfred's face convinced him that this would be a bad idea. All the while Alfred was watching Edward, he was watching him back. Glowering from under his thick bushy eyebrows, he had the look of a man who was not easily fooled, and one who would show his displeasure of being lied to. Edward took a deep breath. He would need to tell Alfred the truth, or at least some of it, he thought.

"Hullo again, Alfred. Yes, I can see that this is irregular. I see the inquest verdict didn't sit right with you either. I mean, it is possible that Miss Jenkins was murdered by a passing pedlar, or vagabond, but I find it highly unlikely. Highly unlikely indeed. So, Miss Phillips here kindly agreed to show me where Miss Jenkins lived. Just in case there was any evidence that had been missed you see... And well, what do you make of this?" He said, moving aside so that Alfred had a clear view of its contents for the first time. "Highly irregular I'd say. And I can't help but think it might relate to the matter that the good Reverend was alluding to earlier. Deliberately he tried to exclude Nesta from the conversation, in the hope that Alfred would then dismiss her as being irreverent. Edward considered that if he and Nesta had decided that Agnes must have been murdered by a local and come to check for evidence of their identity then Alfred might be here on the same mission. Or equally, he might be here because he knew only too well who the killer was and was determined to remove any evidence of his own guilt.

Alfred's eyes narrowed. He had heard Sir Cyril talk for hours about the new doctor, and how he had arrived with grand plans for a charitable hospital. The idea of the hospital had fired Sir Cyril's imagination. He was determined to see it completed knowing how much it could improve the lives of his tenants and workers. A somewhat old-fashioned man, Alfred knew that many of the locals disliked Sir Cyril who could be high handed and quick to take offence, behaving at times like a feudal overlord of times gone past. However, Alfred knew that he also cared deeply for his workers and tenants and took a keen interest in their welfare. Sir Cyril had spent much time and money trying to improve conditions for his tenants over the years, from building new cottages, like the one that Nesta had grown up in, to donating money to the small school. He did much to make the locals lives better for scant thanks. He had despised Agnes and her folk healing, but was powerless to prevent people from seeing her, particularly as there had been no alternative for those who couldn't afford Dr Thomas' high fees – which was just about everybody thought Alfred. Now this new doctor had come and was willing to treat the poor as well as the wealthy. Everybody was talking about how he had treated Jane Andrews without payment, and he was generally regarded as being a good doctor, if rather abrupt. However, Alfred knew that a highly trained and well-educated doctor was unlikely to take on the small practise in Coleford if they had any other options. So far, all Alfred's digging had discovered that the purchase of the house and practice had been arranged with almost indecent haste, suggesting to Alfred that Edward had needed to leave London quickly. What exactly had forced him to give up London, Alfred had yet to discover. However, he was confident that with time he would find out the doctor's secrets. After all he thought, smiling to himself, he always did.

Looking at Edward with the young, pretty Nesta, Alfred thought he could guess why the doctor had been forced to leave London. He pursed his lips in disapproval. While he knew that it was common enough for a master to carry on with his maid. Alfred knew all too many young women who had headed out to work in service full of hope, only to have to return home in disgrace, their good names ruined. Either forced into a marriage they didn't want to some obliging sort, or to pass their baby on, to a baby farm or a childless couple unlikely ever to see the bairn again. While the mother's reputation would be in tatters, it wasn't generally held to affect the character of the man at all. Alfred looked between Edward and Nesta. He wasn't sure that he believed Edward's story that they were here to look for Agnes' killer. He thought it far more likely that they had come here for an illicit tryst. However, he did agree that there was something peculiar about Agnes' death. The story that was being put about Agnes falling foul of a group of travelling ner'do-wells didn't ring true. Keeping a close eye on his community and anyone who might affect it, for good or ill, Alfred knew for a fact that no wandering bands had been in the forest since the end of September.

"May hap' you might be right Doctor." Alfred said slowly, weighing each word carefully "How much is there in yon chest?" He still hadn't made up his mind whether or not he completely trusted this new doctor, so he decided he would be circumspect. He could always bring him into his confidence later if he needed to, but hopefully it wouldn't come to that. Alfred could see no reason to share the reason for his visit to Agnes' ramshackle home.

"We'd only just found the money when we heard you arrive. Perhaps we could count it together?" Edward tentatively offered the olive branch and was glad when Alfred nodded his ascent. He had heard tell of Sir Cyril's steward from some of his patients. A good man, everybody said, but fiercely defensive of 'his' workers and tenants and interested in everything and anything that might affect them. If the stories were to be believed, Edward thought he couldn't be sure that if they found that one of the villagers was a murderer, whether Alfred would hand them over to the police and condemn them himself, or work with them to conceal their crime. For all Edward knew, Alfred himself could be the killer, if he had decided that Agnes' death would help the village in some way.

Together the two men carefully carried the awkward box downstairs. Nesta held back, wanting to give them plenty of room to man-handle the unwieldy box. As she started to follow, something caught her eye. Wedged between the bed frame and the cottage wall was a small brown leather notebook which had been hurriedly stuffed down behind the head board. Moving the chest had dislodged it just enough for Nesta to see the corner poking out the side of the bed. She pulled it out. Inside were page upon page of cramped writing. As Nesta flicked quickly through the pages, the poor light in the bedroom made it impossible for her to decipher the tiny writing. Thoughtfully, she tucked the book into her pocket. She didn't want to have to show her discovery to Alfred until she had had a chance to discuss it with Edward first. Hurrying down the ladder, she found Edward and Alfred sat at the rickety table together, carefully counting the coins. Pulling up a stool, she joined them at the table thankful that they had clearly not noticed her absence and began to help count. When they had finished they sat back and looked at each other. Alfred whistled through his teeth.

"Phew! Ten pounds, three shillings and six pence. Where on earth did she get all that from? That's far more than I expected" said Alfred mopping his brow with a rather grubby handkerchief.

Edward looked up sharply. "More than you expected? So, you expected to find something then?" he said.

"Aye, well like the good reverend said, Agnes used to take a bit extra from her patients to keep quiet like. But nothing much, six pence here, a cake there, you know the sort of thing. Just a little bit here and there from them that could's afford it, when times were hard" replied Alfred. He looked pointedly at Nesta "Mostly it'd be a few pennies from the housekeeping to keep quiet about her helping get rid of a bairn to spare a woman shame before she was married like." Alfred was genuinely puzzled. He had had no idea that Agnes' blackmailing activities had been so prolific.

Nesta turned to Alfred from where she had been sat quietly at the end of the table. "I hope you are not casting aspersions on my honour Mr Turner", she said, and although her tone was light and there was a smile on her face, the look in her eyes told Alfred that if he pursued that line of enquiry he would find himself in deep water. Knowing only too well the anger that both Nesta's mother Mary and Aunt Rose could display if riled, Alfred decided that discretion was definitely the better part of valour on this occasion. He remembered clearly the passionate way that Rose had harangued him when he had questioned why Mary had not been seen about the hamlet for a few weeks. Wincing as he recalled the scathing tirade, he looked at Nesta appraisingly. Yes, he thought, she definitely has more than a little of her aunt and mother about her. Normally placid and good natured, when roused they were transformed into screaming harpies using the kind of invective more commonly associated with the basest of fish wives. Wiping his face again with the large handkerchief, Alfred sheepishly apologised to the doctor and to Nesta.

"Now then, what are we going to do with this money? We can't leave it here. Word'll get out and it's too much of a temptation. Where can we store it safely?" Edward mused. He was thinking about whether or not he could take it back to his house. It would probably be safe, locked away in his medicine store, but he was wary of taking it, knowing that if he did whispers of him stealing the blackmail money would almost certainly follow. Any kind of gossip could harm him badly, but being linked, however spuriously, to a woman who extorted money from patients could destroy his practice completely. Patients wanted, needed, to know that their embarrassing ailments would be kept secret. Edward's tutors at medical school had impressed upon him that patients valued skill, discretion, and confidentiality in a doctor, and not necessarily in that order. If it was thought that Edward would gossip, sell their secrets, or somehow use his intimate knowledge against them, they would shun him and travel elsewhere. His practice would fail.

Alfred was also looking at the box uncomfortably. "Well, I suppose we could take it to Sir Cyril's strong room, but he'll be loath to have anything to do with this" thinking much the same as Edward. There was likely to be a lot of gossip surrounding their find, and Alfred knew that Sir Cyril would want to keep it well away from him, lest he be tainted by association.

"What about the Coroner?" piped up Nesta. She understood both men's reluctance to take the money away, but equally, Edward was right. If it stayed here someone would be sure to take it. To her mind the coroner would be an ideal person to hold it. After all, they represented law and order so to her seemed to be the natural choice to hold what could be evidence.

"Aye", Alfred nodded slowly "Dr Rudge might hold it, until it's needed for a trial. And coming from Monmouth, he'd likely not be seen to be connected to it. Good idea Nesta! As it happens Sir Cyril is heading off to see Dr Rudge this afternoon. If I takes it back to the manor with me, likely Sir Cyril can take it with him in his coach. That'll do nicely." Alfred consulted his large turnip watch. Stuffing it back into his waistcoat pocket, Alfred picked up the box with some difficulty. "It's eleven o'clock already. Sir Cyril is due to leave at twelve noon, so I'd best get this up to the Hall if we're going to send it in the coach. Good day to you, Doctor, Miss Phillips." Inclining his head towards them in greeting, Alfred hurried away.

Nesta let out a sigh of relief. Turning to Edward, she put her hand in her pocket to remove the note book. Just as she started to pull the book out she stopped. Was that the sharp crack of a dry stick snapping? Listening carefully, she shot Edward a warning glance that he should keep quiet. Nothing! Nesta started to relax. I must have imagined that stick snapping she thought, I'm so on edge, which isn't surprising really. She was just putting her hand in her pocket again when she heard the leaves outside rustle, this time right underneath the window. Quickly, she stood up and put her head outside the window, but not quite quickly enough to catch whoever had been lurking there. She just caught a fleeting glimpse of a person dodging into the undergrowth. Edward came to stand beside her.

"What was it? Some kind of animal? A deer maybe?" he asked, silently berating himself for bringing her with him. It was unfair of him to ask her to accompany him to search

Agnes' cottage. After all he had had no idea what they might have found there, and it might have been dangerous.

    Nesta turned. "There's no deer in the forest! Not anymore least ways, the Verderers been hunting them down, even Pete can't find them anymore. Besides," she added scathingly, "when you ever seen deer listening under windows and leaving footprints like that!" There in soft mud outside the window was the clear footprint of booted foot.

Chapter Fourteen

Between the demands of Edward's patients and the long list of chores that Miss Bates had asked Nesta to complete, it was late evening before Nesta had a chance to show Edward the journal she had found up at Agnes' cottage. The hall clock was striking nine o'clock before she was able to finally hang up her apron on the hook on the back of the kitchen door. Nesta stretched, easing her aching back. It had been a long day, and she had only just finished setting the kitchen to rights after the evening meal. A pile of pots and pans were neatly stacked drying on the drainer and the table and floor had been freshly scrubbed. A full kettle sat ready on the range so that Nesta could have boil water for tea without having to first collect water from the pump in the yard outside.

As she began to head up the stairs to her attic bedroom, Nesta saw a glimmer of light shining out from underneath the door to the doctor's study. Remembering that she had not yet had a chance to discuss the book that she had found with him, Nesta knocked tentatively on the door, loath to disturb him when he was working. Nesta had quickly learnt that he hated to be disturbed when he was engrossed in medical problems and would make his annoyance only too clear. Hearing a chary "come in", Nesta took a deep breath and entered the room.

Edward looked up from his work to see Nesta standing in the doorway. He had returned from Five Acres to find several patients waiting for him, and while most of the problems had been minor and easily remedied, he had been particularly vexed by the case of a young boy with a sore throat. While Edward was at first ready to dismiss it as a simple case of tonsillitis with the patient brought to him by an over anxious mother; consulting Dr Thomas' extensive patient notes he had soon realised that the boy had suffered numerous attacks over his short life. Each time he had been sent away with a prescription for laudanum. Unlike many of his profession, Edward did not hold with the modern approach of treating all ailments from the common cold and diarrhoea to post surgical pain following amputation with morphine either in its pure format or mixed with alcohol to form tincture of laudanum. Now he was consulting one of his medical text books, looking for the description that he remembered from his days in medical school of removing the tonsils to prevent their repeated infection. He had asked the mother to return in the morning to discuss her son's treatment and wanted to make sure that he could explain to her clearly the procedure.

"Yes?" he said testily, keen to return to his reading. Continuing to flick through his books he saw Nesta approaching him "Well, what is it? Can you not see I am busy here?"

"I found this up at Agnes' place earlier, stuffed behind the bed. I was going to show you earlier, but didn't like too, what with us being spied upon. I think it's some kind of diary, or journal, but I can't make head nor tail of it." Nesta cautiously handed the book over. "It must be something important though. What else could Alfred have been looking for up there?"

Edward turned the small book over and over in his hands. It was a battered leather journal, small enough to fit into a pocket, but large enough that each page could hold a full day's news. It looked much like the journals he had seen his sisters use as diaries, recording the day's events and tribulations with excitement. The cover had a well thumbed and battered look to it, with the corners turning back slightly, and the leather covering the spine well creased. Inside the pages were creased and dog-eared, some bearing marks from water or food. As Edward flicked through the book, he saw page after page covered in tiny, crabbed writing. It was packed so close together, and covered with so many ink splats, that it was difficult to even make out the letters and numbers. Straining his eyes in the dim lamplight to decipher even the smallest part, Edward tried, and failed, to understand anything written in the book.

"Can you understand it at all Doctor?" asked Nesta. "I can make out the initials, and there are clearly some sums of money, but beyond that... It's like she's written in code, the words don't make any sense, or leastways they don't to me." Chuckling quietly to herself at the thought of the reaction of her former schoolmaster to any writing presented to him in such a state, Nesta stood smiling shaking her head gently. "In't her writing awful though? The master would have summit to say if I'd tried to hand in work like that I can tell you!"

Edward was pleasantly surprised. "You went to school? You can read and write?" Thinking it unusual that anyone, let alone a girl, from an impoverished household would have attended school at all.

"Aye, I can read, and write, and figure numbers, and recite my catechism too!" Nesta replied indignantly. "Go to school, 'course I went to school! We're not heathens out here!"

Edward held his hands up in a gesture of peace. "I'm sorry Nesta, it's just that, back home in London it's unusual that's all. Many of my former patients couldn't read or write. There are schools, but many can't afford the fees, or the parents need their children to work, to earn a wage, so the children don't go. I meant no offence. Please forgive me."

The hostility left Nesta. "Aye, well a few years ago, you'd have been right. There was no schools, or what there were, were hard to get to 'cause the roads were so bad. Grandma and grandpa, they didn't go to school like. But then

Mr Procter came, and he built Christ Church and the Forest School. Da went to school, and so did Uncle Samuel. And so did I." She finished proudly. Edward looked at her, he was genuinely surprised that Nesta had had anything more than a very basic education, and expected that she would have been working, in some capacity at least, as soon as she was able to. He was pleased. Not just that she was able to read and write for her own sake, but also that it made her considerably more useful to him. He wondered whether he would be able to teach her to carry out some of the more basic tasks such as making up and dispensing prescriptions. An intelligent and literate helper could be very useful to him indeed, particularly when, if, the new hospital was founded. Looking back at the book, Edward decided that he would set Nesta a task to test her a little. He handed the book to her.

"It's too difficult to try and decipher Agnes' appalling handwriting and the words at the same time. If I give you some paper and pen, can you try to copy out the book in a fair hand? That might give us more of chance of understanding what she has written."

Nesta smiled, taking the book from him. "Of course, sir, shall I start now?"

Looking at Nesta, Edward could see the tiredness etched on her face.

"No, it's been a long day. Tomorrow will be soon enough. I suggest we both retire. I'll find you ink and paper in the morning. We'll have to think of something to tell Miss Bates as well. I don't think that we should tell anyone about this book. Not yet anyway." Taking the book back from a reluctant Nesta, Edward placed it in the drawer to his desk and locked it securely. He then gently shooed Nesta from his study, locking the door firmly behind them. As Edward followed Nesta upstairs, he couldn't help but appreciate her graceful figure. When he headed towards his bedroom at the front of the house, Nesta turned to him to bid him a goodnight. Looking into her bright eyes, he felt an almost overwhelming desire to lean forward and kiss her. He quickly muttered his goodnights and hurried to his room, closing the door firmly behind him and leaning back against it. Kind, intelligent, literate and pretty, he thought. Nesta would make someone an excellent wife. But not him. They were separated too far, both in station, after all he was a Doctor, and her a maid, the daughter of miner, and in experience. Edward imagined the reactions of his parents if he introduced them to Nesta as his wife. They would be horrified. Or would they? After all, his parent's marriage had caused something of a family scandal at the time. His father George was a sailor. The son of a tailor, he had left the family business to go to sea as a midshipman in the Royal Navy. There he had worked his way up without patronage on merit alone. Serving as a lieutenant on a naval frigate patrolling the coast, he had met Edward's mother Jane when he captured and boarded a French privateer. Expecting to find a hold full of brandy and fine French lace, they had been most taken aback when lifting the hatching they had instead found several frightened civilians. It had been bad enough for her to have been taken prisoner when their ship was set upon at the end of a long voyage back from her father's holdings in the West Indies. Confined to the ships hold as a battle raged overhead had been a horrifying experience. When the hatches were finally raised, not by a privateer, but rather by a dashing naval lieutenant, it was, as his mother said, enough to turn any young girls head. It had been love at first sight for both of them. They had married as soon as they could in a small church in Plymouth, the frigate's home port. His grandfather, a minor Lord, had been less than impressed to find that his youngest daughter had married a young lieutenant with no connections. He had cut the couple off for a while, all the time expecting Jane to come crawling back home in disgrace. That she hadn't remained a source of wonder to him. As time passed, and George was promoted to Post Captain, commanding a frigate of his own, his opinion had softened, and Jane had eventually been welcomed back into the family. Edward had fond memories of visiting his grandparents Devon estate as a child, playing in the fields and woods with his many cousins. Yet however many balls and soirees his cousins invited him to, he had always felt something of an outsider. He knew that some doors would remain firmly closed to him. Talking to his grandfather one evening, he had learnt that his future was all mapped out for him. He would join the family shipping firm, and with hard work and diligence, he could become a trusted manager, running the company for his oldest cousin who would eventually inherit both the money and the title. The idea of working for a cousin, being dependant on him, and like a faithful hound, being expected to be suitably grateful for any favours that he dispensed, convinced Edward that he would need to learn a profession. Something that would mean he would be accepted in his own right, rather than merely following on his cousins' coat tails. A chance meeting with a former shipmate of his father's – a man who had served as surgeon on several of his father's ships – encouraged Edward to embark on a career in medicine, a decision he had not regretted. Living in rented rooms in London, he had worked both at St Thomas', and in private practice. His career had been progressing well, and his private practice expanding to include some well-known society figures, his future looked golden.

That was until *she* came along. Edward felt the bitterness well up inside him again, as he considered yet again how her lies had ruined him. Patients had quickly dropped him, and friends and acquaintances snubbed him, turning their backs to him when he tried to greet them and refusing to accept his cards. A petition had even been raised at St Thomas's to have him removed. Rather than face the ignominy of dismissal, Edward had chosen to resign hoping to preserve what little dignity he had left. Yet, was it such a bad thing he thought. Here he was with a large house, a comfortable living, the chance to establish his own hospital and make a real difference to the local people. He was, he admitted, happier now than he had been in a long time. A small voice whispered at the back of his mind, and there was Nesta.

Chapter Fifteen

Friday 14th November, 1851.

The next day, Nesta rose early and hurried to complete her chores. By the time Miss Bates had stirred herself and made her way sedately downstairs, Nesta had already prepared and served Edward's breakfast, and was busily tidying the kitchen. A pot bubbled on the stove, full of a thick, warming stew for their lunch, and bread rose in its tins. For the first time since she had arrived, Nesta saw Miss Bates give her a genuine smile of approval. Walking to the stove and carefully lifting the lid of pot with a fold of her apron, Miss Bates stirred the stew gently. Instantly the kitchen was filled with a rich savoury smell. Miss Bates let out a sigh of appreciation.

"My Nesta, you have been busy. And this smells delicious!" she said warmly, peering into the pot, Miss Bates tried to identify the different ingredients of the stew. "What's in here? I can see carrot, and parsnip, and tatties of course, and is that a bit of scrag end? But I can smell something else. What is it?"

Nesta looked up and beamed with pride at the praise for her cooking. "It's just a few veggies that were lying around the scullery, a bit of mutton, some barley, but what you can smell is the chickweed. Mother always adds some when she can find it, and Uncle Samuel brought us some this morning." Seeing the blank look on Miss Bates face she continued "Doctor James asked Uncle Samuel to come and cut back that big old chestnut in the garden. Doctor James says it's blocking the light to his study, so he wants it taking down".

"Oh aye. He mentioned he wanted it going. Well I dare say he knows best. What poor old Dr Thomas would say I don't know" replied Miss Bates giving a prodigious sniff. Carefully returning the lid to the pan, she sat herself down at the table and poured a cup of tea. "Now then lass, I can see you've got lunch well in hand, and the kitchen is all cleaned. Have you started on the dining room yet? And I think it's high time that the hall floor was scrubbed. Yes well. I've got some errands to run. I need to see the butcher. That hogget he sent us. More like mutton, tough as old leather it were. Well, I'll just have a bite of breakfast and be off. Once you've finished up in here, you can move onto the hall."

"Yes Mrs Bates." Nesta gave a small curtsey and headed off to the scullery to collect scrubbing brush, coal soap and bucket. As she filled the metal bucket half full of hot water from the range she sighed inwardly. It was all very well Miss Bates telling her to scrub the hall floor - and she was right, it did need doing - but her back was already aching and her knees were sore. Still she thought, it was easier work than being up at the pit. At least she was in the warm and dry. Well, nearly dry anyway – looking down at the hem of her skirts she could see that she had already managed to soak them. Carrying her heavy bucket of water, she moved onto the hall, beginning by the front door so that she could work her way back towards the kitchen. As she scrubbed, her mind strayed to Agnes' diary. Aimlessly she wondered what secrets it would contain and whether it would give a clue to who her murderer was. Although she glowed inside with pleasure that she was to be entrusted with copying out the diary, she still felt slightly aggrieved that Edward had presumed she was illiterate. Most of her friends and neighbours were able to read, if only a little of the Bible and enough to sign their own names. It was only a very few that still had to make their mark as a cross rather than write their name. And those were mostly itinerates who passed through in the summers, or some of the older folk living up in the encroachments. Although Nesta was proud of her ability to read and write - and knew she was better than most – she didn't appreciate quite how unusual she was.

Scrubbing the floor, her mind far away, Nesta began to quietly sing. A gentle, lilting tune that her mother often sang to herself while she worked and had taught her to sing, just as Mary had learnt it from her mother. Although Nesta didn't understand many of the words, she knew enough of the old forest speech to know that it was a song of the hills, the valleys and the forest, in old forest speech. Somehow whenever she sang it she found herself transported to the deepest reaches of the forest, back in time before the enclosures when deer and other animals ran free, as the first people came and found a land rich in plants, minerals and animals.

Working away in his study, Edward heard the gentle sound of singing from the hallway. Soft and calming, he found himself putting down his pen to listen. Finally, he could resist the temptation no longer, and went to peer out of his study door. There he saw Nesta with her back to him, skirts pulled up to keep them from the wet floor, scrubbing away. He smiled, listening to her beautiful voice; the more he saw of her, the more he came to appreciate her qualities. Although she had not yet worked for him for a full week, Edward could not imagine the house without her cheerful presence. The house was already cleaner and more welcoming. She was an excellent cook, and even Miss Bates seemed to have unbent slightly, pleased to have had so many of the household tasks taken away from her. Surprised that she should be literate, Edward was hopeful that she could also take on some of his more mundane paper work, perhaps even be trained to make up prescriptions. He smiled at his good fortune to have found such a helpful, useful maid, her lively presence having done much to ease his sense of isolation and loneliness. His thoughts were interrupted by the harsh sound of Miss Bates voice.

"Dr James! Is there something you require?" she asked, bristling with indignation. Miss Bates had just come into the hall to check on Nesta, and to tell her that she was off to the see the butcher, when she had found Dr James standing in the doorway to his study staring at Nesta working with her skirts all hitched up. Miss Bates had no doubt that Nesta was unaware of the attention and surprised herself by feeling oddly protective of the young girl. Both Nesta and the doctor started. Edward went bright red, realising that he had been staring at Nesta. He cleared his throat nervously. Unwilling to explain that he had been thinking about the quality of Nesta's cooking, he quickly searched his mind for an excuse to have been there. Of course! The journal that Nesta was to transcribe. Now how to ask her to make a start without alerting Miss Bates to the fact that they had Agnes' journal?

"Um, yes Miss Bates. Nesta, once you have finished the floor, would you come into my study. I'd like you to start on that additional task that we discussed last night" he said looking at Nesta meaningfully, trying to remind her not to mention the journal in front of Miss Bates. Unfortunately, his cryptic remarks only served to worry Miss Bates further; she glanced quickly at Nesta to see how she was taking the doctor's new request.

"Yes Doctor" Nesta replied uncomfortably. She had gone pink to think that both Miss Bates, and the doctor had heard her singing. She had often been told that she had a good voice, regularly being singled out by the Rector to sing solo hymns on special occasions in church. It was more that she had been singing *that* song. It was a beautiful, but very old fashioned. Much better if she had been singing one of the modern songs that came out of the music halls. Something more sophisticated, like "Lay a Garland", something that would show Edward that the forest folk could be cultured.

Lips pursed in disapproval, Miss Bates looked between the Doctor standing guiltily in the doorway, and Nesta pink with embarrassment on the floor before him. "Hmpfh! Special task indeed! Well I must say, I expected better of you Nesta! Whatever will your mother say, carrying on like this? Thought you had more sense lass!" Nesta was even more confused. Puzzlement at how Miss Bates knew about her task at copying out the journal, turned to sudden understanding as she realised that Miss Bates thought she was going to be providing a different, altogether more intimate service for the Doctor. Horror, mixed with shame, and she started to splutter her denials, her face going redder than ever. Edward squirmed with embarrassment, torn between wanting to explain about the journal to Miss Bates to protect his and Nesta's reputations, and not wanting to explain how they came to have Agnes' journal in his desk drawer. Miss Bates interpreted his uncertainty for guilt. She gave him a withering look, and sniffed prodigiously, somehow managing to convey her complete distain and disapproval with that single sniff.

The force of emotion in Miss Bates' glare took Edward quite by surprise. He had never been found himself confronted with such derision. Eyes wide, he stared at her, shocked that she would think he would use his position to corrupt Nesta. At first he was angry, thinking only of the slur on his honour, then he looked at her more closely. She had gone deathly pale, sweat beaded on her forehead and even from a distance Edward could see a great vein pulsing on her temple. Wide-eyed, she looked slightly manic, as if only she was only just holding in a great well of emotion. Fearing that she might collapse if pushed any further, Edward went to her. Taking her hands in his, he looked straight into her eyes, speaking kindly and gently.

"No! No, Miss Bates, you have entirely the wrong idea. I am not.... My intentions are purely honourable towards Nesta I promise you. I am not the kind of man who would take advantage of his maids so callously." Looking closely at her, he could see that she too was haunted by her past. Turning quickly, she hurried off to the kitchen before the tears that she had been fighting back could at last overwhelm her. Edward watched her go; he had been surprised by her outburst, not just that she would cast him as such a cad, but also that she would care enough about Nesta to try to protect her. He was well aware that in many households an outburst like hers, however justified, would result in her being instantly dismissed - likely without the references required to secure a new post. As Nesta tried to follow her, Edward reached out and touched her arm.

"No Nesta, not yet. Give her a little time to compose herself. Please finish the floor. Then if you could join me in my study, you could begin to transcribe the diary. We must find out what it says." With that, Edward returned to his study, shutting the door firmly behind him. Always worried when confronted with such raw emotions, he felt strangely discombobulated, both surprised at the role in which Miss Bates had cast him – did he really appear as a sexual predator? - but also that she cared enough about Nesta, who she had viewed as poaching a job that rightly belonged to her niece, to leap to her defence, possibly at the risk of her own livelihood. Sitting down at his desk he mused that while he understood how the body worked, the ways of the human mind were still uncharted territory to him.

  Having finished cleaning the floor at last, Nesta stood up and stretched her back. Carefully she carried the heavy bucket of dirty water out through the back door to pour it away into the open sewer that ran down the middle of the alley to help wash away the rubbish. Pouring the water, she wrinkled her nose, it was definitely smellier here in the town she thought when compared with her home at Berry Hill. There was much less waste there. Scraps of leftover food were fed to the pig, odd bits of peel and carrot tops would be composted for use in the vegetable plot, and drains swilled with the leftover washing water. The communal earth closet was set right back by the pig sties. It was smelly, but also confined to a small area. Here, everyone dumped waste into a small open sewer that ran down the back alley behind the houses. That there were many more households, and that the sewer had to run some distance before it was finally discharged into the brook, meant that the smell was considerably worse, even now in November, when lower temperatures and generally wetter weather helped to keep the worse of the smell at bay. In the height of summer, the smell would no doubt be unbearable. Returning to the house, she saw the shadow of a man approaching her quietly from behind. The arm of the shadow raised, and Nesta turned quickly dropping the bucket with a clatter as she did so. Thinking she was about to be attacked, she braced herself for a blow. A scream died in her throat as she came face to face with a tall, dark haired man.

"Uncle Samuel! Oh you gave me a fright! How are you getting on with the tree?" she asked breathlessly. As she bent to pick up her fallen bucket she caught a fleeting glance of a person darting through the open side gate into the back alley her view of the gate, nearly, but not quite entirely blocked by her uncle's bulk. Clearly Uncle Samuel had been meeting somebody in the doctor's back garden that he didn't want Nesta to know about.

"I'll be done soon. I'm just taking a quick breather. No chance of a cup of char is there love?" he asked, directing her back into the kitchen and away from the alley.

"Yes, Uncle Samuel. Come on in" she said opening the door to the warm kitchen. Samuel sat himself down awkwardly on the stool by the range, turning his hands towards the warmth. Nesta busied herself with the tea pot. She also started to lay a tray, ready to take a cup of tea through to Doctor. As she did so Miss Bates came into the kitchen, busily tying her bonnet under her chin.

She nodded to Samuel, "Mr Phillips" she said.

Starting to stand, Samuel replied "Good morrow to you, Miss Bates".

Greetings somewhat uncomfortably exchanged, Miss Bates turned to Nesta, "Right, I'll be off now Nesta, you mind you take the doctor his tea now. And don't you be warming your hands too long Mr Phillips. You'll be getting chilblains if you don't take care." And with that she bustled out of the door.

Nesta picked up the tray and took it through to the doctor's study. She saw that he had set up a small table for her in the window at the far end of the room, on the table sat the dairy and a fresh pad of paper.

He looked up and smiled. "Ah Nesta. Thank-you. I have put everything you need on the table. I may have some patients later, but I trust that I can rely upon your discretion? Confidentially is everything in medicine. People, they, well they tell you things they would tell nobody else. I may need to ask you to leave if anyone wishes you to. Please don't be offended if they do, it's just that they might have something to discuss that they find particularly embarrassing."

Nesta sat at the table in the window. She hadn't expected to feel so nervous and so excited, to be starting work transcribing Agnes' journal. Excited that she might find some important clues, she was also nervous that she might discover something that she would rather not know. Doubts gnawed at her. She knew that various friends and relations had visited Agnes over the years for help. Some of them, like her mother using her as a midwife, had been open and honest, but Nesta was sure that there must have been plenty others that visited Agnes for more questionable treatments. Looking through Agnes' journal felt almost like spying on her friends and neighbours to Nesta. That she might find out peoples darkest and most hidden secrets, ones that they had paid good money to conceal, made her feel like she was complicit in Agnes' blackmailing schemes. Nesta rubbed her face with both hands, trying to reconcile her shame at prying into others secrets on the one hand, with her desire to catch Agnes' killer on the other. As she glanced across the room she saw that Edward had stopped writing, and was watching her, his bright blue eyes shone with pity and disappointment.

"If you don't feel that you can transcribe the journals, just say Nesta" he told her kindly. While he was disappointed, he thought that it's not really surprising that she can't read and write properly. It was a shame of course that she'd overstated her abilities. A literate helper would have been a boon, but maybe in time he could teach her, or employ a secretary he thought. "Many people find reading and writing difficult, it's nothing to be ashamed of."

"It's not that I can't, Doctor, it's, it's whether or not I should! What if I find out something I'd rather not have known? How will I be able to look my friends in the eye if I know that they have got rid of a bairn or have some kind of...

sinful illness? Why if I read this, then... then... I'm no better than she was!" she blurted out. Edward was taken aback. It had never really occurred to him that they shouldn't read the journal. Yes, people had gone to some considerable lengths to keep the contents hidden from the general public, but that was true of so many things. Of course, ideally, they would just be able to burn the journal as the spiteful tittle-tattle that it was, but he felt sure that a clue to the identity of the killer would be within those pages. Thinking hard, Edward could come up with no other way in which they could learn who had a sure motive to kill Agnes. After all, it's not like they could go around and ask people to tell them if they had ever been blackmailed by Agnes. Nobody would ever admit to it.

"But of course, we must know the contents of that book. It's the only way we will ever catch Agnes' killer. Besides, if they killed Agnes, what's to stop them killing again? It's distasteful yes, but it needs to be done. It's for the greater good. It's not like we're going to use the information for our own gain, not like Agnes did."

Somewhat mollified by his arguments, Nesta reached forward and took a sheet of paper from the top of the stack. Checking the pen had a good, fresh nib, she dipped it carefully into the inkwell, and first wiping the excess ink off on the side of the well, she began to write. The task was harder than she had expected. Agnes' writing was small and crabbed. All long lines of steeply sloping writing tightly squashed together with little punctuation and few gaps between words. As she became more familiar with the style, Nesta became faster and faster at copying it out, however, she soon discovered that despite her misgivings, she wasn't likely to learn any secrets from Agnes' journal. Reviewing the first few pages that she had copied out, she soon realised that they were complete gibberish.

Nesta groaned with frustration. It didn't make any sense! Some of the words were familiar, but others she didn't recognise. There also appeared to be several abbreviations, some of which were common, but others were of Agnes own devising, and the spelling was appalling. A few words Nesta could perhaps hazard a guess at, but there were many other words, where she had no idea whether they were abbreviations, English words spelt incorrectly enough that she couldn't understand them, or in another language altogether. Another language! Was that it, she thought excitedly. Nesta dredged her memory, she was sure she had heard once that while her mother was a local, Agnes father was from somewhere foreign? Surely it was possible that the books were written partly in her father's native tongue. If only she could remember where it was though, but the memory was fleeting and elusive. Nesta's train of thought was interrupted by the sound of the door bell. Heading out into the hall, Nesta found that she was still holding the journal. She placed it down on the side table, smoothed down her apron with her hands, and opened the front door. There on the top step stood her cousin Jane, Frederick just visible, peeking around her skirts.

"Good morrow Nesta" she said, "is the Doctor available?" Nesta smiled a greeting and explained that the doctor was in his study. Welcoming Jane into the hallway, she helped Jane to remove her coat and hat, hanging the coat neatly on the stand by the door. Chattering away, Nesta turned too fast, catching the journal with the sleeve of the coat, so that it fell to the floor. Seeing the book on the floor, Jane bent down to pick it up and return it to its place.

"Careful Nesta, you always were clumsy" Jane chided. As she looked at the book that she had picked up, the colour drained from her face. Gingerly turning the book over, as if it was a bomb that might explode at any moment, Jane starred from the journal to Nesta with muted horror. With a single agonised "No!" Jane fainted dead away in front of her. Nesta watched Jane collapse as if in slow motion. She reached out her arms and just managed to catch her before she hit the cold, hard floor tiles.

"Doctor! Edward! Please help, quickly! Frederick, you go off to the kitchen. Fetch a glass of water." Nesta shouted, lowering Jane to the floor as gently as possible. Nesta was sat on the floor, Jane's head cushioned in her lap as Edward came racing from his study. Concern flitted across his face, as he knelt next to Jane. Taking her wrist, he felt for her pulse; it was fast, but strong and steady.

"She's just fainted" he said tersely. Scooping Jane up in his strong arms, he carried her into his consulting room and placed her on the patients' coach. Reaching forward to loosen the stays of her corset, Edward suddenly paused. He thought better of it. While it was necessary to loosen the corset stays to allow her to breathe more easily, it could be misconstrued. He looked towards Nesta who had followed him into the room.

"Here" he said "can you loosen her corset please? It will help her to breathe. I'll just go to the kitchen and find Mrs Andrews a glass of water." With that Edward rushed away to the kitchen. Nesta hurried to do the doctors bidding. Reaching under Jane so that she could ease the laces at back of her dress, Nesta felt the thickening of her waist, her eyes widened. She hadn't known that Jane was pregnant. Not that it was any of her business, she thought. Nesta knelt on the floor next to the couch, gently stroking the back of Jane's hand, and softly calling her name. Jane's eyes began to flicker. She blinked hard several times, and then looked around her, disconcertedly wondering how she had ended up on the patients' couch. As she tried to struggle up, Nesta placed her hands on her shoulders and kindly but firmly, made her lie back down.

Nesta spoke soothingly. "Now Jane, don't you worry. You had a bit of a turn, 'tis all. The doctor has gone to fetch you a glass of water. You just rest here. He'll be back in a minute." She looked towards the door willing him to return. Both Jane and Nesta started as the door was flung open, hitting the wall with a resounding crash. Ornaments wobbled on the shelves, and pictures jumped on their rail. In charged Samuel, leaving a trail of large, muddy footprints and stray bits of twig and leaf behind him. Edward was close behind him, his face red with rage, grabbing at Samuel's arm, trying to hold him back.

"Now see here sir! I really must protest. How dare you invade my surgery without permission! I know that Mrs Andrew's is your cousin and you must be concerned, but still. It isn't proper man! Now I must insist that you return to the kitchen. This instant!" Edward said sternly. While his voice was pitched low so as not to cause Jane any further distress, it was clear to Nesta that he was furious that his patient's privacy had been violated and was only just keeping his temper in check. Samuel continued heedlessly, long days working down the mine hewing coal by hand had given Samuel immense strength. Despite Edward's tall strong frame, Samuel was able to bat aside the doctor's restraining hand as though he were no more than an irritating fly. Normally a gentle man, he had eyes only for Jane. Racing to her side, he shoved Nesta carelessly out of his way, eyes frantically searching for any sign of hurt or injury. Seeing no obvious signs of injury, he took Jane's small hands in his larger work calloused ones.

"Jane. My love! Are you alright? What happened?" he asked her, desperately seeking reassurance. Jane visibly relaxed in his presence. For a moment it was as if Edward and Nesta had ceased to exist to them, their whole world was filled with one another. Even to the naive Nesta, and the unworldly Edward, it was clear that Jane and Samuel's relationship was much more than just cousins. Messages passed silently between the two lovers. Then the moment passed, and they became aware of Edward and Nesta's presence again.

While Samuel looked by turns embarrassed and afraid, while Jane looked up at the doctor and Nesta defiantly. She sat herself up, waving away Samuel and Edward's concerns.

"I am quite recovered thank-you. I had a shock, that's all." She said, quietly but firmly. She closed her eyes for a second, gathering her thoughts. "It's all been in vain, Sam. They've got the bitches' journal." Samuel's eyes grew wide. He looked fearfully at the doctor.

"It's not how it looks" Samuel said beseechingly.

"No? Perhaps you'd like to explain?" Edward asked. His mind raced, unsure of what it was they were supposed to already know. Although he could guess, he thought grimly.

"Me and Jane, we was childhood sweethearts" Samuel began, "we were going to get married, but then I had a falling out with my old man, and I had to go away for a bit. When I got back..."

"I had to marry him, Sam. You know that. I didn't know where you were, they wouldn't tell me. Pa just told me you'd gone, and like as not, I'd never see you again. They told me I needed a husband, and that Pete was willing to take me, soiled goods though I was. Pa said he was a good man. That I wouldn't, couldn't do better, and that if I didn't marry him, we'd be out on the streets. He *made* me marry him!" Jane said, desperate to convince her lover that she hadn't deserted him. That her love had stayed as strong as his own.

"Aye, I know lass. I know." He said affectionately, squeezing her hand. He looked the doctor straight in the eye "But Pete, he was a right bastard. He beat her, constantly. He'd have killed her. Even Uncle Will saw he'd made a mistake. There was summit rotten in him."

Edward nodded "I see. And Fredrick, was he your husband's child?" Jane shook her head crying quietly, "and this child?"

"He's Samuels too. I think that was what pushed Pete over the edge in the end. He knew that it couldn't be his. He'd not...."

"Claimed his matrimonial rights?" suggested Edward delicately.

Jane nodded "Aye, we'd not... well you know... in a long time. The bairn couldn't be his. But I don't know how he found out about it. I hadn't told him." Jane's face became dark as she remembered with horror that last evening with her husband. "That night, he knew. Someone must have told him and he was in a fearful rage. He came storming into the house cussing and swearing. Crashing up the stairs, he dragged me out of bed by my hair, and to the top of the stairs. He threw me down on the floor and started hitting and kicking me. All the time he were shouting how I was a faithless whore, a slut! That me Pa had made a fool of him once, and he wouldn't be taken for a fool again. I knew then that he meant to kill me. I tried to stand, to run, to fight back, but he pushed me. He pushed me down the stairs. That's all I remember until you arrived Doctor."

"You think Agnes told him?" Edward asked.

"She must have. Nobody else knew. I hadn't even told Samuel." Jane said simply "I'm sorry, Sam. But I knew how Pete would take it, I knew what he'd be like, and I was afraid. So, I went to see Agnes, to ask if she had anything. Something that would make me lose the bairn. But she wanted more money than I could get. She must have told Pete from spite because I couldn't pay."

Edward nodded. The whole sorry story was plainly true. But he sensed that there was something else she was keeping back. Something that Jane wasn't saying. He wondered what it could be. After all, she had already admitted to having sexual relations with a man that wasn't her husband, carrying his children, and planning on having an illegal abortion. All of which would earn her the condemnation of her peers and most likely a prison sentence. If she was willing to admit to these crimes, grave as they were, what more serious crime was she hiding? She must be protecting someone he thought, but who? Her lover Samuel? Could he have come in, seen Pete beating Jane and attacked him? Hit him hard enough to have caused the damage to the back of Pete's skull? Or stalked him along the forest paths? Hit him, and left Pete where he fell? Samuel was certainly strong enough, and he had shown himself to have a fiercesome temper.

As Edward pondered and Samuel comforted Jane who was softly crying, both from fear as she remembered that terrible night, and from relief that she had finally escaped her abusive husband, Nesta looked on. She had listened carefully to Jane, but she was sure that something wasn't quite right. Nesta had been a little girl herself when Frederick was born, eight years later she had known him all his short life. She and her siblings had tried to include him in their games. Had offered to take him with them when they went to play in the woods, but he had never wanted to come, preferring instead to go off on his own, or stay at home, quietly playing a convoluted game of his own devising in the corner of the kitchen. Nesta knew that he often skipped school to wander seemingly aimlessly around the forest. Secretly, Nesta had always been glad when he stayed at home, thinking him a bit of a baby who was scared to leave his mother. Now she felt ashamed, understanding that Frederick was probably worried that Pete would hurt his mother, and hoped to protect her by staying close. Since the death of his father, Frederick had become even quieter and more withdrawn, spending more and more time wandering the forest paths alone.

"Where was Frederick?" she blurted out. She knew that the small boy would never have managed to sleep through the row that Jane described. Jane turned to stare at Nesta like a rabbit caught in the lamp light. Fear, not for herself but for her son, showed clearly on her face.

"He were, he were in bed. He knows to keep out of the way when Pete is one of his moods. He knows he can't stop him, and if he tries, he'll just get a beating too. So, I told him, I made him promise. If his Pa was in one of his moods then he had to keep out of the way, no matter what. And he did, he's a good boy is Frederick. Brave too, he went out to fetch help for me, even though he's a-feared of the dark." She turned to Samuel and smiled up at him. "He's a good boy, your son."

"So, Pete just left you for dead on the stairs, and went on out into the night? And while he was out, he somehow managed to hit his head hard enough to crack the skull bones, fall over, and die. Face down, you said you found him didn't you Mr Phillips? I don't suppose you put him there?" Edward stared hard at Samuel. Although he, like many other men, regarded men who beat their wives with distain, it was still legal for them to do so; and he would hold no truck with a man who killed his lover's husband, whether he was a wife beater or not.

Samuel looked at Edward in surprise. "No Doctor, it wasn't me. Don't get me wrong, I've a temper on me, and I'd have done in a heartbeat if I'd seen him hurting Jane. But to kill him in cold blood." Samuel shook his head "No Doctor. That I couldn't do." And he bent and squeezed Jane's hand.

"Hmmm. Well someone caught him a substantial blow to the back of the head. He didn't do it falling, unless he managed to get himself up, stagger on and then collapse. Where was it you said you found him again?"

"He was up behind the gale, in that scrappy bit where we dump all the rubbish. Thomas found him. He'd just gone for a piss – begging your pardon – he fair near fell over him he said. Thomas came charging back to the gale, and we all went up to help carry him back, Uncle William, that boy of his Bertie, Thomas, and me. Well we got him into the hut and sent Bertie off to fetch Agnes. He were still breathing then, making a terrible row he were. Well we could tell he weren't long for this world, so Thomas, he ran off to get Jane. By the time you'd got to us Doctor, he was gone. But I didn't help him go. My hands are clean." He said looking at Edward defiantly.

A small voice interrupted them from the door to the hallway. Edward realised that with all the kerfuffle, he had forgotten to shut the door behind him when he came into the room. There standing in the doorway was Miss Bates, holding a tray laden with cups and saucers. Steam twisted from the spout of the teapot tucked away under a practical knitted cosy. Frederick stood with her holding a plateful of biscuits. He took a step forward. Pale and nervous, he was nevertheless defiant. He was going to tell everyone what had happened the last time he saw his father. Looking around at the serious adults within, Fredrick's resolve faltered. Biscuits scattered unheeded across the floor as he ran to his mother and buried his head her side.

Between the sobs he blurted. "I did it. I killed Pa. I were peeping round the edge of the door, scared to watch, but I couldn't look away. Pa threw me Ma downstairs. You landed with an awful crash; and I thought you must be dead! Then I saw you move, and Pa ran down the stairs, and kicked you. Kicked you while you lay there, and all the time he were shouting at you, and using bad words. I couldn't let him keep on, I had to stop him. I grabbed the pot from by the bed, and I hit him with it. I hit him as hard as I could, right on the back of the head as he bent over you. He kind of staggered a bit and turned. He tried to grab me, but I pulled free, and into the kitchen. Then he said he were going to get me. He said I were nowt but a cuckoo and he were going to kill me, like he'd killed you. I ran out of the open door. He tried to follow me, but he couldn't keep up. I ran and I ran. I thought I'd try to find Agnes, so she could make Ma better. But the Doctor found me instead, so that was better." Finally, having told the grown-ups everything he subsided. Equal measures of relief that he'd told his secret, and fear as to what would happen next, coursed through Fredrick. He knew he shouldn't have hit his father, he shouldn't have killed him, but equally he was sure that if he hadn't hit him, his father would have murdered his mother. Turning beseechingly to his mother, Fredrick asked "What will happen to me? Will I hang? Will I be sent away?"

Jane held him tight and sobbed. "No Fredrick, no. They won't take you away, I won't them. Oh Fredrick!" She looked up at the Doctor. "Please don't let them take my son" she begged.

Edward meanwhile was lost in thought, pacing back and forth in front of his bookcases. Fredrick's account of hitting his father would explain how Pete's skull had come to be damaged, but was that enough, or had somebody else come along and hit him as well? He pondered; he knew that patients with serious head injuries did sometimes continue on about their days seemingly fine, until they suddenly collapsed later on. However, was that what had happened to Pete, and did Fredrick, who if he was perfectly honest was a rather malnourished, frail little boy, have the strength to inflict that kind of damage? Edward sighed; Fredrick probably had at least contributed to Pete's death, but he would be surprised if a blow to the head delivered by such a scrawny specimen as Fredrick would kill a healthy man. Unless he had been drinking of course, and if he remembered correctly, Pete had reeked of ale. If Fredrick had hit him in the right place and if Pete had had some kind of underlying weakness – an unusually thin skull maybe – then that on top of his probably considerable alcohol consumption might have been enough to cause him to collapse and later die. If the blow to the head had perhaps caused some kind of intracranial bleeding, then yes, maybe that would have done it. He looked at the small boy, kneeling on the floor besides his mother who still sat on the patients' couch. His face was hidden, buried in his mother's skirts. Jane sat, bending down towards him, and muttering reassures in his ear, her hand spread wide on top of his head, ruffling his curly hair. Behind Jane stood Samuel, clearly troubled, a large calloused hand rested on Jane's shoulder.

A cough from the door reminded them all of the presence of Miss Bates. Her sharp voice rang out across the consulting room.

"Well now, this tea is getting frightful cold. Nesta, go back to the kitchen and fetch another three cups and saucers. Quickly mind. Mr Phillips, I would thank you to remove your boots, God knows you've trampled enough mud through this house, but I don't see as you need to bring in anymore. Nesta will have quite a job cleaning all that up, and as for the rug! You've practically turned it into a field." Samuel stared sheepishly at his feet, and began to remove the offending boots, muttering his apologies, and clearly embarrassed to be at the end of Miss Bates sharp tongue. However, as Nesta left the room, chivvied along by Miss Bates, she saw the effect that her words had had. Yes, Uncle Sam was embarrassed, but Jane was trying hard not to smile at his discomfiture, while Fredrick was openly giggling to see Uncle Samuel being told of by this small woman half his height. Collecting cups and saucers, and a fresh pot of boiling water to top up the other, Nesta reflected that Miss Bates, while she might appear prickly and standoffish, was, underneath, really rather a kind lady.

Several hours later Edward collapsed into the leather wing-backed chair with a groan. A fire burned merrily in the hearth, and a small glass of his favourite brandy stood on the small walnut tripod table besides him. Reaching for his glass and taking a long slow slip, he felt the fiery liquid course down his throat, its warmth spreading throughout his body. It had been a very trying day. The revelation that Jane had been engaged in a longstanding affair with her cousin had come as something of a surprise to Edward. As had young Fredrick's confession to having murdered Pete, the man he thought was his father. Even if as it turned out his father was in fact Samuel. More used to the strict moral code of the aspiring upper middle classes in London, Edward was shocked at how easily everyone else had received these revelations. The news that Samuel had not only cuckolded, but also impregnated, the wife of a close acquaintance, if not actually a friend, had been greeted far more calmly by Nesta and Miss Bates than Edward had expected. While affairs were certainly not unheard of amongst of the ranks of the professionals, traders, and minor nobility that Edward had mixed with in London, they were discreetly hidden. Women who were found to have had sexual relations with men other than their husbands, were generally viewed askance and shunned. Their reputations irreparably damaged. They would be seen as a threat by other women and an easy target for more predatory men. A man who indulged in an affair would be tolerated, provided of course that he was discreet, and the mistress kept away from social gatherings. However, if the woman was another gentleman's wife, sister or daughter, he was risking being called out, no matter that duelling was illegal. Some slights could not be ignored.

And that was only one of goodness knows how many sordid secrets concealed within the books pages. Edward flicked listlessly through the pages without enthusiasm. Throwing it down on the table beside him he took another sip of brandy. Edward's head began to nod, and he lolled in the chair, the soporific atmosphere getting the better of him. As the clock in the hallway chimed nine, Edward dozed. He didn't hear the sound of a window being carefully and expertly opened from outside. The quiet rustling as his study was searched. He slept through the soft pad of bare feet creeping cautiously down the hall and into the room, drawn there by the soft light of Edward's table lamp. The intruder moved forward warily, watching Edward for any sign that he might wake up and sound the alarm. But on Edward dozed. Quietly the intruder snuck forwards, until standing behind the wing back chair, they spotted the battered leather journal. Carefully taking it and slipping inside a coat pocket, they slipped away, back across the room. As they slipped through the door, the intruder knocked it gently. That gentle creak penetrated Edward's subconscious, and was enough to make him stir. He woke bleary eyed just in time to hear the groan of a squeaky floorboard in his study. Sensing something was wrong, he headed into the hallway. There he saw that his study door was ajar. Chiding himself – it was his habit to shut and lock the study when he was not inside it. As he approached the door he felt a cold breeze. Quickly he ran across his study, knowing that the window had been firmly closed earlier. He looked out into the night, searching the garden for signs of the intruder.

But he realised he was too late. The garden was a pool of darkness. The intruder could be anywhere, hiding in the bushes, climbing over the walls into the neighbouring gardens, or slipping silently through the back gate and on, through the maze of alleys, gardens and tracks which made up Coleford. Looking around the garden one last time, Edward shut the window firmly. Looking at his desk, he could see that the papers had been riffled. The bookcase too looked as though it had been rummaged, with books removed, and returned haphazardly to the shelves. As yet it didn't look as though anything had been taken. He strode through the house checking on his valuables. As he surveyed his drawing room, he wasn't aware of anything that had been taken. The silver candlesticks, a present from his grandfather on his becoming a doctor, still stood on the mantelpiece, while his pocket watch, which he had earlier removed still hung on its stand. Nothing of any value had been taken. Maybe he had woken as the would-be thief entered, rather than left the room. Glancing round the room one last time, Edward became increasingly sure that nothing had gone. Reaching for his glass to have a slip of restorative brandy, he suddenly realised that the book, Agnes' journal was missing. Quickly he looked around the floor, even going so far as to get down on his hands and knees and look under his chair, but all to no avail. The journal was gone. He had put the book on the table along with his glass, intending to look through it, but clearly the thief had got there first. As the journal was the only thing taken, it occurred to him that the thief and the murderer might well be the same person. The sudden realisation that a cold-blooded killer had probably been in his house, while he dozed in his chair, woke Edward up as if a bucket of cold water had been tipped over his head. Suddenly feeling the need for company, Edward made his way to the kitchen, hoping to find Nesta to tell her this latest development.

When Edward reached the kitchen, he found a scene of quiet domesticity. Miss Bates was sat in her grand wicker throne, straining her eyes to sew by candle light. Nesta was at the large sink, still scrubbing the pans that had been used for dinner. On the stove, a pan of milk warmed ready to make cocoa. As he opened the door, the milk began to bubble, and then suddenly to boil over. Edward strode forward, quickly lifting the pan from the heat and setting it down on the kitchen table. Thinking he'd just done a good deed, he was surprised to receive a whack from an irate Miss Bates, who barging him out of the way, carefully picked the pan up and placed it down on an old iron trivet. Edward's eyes blazed, angry to have been treated like a small boy who had got underneath the cook's feet, but before he could issue a stinging rebuke, he was found himself on the receiving end of a tirade.

"Now look what you've gone and done! That won't scrub out, you mark my words, we'll be having to get Mr Phillips round to sand it, so we will. Did your Ma never teach you never to put hot things down on the table! And let's look at that hand of yours. That'll be needing buttering no doubt, picking up a hot pan without a cloth to protect it. No sense some people, I tell thee Nesta" grumbled Miss Bates, and Edward, doctor and master of the house or not, found himself bustled to a seat, and his hand inspected by both Miss Bates and Nesta, who agreed that while it looked sore, it wasn't as bad as all that, and a damp cabbage leaf was all that was required. Edward found himself meekly accepting their ministrations, in a way in that he hadn't since he was a small boy. Their fuss was oddly comforting. Finally, once Nesta and Miss Bates were satisfied and sat back at the table with fresh cups of cocoa, he was eventually able to tell his story. Both women were shocked that an intruder had been into the house and demanded to know what had been taken. Edward became cagey, not wanting to reveal to Miss Bates that he and Nesta had recovered Agnes' journal. Even if they had managed to lose it again before they had a chance to read it, he thought wryly.

"It was a book, a small leather book. It had no real value" Edward said dismissively, trying to distract Miss Bates away from it.

"Ah. You mean Agnes' journal do you? So you had that then did you? Well, I won't say I ain't glad that that's gone from the house, evil thing, it never brought no good to anybody. But you're quite wrong to say it's worthless, that book was worth a lot of money, well it would if you were that way inclined. Like there's not a man, woman, or child in these parts that Agnes didn't have a comment on. A hoarder of information was Agnes. She'd write stuff down in that little book and bide her time till the time were right, then she'd bleed you dry. Evil bitch. God rest her." Miss Bates said bitterly, crossing herself. Enjoying Edward's look of surprise, she continued "There were much consternation as to who'd managed to get their hands on that little book in town this mornin' I can tell you. Aye, and what they'd be doing with its contents. Old Alfred was right vexed they say when he couldn't find it up at the cottage t'other day. Thought was whoever killed her must have taken it with them. There's plenty worried that they'd be getting a visit from murderer like, hoping to take over from where Agnes left off."

"Did everybody know about Agnes', erm, *activities*?" Edward asked. He'd supposed that Agnes would have kept her blackmailing to a select few, so as to reduce the likelihood of discovery. It hadn't occurred to him that it could be so widespread in the community. The list of possible suspects, and people with a grudge against Agnes, had suddenly become much longer. "If her blackmailing was so well known, why didn't the police do anything?"

Miss Bates pulled a face "Well, I don't suppose everyone knew. Most folk would be like to think it were just them she were blackmailing, and they'd want it kept quiet like. Less anyone asked what it were that Agnes knew. Most people found out only after she'd gone. Too many folk was relieved that she'd died see. And someone tells their neighbour, who tells a cousin, who mentions it to their old ma. Word soon gets about. Peoples' secrets ain't usually as secret as they'd like to think, community like this. Take your Uncle Samuel, Nesta. Everybody knows that his 'Prayer Group' is a bunch of lads what goes off rabbiting, but nobody says owt, and that's as it should be. As for the police. Well, we don't see 'em too much, and nobody much'd talk to them, them being foreigners like. Folk remember what happened to Warren James and the t'others. All 'cause they stood up to stop the enclosures." Miss Bates said sadly. "Anyways, the thing is who knew you had that book, and who climbed in to get it?"

Chapter Sixteen

Friday, 14th November, 11pm.
Purple Hill, Forest of Dean.

The fire burned fierce and bright casting weird shadows as the flames flickered and swayed, lighting the trees then sending them back into sudden darkness. A man and woman stood by the fire, their cloaks pulled tight against the cold November night. Frost sparkled on the damp foliage, and the wind whistled through the trees, making the night feel even colder and more eerie.

The woman stared up at the moon and pulled her cloak tighter about her. Stamping her feet against the cold, she turned to her companion.

"When is she gonna get here? I'm fair freezing! Can we not just rid of the thing and have done?" she demanded impatiently.

"No! You know the agreement, we wait. We burn it together. Then we'll be free." He replied, snaking an arm around his companion's waist, and pulling her close to him. A sharp crack rent the silent night, a branch being snapped by a carelessly placed foot? "Hark! What was that?"

They stood in silence, each trying to breath as quietly as possible, listening intently for the slightest sound. But neither of them heard anything else. They had just begun to relax, when they heard quiet footsteps from behind creeping towards them. Ice crackled underfoot, and a small, slight figure slipped into the glade. The newcomer stood still, looking carefully around before steeping out of the trees into the full light of the fire. Swathed in a long dark cloak with its hood up and a fur muffler pulled tight, the figure was faceless and anonymous. The voice that emerged was quiet, muffled by the thick fabric, although still clearly, unmistakably, the voice of a woman.

"Where is it?" the voice hissed "Give it to me! Quickly now"

The man stepped forward, drawing the slim volume of Agnes' journal from his inside pocket. Hesitantly he edged towards the woman and placed in her imperiously outstretched hand. A smile crept across her face, unseen under the shadow of her cloak.

Looking at the man and woman, she fixed them with a basilisk gaze. "Have you read this?" she demanded.

"No. No ma'am." The man and woman replied in unison, unnerved by the malevolence of the woman's cold voice. She continued to stare at them for what felt like an eternity, judging quietly for herself the truth of their words.

"Good." She said at last. She was relieved, gratified to see fear etched clearly onto their faces. Her left hand, which had stayed hidden inside the folds of her rich cloak, relaxed its grip on the handle of the long thin dagger that was held inside a carefully concealed pocket. Walking towards the fire, she cast the book into the flames.

"There. It is done." she said. Relief flooded through her. Turning, she picked up a large fallen branch and prodded the journal deeper into the flames. The three stood in silence watching the book, the possessor of their secrets turn slowly to ash. The man and woman edged closer together, reaching out, he took her hand and squeezed it tight. It was over.

He turned to his companion "We're free" he said with a grin. "Everything is going to be alright now." Newcomer smiled, her hand grasped the dagger again. It would be easy, so easy, to slit their throats she thought. Slit their throats and leave them on the fire to burn. Her hand gripped the dagger tighter, and she began to pull it free. But no! Why should she kill them? They knew nothing about her. Her only meeting with them arranged in a dark alley. She had taken great care to remain always in the shadows, her voice disguised. She was certain that they had no clue as to her identity. Besides there was no proof, the only evidence of her perfidy was burnt. No-one would ever know the truth now Agnes was dead. She smiled to herself as she remembered slipping the slim blade up and into Agnes' chest, killing her as she hunted for herbs and roots in the moonlight. Now the book was ash. Better to let them live. Let them live so that they looked guiltier than her. She could always point the finger if she needed too. No-one would ever suspect that she was the killer.

Not knowing the danger that he was in, the man touched the killer lightly on the arm.

"Here, we got you the book. We kept our side of the bargain, now where's the cash you promised?" He asked.

The killer turned her cold stare on the man. He could see madness in her eyes. His instinct was to run, to put as much distance between him and this malevolent fiend. But still he held firm. The money had been promised and was his by right. Besides, it would come in mighty useful with the bairn on the way. The killers hand moved slowly under the cover of the cloak. Reaching deep into a pocket her hand gripped a small cloth purse. She withdrew it slowly, making to hand it over, but then stopped.

"Remember Samuel. Remember Jane. I know you. I know your child. If you breathe so much of a word of this to anyone I will kill you both. But not before I've killed both Frederick and your unborn babe. Do you understand?"

The barely suppressed rage her voice was enough to convince them that this was not an idle threat, and they quickly muttered their agreement, keen to put as much distance between them and this cold-hearted killer as possible. Slowly, reluctantly the purse was handed over. Taking it, Samuel secreted it in a pocket. Then touching his hand to his head in a salute, he muttered a farewell. Taking Jane firmly by the hand, they made their way quickly and carefully back towards Berry Hill acutely aware of the danger that they were in. Glad to be away from the killers brooding presence, and to have escaped with their lives they made their way as down the hillside as quickly as the pale moon would allow.

    The killer watched them until they were out of sight. Then she returned her gaze to the flames. It was a shame that the book had to be burnt, she thought, but she needed to be sure that nobody would ever find out her secret. The book had held too much information. A clever man like the doctor might have pieced it all together and then she would have been ruined. Better it was gone. She smiled quietly to herself, remembering Agnes' demands. Agnes had been so confident, so sure of herself, so used to extorting money from folk that she had never even considered that she might have made a mistake when she tried to demand money from *her*. The killer gently stroked the blade of her dagger, remembering how easily it had slipped between Agnes' ribs. She savoured the memory; the look of shock, and then fear on Agnes' face as she had seen her death approach. The noise she made as the blade slipped effortlessly between her ribs and up into her heart, the way her father had shown her. Smiling still, the killer turned and walked back the way she came, vanishing quietly into the woods.

Chapter Seventeen

Saturday, 15th November 1851.
Coleford

Edward sat at the breakfast table feeling dejected. Before him his favourite kippers lay untouched on the plate, his coffee cold in his cup. He had slept fitfully, his mind in turmoil. Alternating between anger that his home had been invaded, and horror that he had drawn a ruthless killer to his home, acutely aware that he could have been murdered where he dozed. He had attracted the attention of a murderer and they could all have been killed. And all of it was for nothing. The journal, and all hope of identifying the killer had gone. He sat alone, toying with a triangle of toast, his eyes heavy with lack of sleep. Suddenly alert, he pushed back his chair. He could hear his study door being slammed, feet running across the hall towards him. The killer must have returned! He looked around in desperation for a weapon, something, anything, he could use to defend himself. The door swung open, crashing back against the wall behind. Edward cringed. Mustering his courage, he stood up straight, determined to look his killer in the eye. There stood Nesta, crumpled papers in her hand, breathless with excitement.

"It's my notes Doctor. They didn't take my notes." She said, eyes shining. "The fair copy I made of Agnes' journal." She went on, seeing the look of complete confusion on Edward's face. Nesta felt more uncertain now. She had been surprised to find her transcription still on the table where she had left it the day before. Nesta had expected that it would have gone along with the journal, but clearly the thief had either missed it, or more likely, simply hadn't known about the copy Nesta had made. Nesta spread the pages out on the table, as Edward brushed aside his cup and plate, breakfast forgotten. Together they poured over the pages. However, staring at the words and symbols, they made no more sense to today that they had yesterday. Some initials Nesta recognized, and a few words, particularly names of herbs, Edward was familiar with. But large parts were incomprehensible. Nesta stared and stared as if somehow it would make the words make sense to her, but they didn't. Still they made no sense to them, like a language neither of them spoke.

"I'm sorry Doctor. I must have copied it wrong. It's like it's a different language. I keep thinking I can get a bit of it, and then it makes no sense again. It's familiar, but not somehow. Oh I'm sorry Doctor. That doesn't make sense!" Nesta flung herself down into a chair, tears of frustration prickled her eyes.

"You're right Nesta. Some words I understand – pennyroyal, Monk's Hood, I understand them well enough, but others? They're gibberish! I mean 'George's hummuck as gun right rasty. Told ee t'at wud pizzun ee, but wudst ee lizen?' Then the line below 'George jud. Told ee.' What's that supposed to mean?" With that Edward flung down the paper in exasperation.

Nesta grabbed the paper. "What did you say Doctor? Read it again, that bit about George"

Confused, Edward read, while Nesta stood still listening, her eyes screwed up in concentration. "That's it. It's how the old folk speak, like me Grandpappy did. It's old forest, you don't hear it as much as you used to, people try to speak posher, but I think I understand. Read it again slowly for me."

"George's hummuck as gun right rasty. Told ee t'at wud pizzun ee, but wudst ee lizen?" Said Edward slowly.

"George's hummuck?" Nesta thought for a moment "that's a leg – has gone right rancid." She translated. "I told him that it would poison him, but would he listen?"

Edward nodded excited "George jud. Told ee. Well I can see that that's I told him, but does jud mean?"

"Jud...Jud..."Nesta muttered to herself, thinking back to sitting listening to her grandpappy talking. "Dead! George's dead. And he is! George Lane cut himself. He didn't get it seen to quickly enough and it festered. He died soon after. Poor old George." Said Nesta sadly. "But that's it. We can work out what it says"

Eyes shining, Edward urged Nesta to sit down next to him. "Here" he said, "I'll read it out, you tell me what it says, and then I'll write it."

They worked on, caught up in the excitement of trying to translate as much of the book as they could. Finally, they finished. They both felt slightly soiled, as if by reading and hearing the secrets of their friends and neighbours they had somehow been prying into their affairs, no better than the worse gossip or peeping tom. Nesta's ears had burnt red at the stories of infidelity. Translating the pages, it was apparent that it was a diary, not just of Agnes' blackmailing, but also of the all the treatments that she dispensed. There was reference to a paste dispensed to treat Alfred's piles, a poultice for one of William's horses, herbs for a teething baby, and the delivery of another. Most disturbing were the references to babies that Nesta knew of as still births. Babies like Nesta's little sister who sadly had not survived delivery, or had died shortly after, but who had appeared in the book along with a price. Nesta thought it seemed odd. Some of the mother's seemed to have been charged a few pence, while others were charged much more, three or four pounds in some cases, far, far more than Nesta would have expected a woman to pay for Agnes' help with a birth, when she saw the grim look on Edwards face and stopped.

"What is it?" asked Nesta cautiously, she knew the doctor well enough by now to know that little really dismayed him.

"I think she was taking babies and giving them to baby farmers." Edward replied softly. "Often adverts will appear in the papers, requesting babies for adoption, and offering to pay for them. It might be childless parents who simply wish for a child to call their own and will love and raise them as their own. But it might not be. My uncle in Liverpool wrote to me of a case he was involved in as a magistrate where a couple were taking in babies and raising them to sell to brothels or to chimney sweeps. Who knows where these poor mites have gone. Agnes hasn't put enough information here that we will ever find out."

A resounding crash echoed around the room, the sound of a full tray being dropped. So engrossed had they been, that neither of them, had noticed the Miss Bates silently approaching them. Turning towards the doorway, they saw Miss Bates, sat on the floor in a daze, surrounded by broken china. Clearly, she had been carrying a full tray of tea things when she had collapsed. They helped her to her feet and gently guided her across the room to a chair. She moved as if she was sleepwalking, in a complete daze.

Finally, she spoke, her voice barely more than a whisper. "Her mother was the same. She'd say she could make babies disappear. Mother's what couldn't care for their bairns, because they had too many, or weren't married, she took them. She'd tell the mother that the babe would be well looked after, that for a fee, a few pounds, they'd be given a new home. That it'd be best for the bairn. So the mother would give them to her willingly. They'd put about that the babe was stillborn, and the mother would take comfort that her child had gone to a new loving home. An' all the time the babe would have been sent off to some baby farmer. They don't care for the young 'uns, they just feed them on sops, an' wait for them to die - which most do - and the mother would be none the wiser. She'd think she'd done right by her bairn. Evil bitch! But Agnes swore that she wouldn't. Said she hated it too, she said she could never sell a baby. She took babies. And all the time, Agnes would be pocketing the money and selling them to a baby farmer!" She spat out the last words, real loathing in her voice. "They won't do it again. Good riddance to the pair of them!"

Nesta was distraught. "Would the mother have known? Or would she have been told by Agnes her baby was dead? Did Agnes steal them?" She asked fretfully "I need to see my Ma. I need to see Ma and Aunt Rose." With that she rushed out of the dining room and towards the front door. Edward caught her as she fumbled with the bolts. He held her wrists tightly and pulled her away, placing himself between her and the door. Trying to get away she beat at him with her hands, tears coursing down her face as she thought about the tiny, well wrapped parcel that Agnes had left with. Nesta was desperate, desperate to find her Aunt Rose and ask if she had seen the baby breathing. Desperate to find out if her baby sister was still alive, sent to some dreadful baby farm. Then, if by some miracle she survived infancy, unloved and uncared she would be sold on to the highest bidder when she could be useful and start work. Nesta wept, imagining all the terrible things that could await her, but determined to rescue her sister if she could.

"Stop Nesta. You must calm down. I will help you find out what happened to your sister. I will help you." Edward said soothingly. Suddenly Nesta stopped struggling, all the fight left her, and she collapsed into Edward's arms, sobbing against his chest. Finally, she stopped crying and slumped down on the hall chair. Taking the proffered handkerchief from Edward, she dried her eyes.

"I'm sorry Sir, I'm such a state! What must you be thinking of me!" she said mopping her eyes with Edward's large spotty handkerchief. "It's just, something felt wrong when Agnes took Ma's babe. It was like she couldn't leave fast enough. I thought she was being kind, taking away the bairn like. But now I wonder..." Nesta's face crumpled again into tears, and she continued to sob quietly.

Edward looked up to see Miss Bates, recovered from her shock, beckoning him from the doorway to the dining room. He moved quietly towards her.

When Miss Bates spoke, her voice was quiet and urgent, barely more than a whisper "'Ere. It's like Nesta could be right, and the bairn might still be alive. Whether Agnes would have taken her with or without Mary knowing, I can't say, but Rose like'll know. For all me and Mary don't always see eye to eye, I'd never have seen her selling her bairn, no matter how hard things might be. I know the gale ain't been doing all that well, and they'll have been right glad to have Nesta out the house, bringing back some money an' all. And Mary was saying only the week before, that she didn't know how they'd manage with an extra mouth to feed. Not with her not being able to work a turn with a little one again. But still, I can't see her selling one of her own. Not one of her own. Rose now, she's ruthless enough to do it. Still, her sister's bairn. You'd have to be cold hearted to do that. We might be out in the sticks, but I've all heard tales of what goes on." She looked at Nesta sadly. "If that bairn has gone to a baby farm, it's like she'll have been left to starve already. For all they tell the mother's their babes'll be well cared for" she added bitterly. As she started to walk back towards the kitchen, she turned suddenly "Still" she said "if you wanted to find out owt more, I'd be minded to ask Rose. Aye, if anyone knows owt, Rose'll".

Edward looked at the still distraught Nesta, torn between wanting to help her find her little sister, and thinking that it might be best to leave well alone. While Nesta was obviously sure that her mother would not have willingly given up her baby to an at best uncertain future, he couldn't quite silence the nagging doubts he had. If Mary had indeed chosen to rid herself of an inconvenient extra child that they could ill afford, then it would do Nesta no good to find out her sister had been in essence sold. On the other hand, if Mary had wanted to keep the child, and she had been stolen away by Agnes, possibly with Rose's connivance, didn't she have a right to have her daughter back? Edward rubbed his face with his hands, unsure what to do for the best. The jangling of the doorbell disturbed his thoughts. Glancing at the clock he realised that it was now one o'clock and time for his afternoon surgery. Stomach rumbling because he had not had any breakfast, let alone lunch, he hurried to open the door and welcome in his first patient. Ushering the elderly gentlemen into his consulting room he began to lose himself back into the world of medicine. All thoughts of Nesta, Mary and her child chased out by the old man's interesting rash. So lost was he in a fascinating new case that he didn't hear the front door being softly closed, nor see the well wrapped figure of Nesta stealing quietly past the front window.

Nesta ran swiftly along the lanes, cutting through dark overgrown snicket ways and down well used tracks as she headed as quickly as possible for her parents' cottage. Whilst the journey was only a few miles, the going was tough as the frozen ground began to melt under the weak November sun. Large puddles left over from heavy rains a few days before covered wide sections of the path. Dark and cold, with a thin film of ice around the edges Nesta was continually obliged to move from one side of the path to the other as she tried to dodge the worst of the mud and water. Approaching one particularly large puddle which stretched right across the path from one side to the other, Nesta paused, then gathering her skirts, she attempted to jump over it. She had almost made it when she landed with a large splash right on the edge of the puddle. Mud splattered her coat and skirts, and her boots filled uncomfortable with icy water. Cursing she continued to run, icy water squelching uncomfortably around her toes, heading unerringly for her parents' cottage.

  It was not until she approached the small collection of cottages that she finally began to slow her headlong dash. Smoke rose from the chimney of her parents' cottage, the back door wide open despite the cold, the gentle sound of her mother singing spreading lightly across the shared yard as she laboured within. Nesta stopped. She felt sure in her heart that her mother would not have knowingly given away her little sister. The memory of her mother's grief was still raw. How could she now disturb her mother's happiness after she had finally found a modicum of peace when in the end she knew nothing more than Agnes had taken some babies and sold them? Whether or not her sister was amongst those taken she couldn't say - she hadn't managed to copy out the last few pages of the journal, and now it was gone. If only she had managed to copy it all out before it was taken, but perhaps she would be able to find the previous night's intruder. Turning to leave she caught a slight movement out of the corner of her eye. It was her Aunt Rose, carrying a heavy basket up the hill towards the ale house that she ran. Suddenly Nesta made up her mind. She would confront her formidable aunt. She must know if the baby was born alive or not. At least then, Nesta would know whether or not there was any baby to search for.

Chasing after her aunt, Nesta quickly caught up with her as her aunt laboured up the hill with her heavy load. Taking the basket from her, Nesta walked up the hill alongside Rose, both were too out of breath to speak much. Finally, they reached the door to the ale house, and slipped inside and through to the kitchen. A rich savoury smell permeated around the room coming from the large pot of stew bubbling gently on the stove, that day's dish to be served in the tap room to any who wanted feeding. Rose began to unpack the large basket on the table; it was full of root vegetables which Rose quickly sorted into piles to be put away in her large pantry once the worst of the mud had been washed off. Nesta wondered where Rose had collected the vegetables from. Rose's own garden stood to the rear of the ale house, and she hadn't collected any vegetables from her mother. It would be unlike Rose to purchase vegetables, or anything that she could make or grow herself, at the market in Coleford, so they must have come from somebody else. Just as Nesta was plucking up the courage to ask, her Aunt looked at her and laughed.

"I can see you're dying to know where these came from Nesta. I've always said your face is like the page of a book, easy for anyone who knows how to read. Old Maddoc gave them to me, to pay off his tab. Poor soul, things are getting tight for him, up there on the encroachment, and there ain't many as wants to employ him as he gets older. Won't be long till he's off to the workhouse, an' he knows it! So I'll take some veggies from him to pay his bill, and maybe I'll find some work for him, for all he's getting too old to dig hard. Bless him." Said Rose, sadly shaking her head. and obviously distressed to think of Maddoc, a man she fondly remembered from her childhood being reduced to a wizened old man, who as soon as he was unable to work anymore would be packed off to the workhouse, there to end his days in penury. In her mind's eye, Rose could see Maddoc sitting by the fire on long winter evenings, whittling toy animals from scraps of wood to sell at Coleford market while she and Mary sat at his feet. Telling them stories of boggarts, hunky-punks, and elves as the cold winds blew through the gaps in the shutters and round the door, and the rain dripped and wormed its way in through the rough thatch roof and turf walls. Despite their dismal surroundings, Maddoc had always had a smile and a joke. No matter how hard times were, he was always willing to help anyone in any way he could.

Shaking off her day-dream and closing a door on the past, Rose bustled Nesta to a stool. When she was sitting down herself in her large wooden carver asked "Now then lass, what are you doing up here? I don't believe for one minute that you've just come up here for a quiet chat. Is it that doctor? Has he let you go, because I'm sure as eggs be eggs this isn't your day off!"

Nesta froze, scared to ask the questions that buzzed around her head, but still desperate for the answers. She paused, several long moments passed in an awkward silence.

Finally, unable to bear it anymore, Nesta took a deep breath "I wanted. I wanted to ask you about the babe. My little sister, that Agnes took away. I know Agnes said she had died, but I heard that Agnes had been taking babies and selling them. Selling them into God knows what, and I want to know, I need to know if she took my sister. But I can't ask Ma, she's only just coming to terms with it, and I don't believe she'd have sold her. She wouldn't have. Couldn't have. So I'm asking you. Did Agnes take my little sister to sell?" As all of this poured out Nesta, she felt herself grow stronger. She was more than a little scared of her Aunt who always seemed so capable, so in control. Rose had always been in her life, often turning up with 'spare vegetables' and 'leftovers' when times were particularly tough for her parents. Like when her Pa had broken his ankle and couldn't work for a few weeks, or now, when the gale wasn't producing quite as much coal as normal because the seam they were following wasn't as good. Nesta treated her aunt as if she was a second mother, and she was loath to upset her, but equally, she was desperate to know the truth.

Rose froze. She stared hard at Nesta. "Who's been telling you tales my girl? Well whoever it is, don't you mind them. It ain't true. Selling babies, whoever heard of such nonsense!" she said, attempting a cheeriness that was belied by the fear in her eyes.

"Don't lie to me Aunt Rose, I'm not daft! I know what Agnes was doing, I've read her journal. Now please, tell me, did she take my little sister?"

Nesta saw her aunt crumple in front of her. It was as if her Aunt had gone, and in her place sat a scared, frail imitation of the strong, confident woman that Nesta knew. Rose sobbed, her face a picture of fear and misery.

"God forgive me, but yes, I talked to Agnes. Your Ma couldn't have raised another child. Your parents could barely afford to feed and house the four of you, let alone another. I knew that Agnes would sometimes take a babe, if the mother weren't married say, or had too many mouths to feed, and give them to another family. When the baby was born, and another girl at that, Agnes took her. Took her and gave her to someone else to raise. Afterwards, I knew I'd done wrong. Your mother fell apart, and I thought if I could just get the babe back, that your Ma would be better again. But when I went to see Agnes, to tell her it was all a stupid mistake, and I'd changed my mind, Agnes just laughed at me. She said she couldn't get the babe back if she tried, and it didn't matter, 'cause she weren't gonna try anyways. Then she started to demand money from me. Said if I didn't pay her, that she'd tell Mary. Tell Mary I'd got her to steal her baby. Your Ma would never forgive me if she knew what I'd done. I wish I hadn't, but I only meant to look out for you, to save you all."

"But it's not for you to save us" said a cold voice. Stepping into the kitchen was Mary, full of indignation. "Things are tight for us yes, but we would have managed. I would have managed. It wasn't your decision to make. She wasn't your baby to take." Walking towards her elder sister who sat frozen in her chair, Mary slapped her hard, leaving a livid red handprint on Rose's face. "Taking my baby, stealing my daughter, was the worst thing you have ever done to me. It was the worst thing that anyone has ever done to me. I have lost her, lost her because of you! To lose a baby like that, you have no idea what it is like. You're not a mother, you don't understand." And with that Mary slapped her sister hard across the face again. Rose just sat there, silently accepting the blows from Mary, mournful and dejected, hunched forward, and head down like a broken woman. Finally the rage left Mary. "I know you did what you thought was best for me and mine, but it was not your decision to make. I'm not a child to be fussed over. You can't save me anymore." She whispered, and with that she reached out and hugged Rose. The two sisters stood, leaning on each other weeping together. Nesta moved on her stool, uncomfortable to have witnessed the argument, and reconciliation between her mother and aunt.

The sound of the stool wobbling reminded Mary of the presence of her eldest daughter.

"And just what are you doing up here missy?" she asked sternly "Well, it's not Sunday, and it isn't your half day holiday. So how comes you to be up here. You've not been let go have you?"

"I heard.... I heard that Agnes had been taking babies, and I remembered how quickly she left after..." Nesta gulped unsure how to approach this delicate subject with her mother without provoking another furious outburst "well, after the babe was born. I wanted to know if she might be alive. I thought I might be able to find her. To bring her back. I thought I could at least try" she finished unsteadily, worried as to her mother's reaction. But Nesta need not have been concerned. Mary smiled fondly at her eldest daughter. Placing a hand on Nesta's head, she ruffled her hair as if she was still a little girl. Mary smiled sadly, a thin, tight smile that somehow did not quite reach her eyes. While the anger, the hurt and betrayal was still plain to see to any who knew her well, the lines of pain around her eyes softened slightly.

"Good girl." Mary said softly. "Trying to find your sister. Well don't you worry. She's safe. And she'll be happy, and well cared for, but she is lost to us. Don't you try to hunt her down. A family have taken her, a rich family, a good family, and she is loved. She is loved so much. But we'll never be able to talk to her, never tell her that she is ours. She has gone."

"But where has she gone? Maybe we could get her back, I'm sure that Dr James would help. Please mother, if you just tell me where she is, and I will get her!" Nesta cried with excitement, desperate, not only to rescue her sister, but to ease her mother's anguish.

"No!" Mary said sharply "No! She is somewhere safe. She is loved. She is cared for. She will be given all of the things that I have longed for for you and your sisters, but could never give you. She will never have to work, never know hunger or want. She is better off there, than with us. Our little lass is gone. Put her from your mind, as I must put her from mine." Large tears travelled unheeded down her face as she gazed bleakly across the room.

Nesta jumped up off the stool and stood, hugging the small frame of her mother. As Nesta stood holding her mother tight, she realised that the tables had turned and for that for once it was her comforting her mother, rather than her being comforted. The realisation made her feel at once grown up and responsible, and she was embarrassed by the way that she had hurried up to the village, without a care for her responsibilities. Nesta knew that soon she would have to head back to the doctor's house and explain herself. The thought of the apology that she must give, while all the while he sat impassively in his chair, made her squirm with embarrassment. But, Nesta considered, the embarrassment of apologising to Dr James, the scolding she was sure to get from Miss Bates, all that was worth it to know that her sister was alive and well.

Chapter Eighteen

Sunday, 16th November, 1851.

Sunday dawned bright and clear. The weak winter sun sparkled on the heavily frosted plants, and ice-encrusted spider webs, so that they looked as if they had been encrusted with jewels. However, few of the early morning walkers stopped to admire the beautiful scene. Coats and mufflers pulled tight, everyone walked with their eyes cast firmly downwards, trying to avoid slipping on the slippery roads. The temperature was still well below freezing, with a bitter easterly wind which promised of more cold weather to come. Parishioners on their way to church turned up their collars against the chill in the air, their breath billowing in front of them like a cloud of steam from a freshly boiled kettle. Nesta laboured hard, eager to make up for her behaviour of the day before when she had run out of the house without so much as a by your leave. She had returned from seeing her aunt and mother with a heavy heart, anxious that she had given cause to the doctor to dismiss her. Instead she had been welcomed back with open arms. Edward had worried all afternoon after Nesta had raced outside and was pleased to have her return to them - despondent, grim faced, but otherwise unharmed. Miss Bates had also taken pity on the forlorn maid, and while she had scolded Nesta, it was clear that her heart wasn't really in the telling off and she was glad simply to have her back, safe at home where she could keep an eye on her.

Nesta scrubbed floors, carried water, and prepared dinner; all the while her mind on her youngest, missing sister. Her thoughts raced as she tried to understand why her Aunt had colluded with Agnes to take the baby. Nesta knew that money was tight at home, and she had often heard her father and Uncle Samuel complain that the coal wasn't fetching such high prices any more. Nasty stuff, her father had called it, it burnt poorly and produced too much soot, so nobody much wanted it to heat their homes. Most people preferred to pay a little more for the cleaner burning coal coming from pits working a better seam. Not only was the coal harder to sell and worth less, it also cost more to extract. The coal was soft and needed extra props to be put in to help hold up the ceilings of the tunnels, they couldn't just leave pillars of unworked coal behind to hold up the tunnel roof. So money was tight at home, her mother had less money to spend at the market, so more and more of the food had been based on what they could grow, gather, or sometimes poach, themselves. Uncle Samuel was a prolific poacher, taking rabbits, pheasants, wood pigeons, ducks, and, before the Verderers had removed them in 1855, even the occasional deer. Nesta's father disapproved of his brother's illicit activities but couldn't deny that they were a useful source of meat.

    Leaving the potatoes she had been busily peeling, Nesta moved across the range where she began basting the mutton joint she had slowly roasting by the open fire to help keep it moist. Nesta hadn't eaten nearly so well until she came to work for the doctor. Dinner at home would usually be cawl, a type of rich savoury stew, full of oddments of vegetables, and meaty bones, broken open to extract the marrow within, which her mother kept bubbling away on the stove ready to give her father a hearty dinner when he returned home from the pit. Nesta had learnt to cook on the small stove in her parent's kitchen. Little more than an open fire, with spaces either side where you could place a kettle or a pan to keep warm. Cooking was limited to things that could be boiled in a large pan or cooked on a flat griddle pan suspended over the flames. She had been so excited to find that the doctor had a large, modern range cooker, with a hot plate, roaster, and boiler. When Miss Bates had shown that, by closing certain valves in the range, she could turn the roaster into an oven to bake her own pastries and breads, Nesta had been ecstatic. Anxious to improve her repertoire of meals, Nesta had begged a battered collection of Mrs Beeton's "The Englishwomen's Domestic Magazine" from Grace, an old friend of her aunts who had been away in service at a grand house in the Cotswolds. Contained with the pages were a whole host of recipes that Nesta had never even heard of before. Her great hope was that one day the Doctor would host a dinner party; then Nesta could apply herself to making all sorts of pies, soups, and creams. But for now I must content myself with roast haunch of mutton, and haricot beans, followed by a boiled raisin pudding thought Nesta. Gingerly she lifted the lid of a large saucepan, checking to make sure there was plenty of water surrounding the pudding steaming gently within.

The steam from pans busily boiling pudding and haricot beans, combined with the rich savoury smell of roasting meat and crept down the passage way and across the hall to the Doctor's study. There Edward, busily working away on his plans for a charitable hospital, felt his stomach begin to grumble. He took out his watch and groaned as he saw it was only eleven o'clock. Dinner would not be served for another two hours. As his stomach gave another particularly violent grumble, Edward gently wiped the nib of his pen and placed it carefully on his inkstand. He would finish his letters later he thought, but right now, he simply must head for the kitchens, and find a little sustenance. As Edward opened the kitchen door he was assailed by a blast of warm, damp air. The kitchen was filled with steam as pans bubbled happily on the stove. Nesta bustled around, stirring this, and basting that; busily preparing the dinner. Seeing the Doctor arrive, Nesta hurried forward.

"Can I help you Sir?" she asked awkwardly, still feeling both guilty and nervous of the consequences of her sudden, unsanctioned departure the day before. Edward looked her, feeling sheepish that he had come in search of a snack. He was well aware of his mother's thoughts of eating between meals and felt rather like a naughty schoolboy as he sought out a forbidden treat. Almost he turned to leave, thinking he would just have to wait for his dinner, but at that moment his stomach gave a particularly loud grumble. Mortified, Edward began to stutter his apologies. Embarrassed for him, Nesta knew that the doctor would be ashamed to have had a grumbling stomach in public, Nesta quickly sought to distract him.

"There's some fresh bread, not long out of the oven if you would like Sir? And a fresh pat of butter I can fetch from the pantry to have with it if you like. Or perhaps you'd like it with the dripping from the roast."

"Bread and butter, I think. If it's not too much trouble." With that Edward sat himself down at the table as Nesta hurried around the kitchen, fetching butter and cutting fresh bread. On the table lay the recipe for roast mutton, and Edward absentmindedly flicked through the dog-eared papers without really reading them. Suddenly he stopped, his eye drawn to an advertisement for Mrs Beeton's Book of Household Management. He looked at Nesta, how much would she like a copy of the full book, rather than the battered copies of recipes that she appeared to be laboriously copying out. Checking the price, 12s 6d, Edward decided at once that he would purchase a copy as a Christmas present for Nesta. His mind raced as he imagined how the surprise and pleasure that she would have opening it, and how grateful she would feel towards him. Whilst 12s 6d wasn't a vast sum of money to him, he knew that it would be a lot to Nesta, and certainly more than her parents would ever be able to afford to spend on her. Then suddenly he felt guilty. He wanted to purchase the book for Nesta as she would enjoy it, and he knew the pleasure that she would get from it, but also, he wanted her to feel grateful to him. He wanted Nesta to feel in his debt, and it was the realisation that he wanted Nesta to feel beholden to him, that he wanted… but no, he thought, that was a door that he must keep closed. He would not allow himself to be compromised again. Nesta swept the papers aside and put down the bread and butter in front of Edward. As he looked up and offered his thanks, Nesta gave him a sweet smile which lit up her face. In that instant he knew that he would have to get Nesta a copy of the Mrs Beeton's Book, he would give her anything she asked of him.

Looking down at the papers again, a mixture of different recipes and household management tips that formed Mrs Beeton's Supplements in *The Englishwomen's Domestic Magazine*, he saw a plan for a dinner party. Drawing the paper towards him, it occurred to him that he could host a dinner for potential benefactors. Having got them altogether, they might be more inclined to support the hospital. It would be much easier than him visiting them separately, and it would help him to get established in the community. Maybe it would also help him to develop his social circle, which at the moment was sorely limited. Mentally he examined the dining room, it wasn't as grand as his parents, but it should be big enough to comfortably seat eight he thought. His everyday dinner service would do at a pinch; he could invest in a grander, more suitable service later. Now all he would need to do was issue some invitations. He would offer the stable boy a penny to deliver them for him and decide on a bill of fare. At that moment Miss Bates came stomping into the kitchen, back from her Sunday morning visit to see her niece Annibiah. Plonking the ancient, empty, basket down on the table she muttered and grumbled away her to herself as she took of her cloak and bonnet. Seeing the doctor sat at the table for the first time, Miss Bates gave a brief curtsey to him.

"Good morrow Dr James. How are you today? I don't know what you must think of me, coming in grumbling away. I've just come back from visiting my niece, poor girl. She's in a mort of trouble, I can tell you. Her current master don't like her, and has been threatening to dismiss her, and without a character, mark you. And then where will she be? In the workhouse that's where, you mark my words. Poor lamb. Hard worker she is, only nobody'll give her a chance." She said, looking at the Doctor pointedly. Edward squirmed. He knew that Miss Bates wanted him to take on her niece as a maid, but he really didn't need two maids and he already had Nesta.

"Hmmm, well. I'm not sure what we can do to help. I'll be sure to recommend her if anyone asks about a new maid" he said half-heartedly, knowing full well that nobody would ask him, a complete new comer to the area, for recommendations for a maid. However, Edward's unenthusiastic offer seemed to placate Miss Bates at least temporarily, and she sat herself down at the table without further complaint.

"Actually" said Edward "I wanted to talk to you, and Nesta, about something. I intend to organise a dinner party. It will only be a modest affair, a few friends and acquaintances here to discuss the plans for the hospital. I intend to issue the invitations today, for next Saturday."

Miss Bates sucked her teeth. "A dinner party? Well Doctor, I can't say it's something that Dr Thomas ever did. Hmmm, well could be done I suppose. There's that set of fine china at the back of the pantry in a box. Dr Thomas never used it, so he had it packed away. Tureens, platters, and so forth. They'll be in sore need of a good wash, but I'm sure me and Nesta can have them cleaned up. And there's some good linen in that press in the attic, well that's if the moths haven't been at it. Now then, you'd do well to consider the dinner menu, in case I need to order owt that we can't find on the market. Even with the train, it'll take the grocer a few days if you want anything exotic. What do you want to serve?"

Edward shook his head "I'd value your opinion Miss Bates, and yours too of course Nesta. I'm not sure what's in season, or what we can get out this way. Nothing too elaborate I think. We'll need a soup, of course, and some kind of fish. An Entree or two. Then perhaps a roast of some kind for the second course, and some desserts. Do you have any ideas Nesta?" Eyes bright with excitement, Nesta drew a small notebook from her pinafore pocket and began to take notes in her steady rounded hand.

"Well, I don't rightly know, never having been to a dinner party, but I've been reading some old recipes from Mrs Beeton. There's some here." Flicking through the papers, Nesta quickly found the one she wanted which gave a sample dinner party menu. "Now how's about this? Carrot Soup, then this Mutton Kidneys a la Francaise, whatever that may be, Boiled beef and vegetables, well that's easy enough, a couple of partridges we can gets. Are there any Blancmange moulds Miss Bates? And I'm sure we can get some apples for this, what do you call it? Apple Compote, whatever that is when it's at home. Desert, well some fruit, the grocer had some good apples and pears. You could order a few of them bon-bons, and some nice almond paste biscuits. Would that suffice Sir? Or is it too much even, I'm not right sure what folk usually offer at this sort of affair."

Edward smiled broadly "That sounds perfect. I'll leave the all details to you and Miss Bates. Thank-you." And with that, Edward retreated to his study, there to write invitations. Planning who to invite, Edward wrote to a few of his fellow medical men; the doctor from Clearwell and his wife, an unmarried surgeon from up towards Ruardean, and another, married this time, from Upper Lydbrook. Sir Cyril and his wife completed the small party. As Edward wrote out the invitations he thought how pleasing it would be to be able to issue invitations in the names of Dr and Mrs James, or even to give over complete control of his social life to a wife. He sighed. Despite the best efforts of his mother, sister and cousin he had yet to find anybody suitable that he would like to marry. His previous love had already been married, and currently the only woman he would consider was unsuitable. Finishing writing the invitations, Edward carefully sanded them, and put them into addressed envelopes. He would ask the stable boy to deliver them as he made his way to church.

Chapter Nineteen

Saturday, 22nd November, 1851.

Nesta rose at 5am. The small fire in the grate of her attic room had long since died down, leaving only ash in the fireplace. Wrapping her blanket around her, she padded across her cold bedroom to the small window overlooking the street. Pulling aside the curtains, the window glass was thick with ice. Wiping gently with the corner of her blanket, Nesta soon cleared a small peep-hole so that she could peer through into the darkness beyond. The dim light of the lantern in the coaching inn opposite gave the street an eerie glow. Everything was covered with a thick layer of snow, the first of the year. Turning away, Nesta dressed quickly, thinking over all the tasks for the day, and wondering if her early rising would be to no avail. Nesta had been excitedly planning the Doctor's dinner party all week, busily washing the dusty dinner service that Miss Bates had found languishing unused in the back of the pantry and mending the best linen which had become a little moth eaten in storage. Looking towards the window anxiously she wondered if the party would be able to go ahead, or if it would have to be re-arranged if guests were unable to travel the forest roads in the snow. Despite the Forest boasting some fine, recently opened turnpikes, the roads were still difficult - if not down-right dangerous - to pass in inclement weather. Heavy rain had reduced some of the paths to quagmires of thick mud, through which the passage of carts and carriages had left deep wheel ruts, now frozen iron hard by a period of prolonged cold.

Nesta thought of Uncle William, who only the day before had arrived on the door stop late at night to ask if the Doctor could sew up a deep gash in his arm. While Edward neatly sutured the long cut to William's forearm, William had explained the whole sorry saga. First, he had been forced by axle deep mud to turn off the forest paths he normally used and instead pay to use the turnpike road. Unfortunately, conditions on the turnpike were not a great deal better. The surface was still slick with thick cloying mud, however there, being more exposed, the mud had begun to freeze. A layer of thick rime covered the mud, giving the appearance of a solid surface; and, so it was for most travellers. Unluckily, one wheel of the heavy coal cart had broken through the surface crust into the liquid mud below, and as the horse laboured to pull the cart, a spoke had snapped. William had then been forced to unload the coal to make emergency repairs, during which he had cut himself on the jagged edge of the broken spoke. Thus a short journey that he normally completed in an hour or so, had taken him most of the day. With day light fading fast, no lamp, and a damaged cart, he had had to abandon most of the coal at the side of the road until he could return to collect it the next day with a properly mended cart.

"If it's still there!" he muttered morosely "That's if some thieving beggar hasn't decided to help himself to it. A pretty penny this day has cost me" he said handing over three pence to the doctor for his work. "No, I won't have another cup o' tea, thankee Nesta. My Jane will be worrying where I've got to, so I'll be back away to her and the bairn. Thankee Doctor; good night to you, Miss Bates, Nesta" and with that, William touched his cap to each of them in turn and headed out of the kitchen door into the night.

Nesta hurried quickly down the stairs into the kitchen. There she quickly stirred the banked fire in the big range back into life, carefully building it back up to a steady blaze. She put the kettle on to boil, then dusting herself down, headed off to prepare the dining room ready for breakfast. Mindful that they might have guests, and keen to help make Edward's dinner party a success, Nesta dusted everything with particular care, before setting the breakfast table. Nesta had just finished opening the downstairs window shutters and cleaning the hallway, when the clock struck seven. Hurrying back to the kitchen she filled the large earthenware ewer with hot water from the boiler ready for Edward's ablutions. Carefully she carried the heavy jug upstairs, trying not to spill any of the scalding water. Reaching his door, she knocked tentatively, and turned to head back downstairs to begin cooking the breakfast of eggs, bacon and porridge. She was just reaching the top of the stairs when she heard the door open, turning back she saw Edward just bending to collect the jug. Naked from the waist up, Nesta gazed at his well toned body, appreciating his lean, well fed physique. Continuing to watch as he picked up the jug and turned back into his room, Nesta imagined how it would feel to be wrapped in Edward's strong arms. Suddenly he looked across at Nesta, seemingly aware of her interest.

"Good morning Nesta" he called seemingly unaware of the effect that his state of undress was having on his housemaid's equilibrium.

"Good morning Doctor" Nesta stammered, embarrassed to have been caught staring at her master in a state of undress, sure that he must have been aware of her thoughts. Staring at her feet, she risked a quick glance up, but found her eyes were again drawn to Edward's lean stomach, and muscular arms. A deep breath, and then she made a conscious effort to look Edward in the eye.

"I trust there are no problems, and all is in order for today?" he asked, his eyes sparkling with mischief. He recognized and enjoyed Nesta's interest, and was revelling in her discomfiture, so different to brazen behaviour of the women in the London saloons. Seeing the laughter in Edward's eyes, and thinking that it was aimed at her, Nesta bobbed a quick curtsey, and turned and fled to the safety of the kitchen.

Edward closed the door smiling to himself. He was aware that he had a fine figure, as yet unspoilt by accident or over indulgence, and was somewhat pleased with the effect that it had had on Nesta. He had longed to reach out to Nesta, to take her in his arms and kiss her, and he was now sure that she would welcome his advances, but he knew that the social divide between them was vast. If he were to take Nesta as his lover, her reputation would be ruined. The strict moral code that prevailed amongst the Victorian Upper Middle Classes meant that while an affair would have little impact on his social standing, it would have very serious consequences for Nesta. Forever she would be tainted as a fallen woman, and shunned by many, while, hypocritically, many men would see her as fair game. It was not even as if Edward could marry her. As a professional with aristocratic connections, no matter how distant, he was so far above Nesta's social status that to marriage would cause as big a scandal as if he simply took her for a mistress. In fact, many of his former colleagues and friends would find that far more understandable.

Edward picked up the water jug from the previous night and standing with his head tipped over the washstand bowl, he poured the icy water over his head and neck. The water was so cold that it felt as if it would freeze his brain. Grabbing a towel, he rubbed his head vigorously, clearing his head of the last remnants of sleep. Now using the hot water that Nesta had provided, he shaved himself rapidly and expertly, deftly removing the last of the night's stubble with his razor-sharp blade. Finally satisfied, he dressed in his second-best suit, and hurried downstairs to breakfast.

Edward entered the dining room to find the table set with breakfast dishes, and the buffet covered with lidded tureens. Cautiously lifting the lid of the first, he was enveloped in the delicious aroma of freshly cooked bacon and eggs. Gingerly he lifted the lid of the next to find it contained his favourite a pair of kippers, lightly fried in breadcrumbs. Taking his plate, he loaded it with food and returned to the table, and the neatly folded newspaper. Sitting down and tucking into his princely breakfast Edward thought, not for the first time, how lucky he was to have Nesta. In a few short weeks her cheerful presence had completely changed the whole dynamic of the household, to the point where even the previously surly Miss Bates, had been known to smile. Yes, Edward thought, life was almost perfect. As much as he had resented his banishment from the bright lights of London society and the exciting developments in medicine which were being pioneered there, Edward appreciated just how lucky he had been. His medical practice was large and healthy, and likely only to increase. His social circle was rapidly expanding, everyone he had invited to his dinner party being only to keen to attend. All he needed now he thought was a wife, and looking dolefully at his cup, a decent cup of coffee. However, as he drank the rather muddy brew which passed for breakfast coffee, Edward found his eye drawn to an advert for *Loysel's Hydrostatic Urn*, which promised, by a process of percolation to provide fresh coffee, without the need for isinglass or egg whites to clear it. As Edward contemplated his rather muddy drink, he resolved to place an order for one straight away. He longed for a cup of good strong cafe noir, or cafe au lait, which he had drunk so often visiting the saloons of London. If he could replicate that coffee here, rather than the rather weak, watery coffee Nesta provided, he would be a very happy man.

The day passed quietly, with snow lying thick on the ground, and more falling steadily, Edward didn't have many patients visiting him. As lunchtime approached, Edward got up from his desk from where he had been dealing with his correspondence and walked over to the front window. Looking up and down the street, all was white, with smoke rising from every chimney. Even the main road had lost its usual dismal appearance as a carpet of straw, mud, and worse, to be covered instead in a thick blanket of snow. A few foot tracks, and a single line of wheel marks from a coach marked the only travel that had taken place that day as the heavy snowfall had reduced traffic on the busy thoroughfare to almost nothing. Looking at the state of the street, a principle highway in Coleford, Edward thought it highly unlikely that anyone would brave the dismal weather to attend his dinner party that evening. Sadly, he headed towards the kitchen to warn Nesta that it was unlikely that anyone would come to sample her wares that night knowing that she had been looking forward to the occasion with as much relish as he had. Thus he was already in the hall when there came a frantic ringing of the bell, and someone began beating on the door as if their life depended on it.

Answering the door, he was immediately grabbed by Annie, the pinch-faced nursemaid to Sir Cyril's infant daughter.

"Thank God I've found you! We need you to come immediately. It's Victoria, she's poorly. I don't know what's wrong. Come quickly, oh Sir, please hurry and come quickly" She pleaded, grabbing his arm and almost pulling him out into the snow as he was in his shirt sleeves. Gently Edward shook her off. "Of course I'll come" he said "Let me just prepare a few things, it won't take a moment." And with that he hurried back inside the house to collect his medical bag and a thick coat, followed doggedly by Annie extorting him to hurry. Taking a stout walking stick from the rack by the door, Edward headed outside into the snow. Automatically he began to head down the street towards the coal yard where he stabled his horse only to find himself stopped by Annie impatiently pulling on his sleeve.

"Come on Doctor!" she said with exasperation "Victoria is up here, at the Inn. We was on our way back from Bristol when the snows started. Sir Cyril decided it was too dangerous to continue last night, so we stayed at the Inn here. That's where we need to go." With that she was off, racing through the snow, slipping and sliding until they reached the door of the inn. As they went inside they were hit with a warm fug. The pleasant smells of roasting meats, fresh bread, and the little packets of dried lavender that the landlady had taken to strewing around the place, combined with the less pleasant aromas of unwashed bodies, damp clothing, spilt beer, and poorly drawing fires. Following Annie, Edward smiled and nodded to his neighbours and patients, and began to laboriously pick his way carefully across the room that was packed with men and dogs. It seemed like almost all of the trades around Coleford had shut down as the thick snow stopped even the hardened foresters from venturing out into the surrounding forest and pasture lands.

Eventually they reached the small staircase in the corner that led upstairs to the few rooms available for hire. Here Edward found Sir Cyril and his wife ensconced in a small private drawing room. Lady Annabel was huddled over a small wicker travelling crib, alternating between gently wiping the baby's brow, and drying her own tears on a dainty lace handkerchief. Sir Cyril, who had been standing staring out of the window across the inns yard and towards the forest, turned. His face was grim as he strode across the room to clasp the doctor's hand.

"Dr James - Edward. Thank-you for coming so quickly. It's Victoria, she's in a bit of a poor way I'm afraid. Is there anything you can do for her? She's so fretful." said Sir Cyril, desperation etched into every line of his face.

Lady Annabel looked up, uncharacteristically dishevelled, her face tear-stained and her hair awry, completely at odds to her normal carefully arranged hair, and expertly applied powders. Her eyes hollow, and her voice heavy with despair she begged. "Please save her Doctor. Please save my baby".

Edward walked towards the crib, fearing the worse. When he peered inside he saw Victoria, well bundled in clothes, and her face flushed a deep pink. She tossed and twitched, emitting small mewling sounds. Edward reached in and picked her up. Briefly she opened her eyes and looked at him, before closing them tightly again. Deftly Edward began to remove her clothing so he could better examine her. As he removed the outer layers of swaddling, a foul stench spread around the room. Ignoring the smell, and slight damp patch leaking through the baby's napkin, Edward carefully removed the final layer of clothing. There, spreading across her tiny chest were a few small raised spots. Replacing the covers loosely over the child, he nodded to himself, turning away from the crib to address Annie.

"You can clean her up and dress her now. However, try not to bundle her so tightly. With the fire raging in here it is quite warm enough; she only requires a few light coverings." He said to Annie, slightly exasperated that he should have to give such basic advice to the child's nurse, particularly since he had already warned her once before about the dangers over heating infants. Mentally he resolved to talk to Sir Cyril discreetly about his choice of nursemaid, and maybe suggest that he should look for a different nurse for the baby.

"Sir Cyril, Lady Annabel, it would appear that Victoria has the chicken pox. It's an unusual time of year for it, I grant you, but the blisters are quite unmistakeable. It's not normally anything to worry overly about, although it can be trickier in one so young. Plenty of warm oatmeal baths, and keep her cool is the best way forward."

Lady Annabel shook her head vigorously. "Chicken pox –oh my poor baby!" she cried "Will she be terribly scarred? I can't bear to think of my little one being so, so damaged."

"Now, now, Lady Annabel. There is no cause for distress. Chicken pox is normally a very mild condition. She'll be back to her normal self in no time. However, I must again stress to you the importance of not allowing her to get so hot. She will have a slight fever, and her spots may itch slightly, but she will fair far, far better if you keep her cool. Not cold mind you, but as I have cautioned you before, there is no need to keep her bundled so." Replied Edward kindly, but firmly. Sir Cyril crossed the room and stood with his hand on his wife's shoulder.

"Thank-you Doctor" he said, and meeting Edward's steady gaze "I can assure you that our nursemaid will follow your directives to the letter. My daughter will not be swaddled or over-bundled again." As he said this, Annie looked up, and Edward was surprised by the hatred in her eyes. There was something odd about the whole situation Edward thought. The nursemaid was clearly concerned for the child when she came to fetch him, anxious to return to her charge quickly. However, she was also ineffectual, failing to complete some of the most basic tasks to keep the child happy and healthy. While Annie clearly hated Sir Cyril, he glared back with a mixture of distrust and disgust. Not a happy domestic situation, thought Edward, as clearly Sir Cyril did not like or approve of his daughter's nurse. Annie must have been appointed by Lady Annabel, he mused. Edward prepared to make his good-byes, shaking Sir Cyril's hand, and touching his hat towards Annie. As he raised Lady Annabel's hand to kiss Edward froze. It was warm and clammy, and now he looked more closely at her face he could see that under the tear stains she was flushed, her eyes wide with fever. Edward paused, looking closely at Lady Annabel. A perceptive man, Sir Cyril recognised that something was wrong.

"What is it Doctor?" he muttered in an undertone.

Edward knelt on the floor in front of Lady Annabel, and gently put his fingers to her wrist to feel her pulse. As he expected it was fast and irregular. "My Lady, forgive me. Have you ever had the chicken pox?" he asked gently. Woozily, Lady Annabel shook her head.

"I'm not sure. I don't think so." She mumbled. Sir Cyril looked from his wife to the doctor and back again. His clever eyes showed that he had grasped the situation immediately.

"My dear, I told you to take more rest. Here why don't you come and lie down on the bed a while. Little Victoria will be fine. Annie will take good care of her and be sure to follow the doctor's advice about keeping her cool, won't you Annie?" he said solicitously, trying to encourage his wife to move away from the crib-side. "You have a little rest, and I'll arrange for us to head back home this afternoon. I'm sorry Edward, I'm afraid we will of course have to miss your dinner party, but I'm sure you quite understand in the circumstances."

With many long backward glances towards the crib, Lady Annabel allowed herself to be led away by her husband. Through the closed door Sir Cyril could be heard to continue to fuss about offering blankets and to send down for warm drinks and possets. Edward smiled to himself at Sir Cyril's fussing, staring out of the window so that Annie would not see his barely suppressed laughter. Having settled his wife, Sir Cyril returned quietly and unnoticed a few minutes later. He was surprised that Edward was still in the private drawing room, staring out into the snow. The atmosphere in the room was frosty, the mutual apathy between Edward and Annie evident. While Edward stared out of the window, keeping his back to Annie so that he didn't feel obliged to engage her in polite conversation, Annie sat in the chair recently vacated by Lady Annabel. Rocking the crib absentmindedly with her foot, her gaze was fixed on Edward's back. Although Edward seemed completely relaxed and oblivious to her presence, Annie was glaring at him with such venom that Sir Cyril was surprised that Edward didn't drop down dead where he stood. He cleared his throat. Both Edward and Annie jumped, Edward to turn around, his face impassive, while Annie's whole demeanour changed to one more befitting a nurse with a sick charge. Her abrupt change of manner from complete disinterest to humble concern ignited a nagging doubt. If he hadn't seen the loathing on her face with his own eyes he would never have believed her capable of such naked hatred. That she could hide her emotions so quickly and completely made him worry slightly about what else she could be hiding. If he was completely honest with himself, he had never been happy with Annie as a nurse and had even discussed her dismissal with his wife. There was something about her that just didn't seem quite right somehow, but for now, he thought, that will have to wait. Once Annabel is herself again, and Victoria has recovered, then I can give Annie notice, but until then, I need her to look after Victoria. At least there is no doubt that she dotes on her, he thought.

"Edward, thank –you for staying, but Lady Annabel is dozing, and as you can see Annie has everything in hand here with little Vicky." said Sir Cyril with an expansive gesture sounding far more jovial that he felt. "Now, I need to speak to mine host about organising some transport home for us, and then we'll be off."

Edward cleared his throat uncomfortably. He knew that he risked offending Sir Cyril, but he needed to speak up. "I'm sorry Sir Cyril, but I really must counsel against it. The snow is still falling fast; my maid told me that even the turnpike was almost impassable last night. By now it will surely be blocked. A fit man might get through, but not an ill woman with a sick baby. It would be foolish to attempt such a thing, as your physician, and as I hope, your friend, I must implore you not to risk them in this way." Said Edward firmly.

Sir Cyril rubbed his face with his hands. A roar of raucous laughter from the tap room bellowed up through the floor boards, disturbing the quiet of the rooms, and causing Victoria to stir and whimper in her crib. A quick glance out of the window convinced him of the truth of Edward's words. He collapsed heavily into a chair. Gripping the arms, he noticed the multitude of stains that covered the upholstery and left his hands feeling vaguely sticky. Looking around the room in despair his keen eyes picked out the cobwebs in the rafters and the small piles of mouse droppings in the corners of the room. He shuddered fastidiously.

"I understand what you are saying Edward, but we can't stay here. It's too, it's too *basic*, for myself, of course I could endure it, but Lady Annabel is delicate. The roads are difficult, yes, but not yet completely impassable. There is no telling how much longer the snow will fall for, if we set out at once we might, should, get home. If not, it could be weeks until a thaw. I don't want my wife to spend a lengthy convalescence in this dirty, noisy, dingy tavern. She needs a few comforts. No, we must leave here as soon as possible."

Edward smiled brightly "Hmm. Well, perhaps you would accept my hospitality instead? My home is not as grand as your own of course, but it is clean and quiet, and Nesta and Miss Bates are on hand to help with any nursing. Why don't you bring Victoria and Lady Annabel to my house? I would be delighted to offer our assistance."

Pausing for a moment, Sir Cyril looked between the doctor, the snow outside the window, and the door to his wife's bedroom. He would much rather head back to his own house, but Edward was almost certainly correct; the snow was too thick to allow them to travel safely. While Edward's house would be a better place for Lady Annabel and Victoria to convalesce, it made Sir Cyril feel awkward to accept the hospitality of someone that he saw as his social inferior. Then again, he thought, he had heard that Edward had been trained at a proper London medical school and had connections to the aristocracy himself, so he was a cut above the average sawbones. Perhaps it would not be too demeaning to accept Edward's offer, and certainly it was the best he could do in the current circumstances. Slowly he nodded his head.

"Thank-you Edward, that is most generous of you. We will come at once. Annie, can you begin to pack please. I want us to move as soon as you and the Doctor are ready."

Behind Sir Cyril's back, Annie glared at Edward. She would rather face the difficulties and dangers of the frozen roads than go to stay with the doctor, but she knew better than to argue with Sir Cyril. As soon as she could get Lady Annabel on her own, she'd make her opinions known. They wouldn't be staying long at the Doctors house. She'd see to that.

Although Edward was grateful for his patient's sake that Sir Cyril had seen the sense in not venturing out into the snow, he was apprehensive about having them to stay in his home. Although the house had several guest rooms, Edward had barely even glanced in them, and rightly suspected that they would take a little time to prepare for visitors, particularly ones such as Sir Cyril who saw themselves as minor aristocracy. Edward chuckled to himself as he made his way as quickly as possible into the house; he knew that his Grandfather, himself a Lord and far and away Sir Cyril's social superior, would have had little time for Sir Cyril and his pretensions.

Coming into the kitchen, he found Nesta and Ms Bates working away industriously. Quickly he explained that Sir Cyril, Lady Annabel, Victoria and Annie would all be coming to stay. Nesta and Miss Bates exchanged a grimace.

"Right lass. Let's make the best of this." Said Miss Bates "We'll put Lady Annabel in the blue bedroom, Victoria can go in the dressing room, so she's nearby for her. Sir Cyril will have to go into the little room at the back, if Lady Annabel is ill, he won't want to be in with her."

"What about the Nurse? Where'll we put her?" asked Nesta.

"Humph. She can go on a truckle on the floor of her mistresses' room. And make sure you go and lock all the dresser cupboards and keep the pantry key close. We don't want the likes of that Annie wandering in and out." Miss Bates warned. Nesta was surprised at the venom in Miss Bates' voice. But then she wasn't anything like as familiar with her wider neighbours as Miss Bates, who it seemed to Nesta, knew everybody within St Breivals, and had something to say about all of them! Nesta had quickly learnt to take what Miss Bates gossip with a pinch of salt. While it was interesting to hear her opinions on people, Nesta had always been taught to wait, and form her own opinions. Miss Bates' good opinion was too often based on her own desires and what the other person could do for her to be considered a shrewd judge of character. She was therefore quite taken aback when Edward endorsed Miss Bates assessment of the nursemaid.

"Quite right Miss Bates," he said "for as long as Annie is in this house, I want you to make sure that you keep the dressers and pantry locked. I hope she will be kept busy looking after her charge and nursing her mistress. Although I would appreciate it if you could help her with this when you can, please remember that it is principally her job. Annie is to be treated as you would any other visiting servant. She should not give you orders, and you do not need to follow any requests that you think are unreasonable. She is not to wander around the house aimlessly, and for as long as she is here, I want you to make sure that the door to my study and consulting rooms are kept well locked. Even if you only leave the room for a minute, you must lock the door behind you. I hope that that's clear." He exchanged nods with Miss Bates, and an unspoken understanding passed between them, before he hurried from the kitchen.

"What was all that about?" Nesta asked when he had left "I've never known him to labour a point like that!"

Slowly Miss Bates looked at Annie, her face grim. "Aye, well, shrewd man, that doctor. I can't say I took to him at first, but he's alright. There's summit rotten about that Annie. I can't tell what it is, but there's summit. So you just take the keys, and you go round and lock everything up. And make sure you keep your keys in your pocket. We don't want the likes of her wandering where she has no business to be!" With that Miss Bates gently shooed Nesta out of the kitchen, before she headed upstairs to begin preparing the little used guest bedrooms.

Nesta hurried around the house, checking that cupboards and doors were firmly locked, and had their keys removed. Then she rushed upstairs to help Miss Bates with preparing the rooms. There was a lot to do. Fire places needed to be blacked, then fires laid and lit, shelves and windowsills dusted, and the beds made up with fresh linen. A small truckle bed was found in the attic for Annie to use in the little dressing room which they intended to use as a makeshift nursery. Nesta ran back and forth to the linen cupboard, finding out clean sheets, and putting spares to one side, ready for if they were needed for the sick bed, while Miss Bates hunted in the attics for spare chamber pots, and an old battered bucket for the baby's nappies.

Finally, after much racing around they were ready. Miss Bates headed downstairs to report to Edward that they were now ready to receive guests, while Nesta returned to the kitchen, having it in mind to make some beef tea, her mother's cure all for any illness. She was just beginning to skim the surface of the tea, removing any scum and fat that had floated to the surface, when the kitchen door was flung open and in stormed Annie.

"It won't do. It won't do at all. How can my mistress be expected to sleep, to convalesce, in a place like this! There are not enough pillows and bolsters for her, and there is no jug of fresh water at the bedside. And what is that you are making? Surely you can't expect anybody to eat or drink that!" ranted Annie as she paced around the kitchen, picking up utensils and replacing them with a grimace, lifting and banging down pans. Nesta, used to dealing with tantrums from her younger siblings, simply ignored her, and continued to skim scum from the beef broth bubbling away on the hob. Eventually Annie reached the door to the scullery and pantry beyond. Finding it locked, she rattled the handle, then turned to Nesta.

"You! Open this door at once! I want to look inside!" she demanded.

"No. It stays locked." Replied Nesta calmly. The broth simmered and skimmed to her satisfaction, Nesta removed the heavy black iron pot from the stove, and carried it to the table, where she gingerly began pouring the liquid through a fine sieve to remove any lumps.

"What! How dare you defy me! I told you to open this door girl, and open it you will!" screeched Annie, her eyes burning with rage. All the time, Nesta continued calmly about her chores, preparing food for a late light luncheon. This infuriated Annie even more and, unused to being ignored, she flew towards Nesta in a fury. Standing close to Nesta, her face only inches from Nesta's, she poked Nesta in the chest with one hard, bony finger.

"I told you to open that door. When your betters tell you to do something, you do it. So let me make this clear, I am your superior in all things. When I give an order, you do it. If I ask you for something, you fetch it. You do not want to cross me, girl, I promise you that. Now give me your keys. I will hold them while I am here." She said, her voice full of malice, spittle dripping from the corner of her mouth where she had worked herself up into a state of red hot anger. Annie thrust out a well calloused hand, the thick sinews showing the strength in her arms.

Nesta took an involuntary step backwards and found herself pinned against the sink. Inside Nesta was quaking with fear. She now understood why Edward and Miss Bates were so wary of Annie. Both must have sensed, or heard, something which revealed her true nature. The act that Annie put on of the perfect nursemaid, kind and attentive, was just that - an act, designed to deceive those that she saw as her superiors. As soon as they had gone, however, Annie returned to her true form, bullying and intimidating those that she saw as beneath her, manipulating people to her own ends. Annie had judged that Nesta, a young girl, not long started in service would be easy to control, however she had reckoned without Nesta's strong character. Nesta was not ready to be bullied and intimated. She would not give up so easily.

"No" she said firmly. Annie raised a hand to slap Nesta across the face, Nesta tensed herself for the blow, closing her eyes and turning her face away, but the blow never came. After a pause which felt to Nesta like an eternity, but was actually only a few seconds, Nesta slowly half-opened one eye. Then opened both with relief. Unnoticed by Annie and Nesta, Edward and Sir Cyril had been drawn to the kitchen by the sound of Annie shrieking. They stood together in the doorway, watching the power struggle within. As Annie bullied Nesta back against the sink, Edward moved, ready to rescue Nesta. Moving quickly, he had been able to catch Annie's hand before she landed a blow. Holding her thin wrist tightly, he was surprised by her wiry strength. However, it was no match for his own greater strength.

Annie turned startled that anyone would lay hands on her. Seeing the doctor and Sir Cyril standing behind in the doorway, Annie quickly went on the offensive.

"Sir Cyril, Doctor, thank goodness you are here! I was making my Lady some beef tea to tempt her appetite when this girl came in. She refused to let me into the store rooms to fetch a little salt to season the tea. Please Doctor, I know it will lift my mistress, just let me get a little salt." She wheedled, aiming to make out that Nesta was being unreasonable.

Edwards face remained impassive. He had seen enough of the incident to know who the aggressor was. Edward cast a glance at Sir Cyril, hoping he would step in. Edward did not want to have to discipline his guest's servants, particularly not in front of him, as he knew that the officious Sir Cyril would consider it a grave insult. However, he was not willing to stand by and see Nesta abused. If Sir Cyril would not, Edward would have to deal with Annie himself, even if it cost him Sir Cyril's friendship, and in turn, put his dreams of a hospital in jeopardy. He was painfully aware that he needed Sir Cyril's support and patronage to make the hospital a reality.

Sir Cyril's face was inscrutable. He had seen the appalling way in which Annie had treated the maid, and in fact, had suspected for some time that Annie was a bully and a petty tyrant amongst his servants at home. Sir Cyril was not a coward, he was brave and courageous, resolute, a kind and just master to his servants; however, he was also completely in awe of his much younger wife and would go to great lengths to keep her happy and content, even if that meant compromising his own wishes. It would be difficult to remove Annie from his household, although he knew that that is what he must do, as she was devoted to her mistress, just as Lady Annabel was devoted to Annie. Previous attempts to broach the subject of Annie's dismissal with his wife had been met with furious arguments, bordering on hysterics. However, trying to slap a maid in a guest's house was intolerable, even Lady Annabel would see that. Sir Cyril steeled himself, he would have to speak to his wife again. Perhaps when she had recovered a little, he would be able to make her see sense about the matter. But for now, to avoid causing her any more distress, Annie would have to stay. However, so as not to lose face in front of the doctor and be thought of as being unable to control his own servants, he would have to publically admonish her.

"Annie. Both the Doctor and I witnessed the whole argument. I know that you started shouting at the poor maid for no good reason. Now I have agreed with the doctor that his staff will fetch meals for Lady Annabel. You can either choose to eat with her, in her rooms, to keep her company, or come down here to the kitchen to eat with Doctor James' cook-maid and house-keeper. It is up to you what you would prefer to do, although you will of course need to let the house-keeper know. If you need anything to help with nursing my wife, or for Victoria, you need only ask, but the Doctor would prefer you not to try to fetch things yourself. The good doctor has lots of potent medicines which need to be handled with care and he does not want you to inadvertently hurt yourself or your charges. So you will go only to the kitchen to ask for things you need. Ask mind you, not demand! Please remember we are guests here. I do not want any repeat of this unedifying behaviour Annie. If I hear of another outburst like this, I will be forced to terminate your employment immediately. Now return to your charges please."

Annie's face turned a deep beetroot as she struggled to contain her rage. She stalked out of the kitchen to return to her mistress. Everyone let out a sigh of relief.

"Edward, please accept my profound apologies'. Completely intolerable behaviour. I am sorry you had to witness such disgraceful behaviour" said Sir Cyril, mopping his face with a large spotty silk handkerchief. Turning to Nesta he said awkwardly "And my apologies to you too of course, erm..."

"Nesta Sir" she supplied with a smile and a curtsey "The beef tea is almost ready Sir, I just need to skim off the fat when it's cooled, and warm it back up ready. Is there anything in particular that your wife likes? I'm not as accomplished as your cook of course, but maybe I would be able to make something to tempt your wife?"

Sir Cyril smiled. Clearly the maid, this Nesta, was none the worst from being harangued by his servant and was still eager to help. He thought hard.

"Well, Lady Annabel is very keen on rice pudding, very keen. I think her nanny used to make it for her, perhaps, that, if the good doctor thought it advisable of course?"

"A capital idea, Sir Cyril, a good food for invalids. Nesta, could you make up some rice pudding, maybe with a little of Miss Bates best strawberry jam?" said Edward, relieved that everything seemed to be calming down.

"Of course, Sir. I'll get on with it right away." Said Nesta giving them a small curtsey and heading off to the pantry to collect some pudding rice and the big earthenware jug of milk which was kept in the cool at the back of the scullery.

Chapter Twenty

Dawn was just starting to break, the sun rising slowly over the trees of the forest. It had been another clear, cold night. The snow which had fallen the previous day had been blown around by the bitter north easterly wind forming deep drifts which blocked most of the roads. The ground covered in a thick, cold blanket and the roads a slushy mess of snow, manure and refuse churned together by the feet of the few pedestrians who had braved the weather to continue their business under the sullen sky. Pinkish-grey clouds gathered on the horizon, threatening yet more snow, and the temperature was still well below freezing. Nesta peeped out of the window in her attic bedroom. A thick blanket from her bed wrapped around her shoulders, her bare feet freezing on the bare wooden floorboards. Moving to the washstand, she found her jug of washing water had taken a thin film of ice. Nonetheless, she used the water to wash rapidly, gasping at the coldness of it, before dressing, placing a clean pinafore over her dress. Thoughtfully, she carried her shoes so as not to make a noise on the stairs and disturb the guests, and so padded down stairs in stocking feet.

Turning across the landing she passed the door to Lady Annabel's room. That door had a tricky catch so that it would often spring open if not firmly shut. So it was that the door was slightly ajar. As she passed the doorway, Nesta could hear sobbing from within. She stopped, unsure of whether to knock and enter to offer comfort and assistance to Lady Annabel, or whether to attempt to rouse Annie, so that she could tend to her mistress. She had just decided to go in herself, when she heard the low hiss of Annie's voice.

"You know what we agreed. If he tries to let me go, I'll tell Sir Cyril everything. After all, what have *I* got to lose?"

The sobbing increased, and disturbed, Nesta backed away from the door to continue to the kitchen and her work. As she reached the top of the stairs, Nesta was aware of someone watching her. Turning quickly, she saw Edward already neatly dressed, standing in his study doorway looking worried. Catching her eye, Edward beckoned Nesta to follow him into his study.

When she went in, shoes still in hand, he was standing in front of an inexpertly banked fire, his face like thunder. "Nesta. I know you had a nasty run in with Annie, but I cannot countenance my staff spying on my guests." His voice dripping with distain. "I cannot, will not, accept eavesdroppers. Do I make myself clear?"

Nesta's face burnt bright red. "Yes Sir. Sorry Sir." She stammered, embarrassed both that the doctor was admonishing her, and that she had been listening to what was obviously a private conversation, no matter how disturbing it was "I didn't mean to eavesdrop Sir"

Edward's eyebrows raised. "So you just happened to find yourself in the doorway to one of our guest's bedroom did you?" He asked sarcastically.

"Yes Sir. Well no, Sir. It was just the crying. I could hear Lady Annabel sobbing, and I thought that maybe she needed something, and Annie wasn't there, or was asleep or something. Then when I went to open the door, I could hear Annie in there. And she was talking to Lady Annabel, and well, threatening to tell Sir Cyril something, so I thought I'd best away. Let them be. I didn't mean to eavesdrop Sir, honestly. But now I suppose you think I'm a gossip as well. Sorry Sir. It won't happen again." Nesta replied wretchedly, upset not only with herself for listening, and for reporting what she had heard – although she had blurted that out without thinking, but also disturbed by the way in which Annie was talking to Lady Annabel, as if Annie was in charge, rather than her mistress.

Edward frowned. Concerned by what Nesta had told him. It did not bode well for Annabel if Annie had some kind of hold over her. Edward was sure that not only would Sir Cyril remove the nurse as soon as possible, but that Annie would be vicious and would hurt Annabel if she could. Since his first meeting with Annie he had been convinced that there was something wrong, as though she had a powerful hold over Lady Annabel. That there was some kind of secret did not surprise Edward

"Put your shoes on Nesta" he said absentmindedly. Nesta put her shoes on and left the study, leaving Edward staring out of his window, deep in thought as to how he could help Lady Annabel.

The day passed in a whirl as Nesta and Miss Bates rushed around trying to make the household, with its four additional members run smoothly. Annie was more of a hindrance than a help. She refused to carry meals up for herself or Lady Annabel, and would demand assistance at every opportunity, expecting to be waited upon. Nesta wore herself out running up and downstairs as she brought a constant stream of beef tea for Lady Annabel, and warm milk for the baby, and taking away chamber pots and soiled nappies from Victoria. Victoria herself was out of sorts and cried constantly, which in turn distressed her mother, and made the whole house fretful. Miss Bates became sullen and withdrawn, while Nesta was exhausted trying to meet the constant demands. Sir Cyril alternated between sitting by his wife's bed as she tossed and turned in a broken, feverish sleep, and pacing up and down the drawing room. By evening the whole household was on tenterhooks. The pressure of ill-feeling, distrust, combined with worry for Lady Annabel, whose fever still hadn't broken, making everyone agitated. By late afternoon, even the morose Miss Bates couldn't stand it any longer. Taking her hat and cloak she'd announced that she was going to church and had yet to return. Dinner was a particularly gloomy meal, with both Sir Cyril and Edward eating in sullen silence. Nesta had served them slices of her rich savoury pie before beating a hasty retreat to the kitchen, unable to bear the atmosphere in the dining room. Pie was a firm favourite with Edward, a meal he would normally eat with gusto, but now pushed the pieces miserably around his plate, his appetite lost to the oppressive tension in the house.

A scream from upstairs broke the silence as it echoed around the house, followed quickly by the sound of heavy footsteps as somebody rushed across the landing and down the stairs. Nesta hurried into the hallway, the front door stood open. Full of foreboding, she rushed upstairs. The rooms were empty. As she hurried back towards the dining room, she met Edward in hallway, shutting the front door.

"Its Lady Annabel" she panted "her and the bairn, they've gone. It must be that Annie, she's taken them!"

Panic ensued. Grimly Edward strode from the room, flinging open doors and searching rooms, checking that they were not elsewhere in the house, unaware of the concern that their departure had caused. Having quickly checked all the other rooms, Edward returned to the front bedroom that Annabel had been using. The bed was rumpled, and clothing was left in untidy heaps, so it was evident that she had left, both in a hurry, and not entirely willingly. A tray of food, now luke warm and congealed stood untouched on the side table where Nesta had left it. Looking into the dressing room, the crib stood cold and empty. Sir Cyril stood in the middle of the room, holding his daughters small doll tightly. Distress marked every line of his face, and he stood, bewildered and broken, unable to process that his wife and daughter were missing.

Seeing that Sir Cyril would be of little use for the moment, Edward took charge. He ordered Sir Cyril to look around, to see if any of his wife's clothes were missing. Sir Cyril stared around blankly. Nesta, quick to understand the doctor's thoughts, to see if they had left willingly or had been taken, looked quickly too.

"I'm not sure Sir, but I don't think there's much of Lady Annabel's stuff missing. But there is a blanket missing from the bed, and little Victoria's warm cloak – that's gone. There's no sign of that Annie either. It looks as if all her stuff has been taken." she reported to the doctor in an undertone. Looking out of the window "it's starting to snow again Sir. And I've had a quick peek out the back. There are footprints in the snow heading for the gate. Towards the forest."

Edward closed his eyes, pursed his lips and let out a long slow breath. "Right" he said "Here's what we'll do. I'll set out to follow these footprints. They can't have got too far.

Nesta, you head round to your Uncle William's, see if you can round up a few men. Then see if you can find out where Miss Bates has taken herself off too, get her to come back and help you. We need to find them both as soon as possible. It'll be bitter out there again tonight."

Quickly, they hurried away, to rouse friends and family to help with the search. Edward pulled on his boots and headed into the scullery where a large lamp was kept. Shaking it to check it was full of oil, he lit it, and pulling on his great coat, hurried out into the swirling snow to follow the footprints from the back door. Sir Cyril remained standing stock still in the middle of the room, clutching the small doll that he had brought for his daughter. He slipped it inside his waistcoat, so that it would be close to his heart, before he grabbed his own cloak and headed out into the storm, racing to catch up with the doctor.

Battling against what was growing into an increasingly strong wind, Edward hurried along the back paths, following the footprints as quickly as he could. Mentally he tried to work out how much of a head start Lady Annabel had. He knew that Nesta and Miss Bates had mostly kept away from the sick room, driven out by the brooding presence of Annie. Something had seemed wrong from when Annie had first entered the house, and he should have been more watchful, aware that something like this might happen. He knew that he would not forgive himself if something happened to Lady Annabel or the baby, however much a small voice of reason reminded him that it was not his fault, not his responsibility for the nurse, certain as he was that it was her that had stolen Lady Annabel and Victoria away. Plodding resolutely through the snow, his head down, and shoulders hunched against the cold. He followed the footprints as best he could through the snow. So engrossed was he, that he didn't hear the footsteps until they were right behind him. Turning quickly he was relieved to see the solid reassuring figure of Samuel. Behind him, peeping out from an old great coat of her Uncles was Nesta.

"Well met, Doctor. It's a filthy night. Nesta found us. I hear you've lost Lady Annabel and her bairn." He said in his long slow drawl. "Well I reckon as you might need some help, and you've been good to Jane, so..."

Edward reached over and shook him firmly by the hand. "Thank-you Samuel. I can't tell you how glad to see you! I think these are their footprints, but I'm not sure."

Samuel looked down at the footprints, then back at the doctor with confusion. "Humf" he said "These ain't Lady Annabel's, they're fox tracks."

The colour drained from Edward's face as he realised that he had lost tracks. Their best, only, hope of finding Lady Annabel before it was too late. "My God. What have I done?!" he cried.

"Don't worry, Doctor" said Samuel grimly "let's head back, we'll find their tracks again, don't you fret." Samuel led the way back, following the doctor's prints carefully. They had only travelled a short distance when Samuel stopped. He crouched looking carefully at the floor he could see the faint outline of another human foot, now half-covered again with the fresh snow that was still continuing to fall steadily. Samuel led the way off the established path, following a small track which head off up towards Purples Hill, and the enclosures beyond. The trail headed over rough ground, climbing ever upwards towards a rocky outcrop.

"Are you sure this is the right way?" Edward demanded "Haughton Hall is the other way."

Nesta patted his arm reassuringly. "Nobody can track like my Uncle Samuel. There isn't an animal that walks God's earth that he can't follow. Now, hush! Let him concentrate."

Onwards and upwards they headed, pushing through wet undergrowth so their clothes were soaked, and they were half-blinded by the windblown, powdery snow. Somehow the darkness seemed to be even more complete as they headed further into the trees. The occasional scurrying from the undergrowth told them that other creatures were about. Stumbling over roots and dead branches Edward felt the first tendrils of fear, his imagination running wild as he remembered every tale of boggarts and bogeymen he had ever heard. Trying to quell his fears by telling himself it was only foxes or small rodents going about their nocturnal business he could hear, he nonetheless tried to keep as close as possible to Samuel, and the dim circle of light from the lamp.

Suddenly Samuel stopped. On the wind they could hear faint snatches of shouting, and a baby crying. Samuel turned, and placing a finger to his lips, indicated that they should edge forwards as quietly as possible. Slowly, carefully they crept forward, Samuel turning down the lamp and shielding it, so that it let out barely a glimmer in the dark night. The voices were closer than they thought, the sound carrying only a short distance on that stormy, windswept night. The trees began to thin slightly, and they found themselves on the edge of an expanse of heathery moorland. Kneeling on the ground, her feet bare and dressed only in a thin, sopping wet nightgown, was Lady Annabel, desperately begging, pleading with a cloaked, hooded, figure.

"Please, please, I'll do anything, give you anything! Just please don't hurt my baby." She begged, weeping her arms raised in supplication.

"Your baby? Your baby! She's not your baby! You're barren as well you know." The cloaked woman sneered back, holding the baby close to her own body. "This isn't your baby. I'm taking her, back to where she'll be properly looked after. Loved. Cherished." The voice from inside the cloak was muffled so that it was impossible to work out who it belonged to, but the bitterness was clear. Samuel was pale; he edged back, murmuring to himself.

"It can't be, it can't be." He muttered, Nesta looked at him. She was surprised to see her big, strong uncle, who always seemed so capable to be backing away from a woman in fear. A sharp, cry; the wail of a baby who is unhappy and hungry, pierced the air, drawing Nesta's attention back to the strange scene in front of her.

At the cry, the doctor raced forwards, stumbling as he tripped and fell on the uneven ground. A knife appeared in the hooded figure's hand, it slashed wildly at the doctor.

"Keep back! Keep away!" The voice hissed, as baby tucked under one arm, they lunged towards him. Instantly recognizing the face, Edward recoiled in shock. Mastering himself, he stepped forwards again, determined to rescue the child if he could. His eyes followed the knife carefully, he was wary of getting too close to the thin, razor sharp blade, which flickered and moved. Out if the corner of his eye he saw a shape moving towards him at speed. Fearing that there might be about to come under attack from an accomplice, he tried to dodge aside. Taking advantage of his momentary lapse of concentration, the knife flicked forwards. He landed heavily on the ground, the breath knocked out of him. Gasping for air, he struggled, finding himself trapped below something heavy. By the time he had pulled himself free, he was just in time to see the hooded figure scramble off over some rocks. About to follow, he realised the figure on the ground was Sir Cyril, gravely injured. His head cradled in his wife's lap, a wry smile on his face, Sir Cyril lay still on his back. Edward paused, torn between chasing after the hooded figure with the baby, and caring for the man who had undoubtedly just saved his life, possibly at the cost of his own. He had just decided that Sir Cyril would have to take his chances, that if he was to stand any chance of recovering Victoria he would need to run now, when he saw Samuel already chasing after her. Doggedly following the hooded figure, he was slowly gaining on them as they headed away, off across the moorland, higher and higher up the rocks. Wrenching his attention back from the desperate chase unfolding on the hillside, Edward turned his attention back to Sir Cyril. To his horror a large, dark red stain was spreading inexorably across Sir Cyril's chest. Already his face was deathly pale, his knuckles white as he gripped his wife's hand. Kneeling down beside him, Edward was aware of another figure by his side, gently Nesta touched Edward on the shoulder. Then she was gone, off into the darkness. His attention fixed on Sir Cyril Edward barely registered either her presence, or her leaving, so engrossed was he. Quickly, gently, Edward probed with expert fingers, searching, searching for the wound. Then he found it. Small, tucked away to one side, it bled copiously. The knife must have nicked a great vessel. Pressing hard, Edward attempted to staunch the flow of blood, but although it slowed slightly, the wound continued to bleed and bleed. Edward knew that without treatment, Sir Cyril would bleed to death very soon. Suddenly inspiration struck. Grabbing handfuls of snow, Edward pressed them against the wound, hoping that the cold would help to slow the rate of bleeding. Slowly, too slowly, it seemed to be working, the blood flow slowed to a trickle. Still, it was nothing more than a temporary measure, he needed to get Sir Cyril to his surgery, needed to sew his wound closed properly, but he knew that even if Lady Annabel and Nesta were to help, they would never be able to carry Sir Cyril's considerable bulk back down through the trees. The immediate emergency past, he finally realised that Nesta was no longer at his side. Suddenly he felt very alone.

A feral scream like that of a cornered, wounded animal rent the air. Together he and Lady Annabel looked up. A dim figure was just visible in the pale moonlight at the top of the rocky outcrop above them. There was some kind of struggle. Down below it was too dark for them to see properly what was happening above. All they make out was the shape of two people, one small and slight; the other larger – the figure of a man. The man reached out, a faint shout reached their ears. Then a scream. A long, terrible scream which echoed around. It seemed to those gathered below that it continued for an eternity, before finally it ended with dull thud as the body landed amongst the rocks just a few feet away from them. Silence fell. A total, dreadful silence.

Lady Annabel leaned forward into Edward's arms. He held her tightly. Her small, slight frame, dressed in only a thin shift which clung wetly to her body, pressed against him. Her body racked with desperate sobs as she cried with fear and desperation for both her husband and child. Her skin felt icy cold beneath his touch. Removing his heavy overcoat, Edward draped it around her shoulders. As he sat, shivering in the bitter wind in just his house coat, he was well aware that they needed to find shelter soon, or they would all succumb to the freezing temperatures. Weighed down with sadness, Edward knew he should get up and investigate the body lying at the bottom of the small cliff. He knew that he should go and check for any signs of life, but in his heart, he knew there would be none. Trying to summon the energy to his tired limbs to make himself move, his ears picked out another sound. The faint sound of a person walking unsteadily over rough ground in the dark. Stones rattled, twigs snapped, and the heavy, uneven tread of a man who is completely exhausted and drained of all energy. Out of the darkness he came stumbling towards them. A large man, scrambling over the rocks, using only one hand to steady himself as the other is filled with a burden, that while light, weighs heavily upon him. A brief flicker of hope stirred in both Edward and Annabel. They looked towards each other in disbelief as the figure came closer. Samuel, carefully, carefully set himself down next to them. There snuggled under his coat tight against his chest was Victoria. Safe and warm. Reluctantly, Samuel handed her over to her mother's eager arms. Annabel took her and kissed her gently on the forehead. Carefully she wrapped her safely inside the folds of doctor's overcoat. Holding her close to share what little warmth she had left. Victoria whimpered slightly but was too cold even to cry. Edward looked at Samuel. The haunted expression on his face convinced him that this is not the time to ask what had happened alone there on the cliff top.

Instead he asked, "How are we going to get them of this hillside before we all freeze?" But Samuel gave no more response than a grunt. Lost in the horror he has just witnessed, despair overtook him, his chin drooped to his chest and he cried huge silent tears. Quickly Edward accepted that it was up to him alone to get them all home safely before hypothermia set in. Annabel was too cold and weak to walk far - she would almost certainly need to be carried, while Samuel had withdrawn into himself. Sir Cyril was most likely already dead. Walking down the overgrown hillside with just the dim light of the lantern would be dangerous enough even if he wasn't already frozen half to death. To attempt it carrying Lady Annabel, and Victoria would be suicidal. He looked around, searching for something, anything that could help them. He had just about given up hope of getting them safely home, thinking that their only chance would be for him to carry Victoria, while Samuel carried Lady Annabel. Sir Cyril would just have to be left. Then to his immense relief, Edward saw small pinpricks of light heading towards them from Broadwell. Excitedly he grabbed the lantern, opened the shutter and turned up the wick. Light streamed out, and he began to shout.

"Up Here! Here!" He yelled. "Come on Samuel, shout out! There are lights, we're saved."

An answering shout greeted him, and Edward was pleased to see a sturdy group of men, each carrying a stout staff and lantern running towards them. As they came closer

Edward recognised a group of men from the local inn, led by Alfred, Sir Cyril's steward.

"Well met Doctor. Lady Annabel. Samuel." Alfred greeted them each in turn. Quickly he assessed the situation, and organised the men, all sturdy farmers and miners, to fashion two stretchers from their stout staffs and a pair of great coats. On to one they loaded Lady Annabel. Lady Annabel refused to release her iron grip on the baby until Nesta approached her. Talking gently and softly to her for a moment, Annabel finally, reluctantly handed over the baby and Nesta tucked her in close to her body in a sling made from a blanket. Sir Cyril was lifted carefully on to the other and covered over with another coat. Finally, they were ready to leave, and the men set off down the slope, carrying their heavy load.

Alfred walked over to the misshapen body lying alone at the foot of the cliffs. Forlornly, he stared down at the once familiar face, now battered by her long fall down the cliff-side. For a moment he stood, contemplating the events that had led up to her death. Wondering what had led a woman he had known well in life to such a terrible end.

"Here Doctor. You'd best take a look before we go." He called sadly.

Reluctantly, Edward walked over to the body. He stared down at the familiar face. The wild eyes open and staring forever in death. The homely face forever frozen in a twisted mask of hatred and fear. Silently he reached down and closed the eyes of his housekeeper. Although he hadn't always seen eye to eye with Miss Bates, he had begun to feel a grudging respect for her. Now he pondered what had set her upon such a destructive path, and what if anything he could have done to stop her. Covering her gently with her cloak, he turned. Wordlessly he walked down the slope with Alfred, setting a quick pace to try to catch up with the men who had gone on ahead. It was much easier going down the rough track to Broadwell, rather than having to retrace their steps, forcing their way through the trees and undergrowth as they had on the way up. The snow had thankfully eased allowing them to travel more quickly under the bright light of the hunter's moon.

At Broadwell, Alfred banged on the door of the inn. Long since closed for the night, the last customer dispatched home many hours before, its shutters and door were all firmly shut against the cold. Alfred banged and banged, continuing until eventually the door was wrenched upon by the angry landlord who demanded who it was disturbing the sleep of god-fearing citizens. His anger quickly dissipated when he caught sight of the stretchers and recognised Alfred. Bringing them into the tap room, he set about relighting the fires to mull ale to get warmth back into them. His wife, eye still heavy with sleep, bustled about, wrapping blankets around them all, and finding some bread and sops to feed Victoria, who, while vocal about her hunger seemed none the worst for her ordeal. Lady Annabel had fared less well. She was worryingly cold. Having raced from her bed in just her nightgown without stopping to put on shoes, her feet were particularly bad and were covered in sores and deep cuts, her toes an unhealthy pale blue. She cried out with pain as they warmed, and blood began to flow into them again. Edward rubbed her feet, hoping to ease her pain a little and help to restore the circulation. Watching a couple of toes that steadfastly remained a disturbing grey, he was concerned that she might have developed frost bite. If so the toes would need to be removed, an operation that Edward was unsure that she would have the strength for.

Sir Cyril was laid reverently on the table in the kitchen, covered over with a fresh blanket. Despite the doctor's best efforts, he had lost too much blood. Seeing his men settled, each with a pint of hot, freshly mulled ale, Alfred went to pay his respects to the man that had been his master for over 30 years. He stood, tankard of ale in his hand, looking down in silent contemplation. Alfred grimaced as he saw the fresh blood spreading across the clean blanket.

"Here, ale wife, we'll need another blanket, this one's covered in blood." He called. Edward, who had been sitting quietly next to Samuel looked up.

"What?" he said. Throwing off the blanket that had been wrapped around his shoulders, he hurried over to Sir Cyril. Quickly he snatched off the soiled blanket and placed two fingers firmly to Sir Cyril's throat. There he caught a faint, but unmistakable, pulse. Bending low over him, he placed his cheek to Sir Cyril's mouth, and looking down the body towards his feet. There, faint but unmistakable was the gentle puff of a breath exhaled, the chest moving slowly in rhythm. Frantically looking around for something to help him, he caught sight of the large knife hanging over the fireplace. Grabbing it, he deftly cut away Sir Cyril's coat and shirt, revealing the pale white flesh below, and the small wound which continued its steady, drip, drip of blood.

"Ere, what you playing at Doctor?" demanded Alfred, grabbing Edward's arm. Impatiently Edward shook him off and continued to poke gently at the wound with the tip of the knife blade. He turned to the alewife.

"I need a needle and thread. Quickly. I need to sew him up." He said urgently. As the woman hurried off to find what he asked for, Alfred grabbed his arm angrily.

"I know you've been through a lot Doctor, but he ain't even cold. Is this the time to be sewing him back up?" he demanded.

"Yes. Exactly- he's not cold! Don't you see?! The wound, it's bleeding. Corpses don't bleed! He's still alive, and there's a chance, just a chance mind you, that I might manage to save him - if you'll just leave me to get on with it." As soon at the alewife returned with her sewing box, Edward upended it on to the table. He rummaged through the odd collection of needles, silks, spare buttons and thimbles, looking for a needle and thread of the right size. Finally satisfied, he threaded the needle with a fine length of silk and began to painstakingly repair the damage to Sir Cyril, gently sewing the cut edges back together again. It was a difficult task, carefully sewing the cut veins back together by only the unsteady light of the inns oil lamp. Finally, his task completed, he sat back on his heals' and wiped his brow with his hands, leaving bloody streaks. Alfred grimaced and turned away in disgust, while the alewife, more practically offered him a clean cloth soaked in warm water.

"Well that were a fancy bit of embroidery, so it were. Do you think the old sod'll make it now?" enquired the alewife affectionately.

"I don't know. I don't know. But he has a chance, so with God's will and a fair wind behind him... Maybe." Edward replied as he slumped exhausted onto the floor.

"Aye, well you've done your best for him. We'll say a prayer for him, never you fear. Now you look all done in. You sit quiet with an ale." She said kindly, patting him on the shoulder as if he was an errant young child.

As the night passed, the storm finally blew itself out and the wind eased. Edward stirred, wondering why his bed seemed so hard that morning. As he gradually came too, he realised that instead of his comfortable bed, he was sat awkwardly in a hard-wooden settle, and instead of his soft sheets, he was covered by a rough homespun blanket that smelt strongly of horse. A warm figure was snuggled into his side, with an arm reassuringly spread across his chest. He breathed in deeply, smelling not only the strong odour of horse, but also the lighter, gentler fragrance of lavender and rosemary that Nesta used to wash her hair. Nesta began to stir, but tired from walking miles in the snow the night before, she merely wriggled before returning to sleep tucked into his side. Looking down at her, Edward smiled, thinking how natural it seemed to be curled up next to Nesta. Gently, so as not to disturb her, he placed a kiss upon her brow.

"Now then Doctor, that's my niece you got there." Samuel's voice, pitched low so as not to disturb the other sleepers and melodious with his soft forest accent, was amused, but nonetheless contained a hint of censure.

"Samuel. I think we need to talk." He said. Edward, normally so private, found that he was strangely unbothered that Samuel had caught his display of affection for Nesta.

"Aye Doctor. I figure we do. I guess you want to know what happened last night, up on the hill. Well, old Doris, she were about to stab you, when Sir Cyril came bowling in from nowhere. I didn't know he were up there with us. He must have followed me and Nesta. But I reckon as he saved your life, pushing you out the way like that. She'd have fair gutted you if he hadn't banged you out the way, even if he did get spitted himself. So anyways, I saw her run off with the bairn, and I thought, well I thought I couldn't be having that. I went after her. God but she were quick on her pins. I didnae know she could move like that, up and up she went. By the time I caught up with her, she were right at the top of the cliff. Recon' she hadn't noticed me come up behind her, not 'til then. Raging she were. Raging that no-one could have this bairn. I thought she were going to jump and take the babe with her. I grabbed her. Somehow, I managed to get the bairn off her, though she fought like a wild cat. Scratching and biting she were, shouting that she were hers. That they hadn't been looking after her properly, so she were going to take her, she'd keep her safe. Screaming that Agnes never should have taken her, and now she were going to take her back. Full of anger she was. Anger, and spite, and hatred. Then she just seemed to step back, and I grabbed, and that was it. She was gone and I had the babe in my arms." Samuel stopped. By nature introspective, he found it difficult enough to speak of his emotions normally, keeping them bottled up inside. But today the flood gates had opened, and everything, the emotion, the fear of the night before was pouring out of him. "She just fell. You understand don't you doctor?" he pleaded, a haunted look in his eyes.

"Aye. I reckon she just fell, don't you Doctor?" Edward and Samuel, engrossed in their conversation hadn't noticed Alfred quietly coming in through the front door, shaking snow off himself. He sat down heavily on the bench by Samuel. "So little Vicky's a cuckoo then. Well, can't say as I'm surprised really, fifteen years they been married, and still no babe in the crib." He sucked his teeth, paused and continued. "Anyways, I've organised for a cart to come to collect Lady Annabel and Sir Cyril, to take them back to Coleford. Nesta said to have them taken to your house Doctor?" Edward nodded his assent

"Aye, well. I'll get some of the maids from the estate to come give young Nesta a hand. Bless her, she works hard, but likely a bit of help wouldn't go amiss. An' it's stopped snowing. Soon as its proper light, we'll head up. Bring the body back down. We can take her to the church. Reverend can pop her in the bones house for now, then once the grounds thawed a bit, we'll reopen Agnes' grave and stick her in with her sister. An' good riddance I say." He chuckled sadly to himself "They'd always hated each other in life, couldn't stand to be together. I reckon it'll serve them both right." Seeing the look of complete confusion on Edward's face, Alfred decided to explain. After all, if this Doctor was going to stay and be a part of his community, he would need to understand the complex undercurrents of forest life. The ties that linked them, miners, merchants and farmers all, and bound them together. Ties of blood, and ties of friendship, which worked and weaved their way between them all.

"So there were old Agnes. She were a midwife, a wise woman. She lived in a battered little cottage up on the encroachments. Well her an' her man, they had two daughters, twins. One named Agnes, for the mother, the other Doris. Like chalk and cheese, they were, and fought like a cat and dog from the moment they were out of their mother's womb. As they got older, Agnes grew more and more like her mother, while Doris, she grew more and more away. She hated living in that tiny encroachment cottage, so as soon as she could, she upped and left. Went to work in some big house, over Monmouth way if I recall. Changed her name and everything. Oh, she'd come back every now and then to see her mother, tell 'em how well she was getting on, and generally lord it over them a bit, but mostly she was away. Then one time she came back and stayed a few months. Word was, she was in the family way, and there were them that said it was the old Lord's child, but whoever's it was, she were back here, with no character and a full belly." Alfred shook his head sadly "Well, after her confinement she just vanished again. Word was the bairn had died, and she'd gone off back to Monmouth way where she worked in some big house. That must have been, what all of twenty years ago now? Pretty young thing she was in her youth, but full of airs and graces. Didn't see her again after that for a fair old while. She didn't even come back to see her Ma buried. Then when Doctor Thomas should come here, who should he bring as his housekeeper? Well, things settled down, and somehow, Doris and Agnes seemed to get a bit closer for a while. They spoke to each other if they saw each other, but they were never what you'd call bosom friends. Civil I guess. Still had some right to dos, but for the most part, they rubbed along together. I don't know what happened to cause them to fall out this time. But I'd lay a guinea to a farthing, that Doris did for Agnes. Her own sister." He said shaking his head.

"It were the bairn." Samuel said "She told me. She said "Agnes shouldn't have taken the bairn. She promised me she wouldn't steal any more babies." I mean everyone knew that if you didn't want your baby, Agnes could make it disappear. She knew someone in Monmouth as would always take a healthy baby, find it a good home, split the money with the mother. But Agnes must have got greedy, taking them that was wanted as well. Saying they'd died when they ain't. An' Doris, well she wouldn't stand for that. So she killed her."

"A sorry tale. But what to do now?" mused the Doctor.

"We take Lady Annabel and Sir Cyril, nurse them back to health. Alfred will collect Miss Bates body, and the reverend will bury her quietly." Nesta sounded resigned, as if resolved to a difficult decision. She sat up, her hair tousled, her face soft with sleep, eyes dark rimmed. A soft cry came from the basket by her side, and she reached in and picked up Victoria. Nesta smiled down at her baby sister sadly, rocking her in her arms and shushing her gently. An unpleasant aroma filled the air. Wrinkling her nose with disgust, Nesta carried the baby away to the kitchen, hunting out the alewife and a clean cloth for the baby.

"She's a natural. Just like her mother. Make someone a good wife, so she would. Aye, and a good mother when the bairns come along." Samuel said watching her go. Edward got the distinct impression that he was being ever so slightly mocked and began to blush. To hide his discomfort, he stood up, and headed over to where Sir Cyril was lying uneasily on a bench. Carefully he lifted the blanket to inspect the wound. Red around the edges, the wound looked raw and painful, but there didn't seem to be any further blood loss and for that he was grateful.

Chapter Twenty-One

Friday, 4th December 1851.

It was nearly two weeks before Sir Cyril regained consciousness sufficiently to speak. Then his first question was about Victoria, his second for his wife. Nesta, who had been carefully spooning beef tea into him, sighed with relief. Reassuring him that all was well with Lady Annabel and Victoria, she stayed with him until he slipped back into an uneasy sleep. From that point on, he made rapid progress, quickly developing a hearty appetite and a fondness for Nesta's stew. Lady Annabel herself had been rather wane and inclined to pick over her food. It was taking time to recover both from the chicken pox, as well as her ordeal in the snow. Thankfully, her feet seemed to be healing well, and Edward was pleased that his hot bread poultice was easing the worst of the pain. Despite Edward's earlier worries, it looked as if she would keep all of her toes.

Time passed. Good to his word, Alfred organised Doris Bates' funeral and internment alongside her sister Agnes. As the grave was refilled, more than one member of the congregation was heard to breathe a sigh of relief that the blackmailing sisters had be finally laid to rest. Of the third member of the family, Annibiah, there was no news. Despite Alfred circulating both her description and that of some distinctive pieces of Lady Annabel's jewellery that she had taken, no one reported seeing hide nor hair of her. Her complete disappearance was attributed to her leaving the area altogether, certainly she had stolen enough valuables to pay her fare to London, or even America if she should so choose. Common opinion was that she was long gone and good riddance! What with the inquest, funeral, police investigation (such as it was) and nursing both Sir Cyril and Lady Annabel, November slipped into December in a whirlwind of activity. It was nearly Christmas before Edward judged that Sir Cyril and Lady Annabel were well enough to return home. Wanting to ensure that the house was prepared for them, with fires lit, and staff ready to welcome them home, Edward sought out Alfred. It was agreed that the steward would send the coach for them in two days, time enough to ensure that everything was aired and ready at the house.

   Edward was surprised upon his return home from his talk with Alfred to find Sir Cyril and Lady Annabel sat in his drawing room; drinking tea and talking rather awkwardly with Nesta. Everyone seemed relieved when he entered the room. Explaining that the preparations for their departure in a few days were all in hand, Edward was about flee the awkward atmosphere and beat a hasty retreat to his study, when the doorbell rang. A borrowed maid showed in Thomas, Mary, Samuel and Jane, all looking worried.

Sir Cyril tried to stand to welcome them but failed. "Thank-you for coming. As you can see, I'm still not fully recovered." He said ruefully "I want to thank you, Samuel, personally for rescuing our daughter. It was a great thing you did, and I can never thank you enough. But I, we, also wanted to talk to you about that night. There are some things we still don't fully understand."

Samuel turned his cap over and over in hands uneasily. Not used to being in the august company of his landlord, he was uncomfortable enough to begin with, let alone as the conversation was heading down a path he'd rather not follow.

"So, to start at the beginning. My husband and I were desperate for a child. We called on Doctor Thomas, we tried everything, but nothing seemed to work. I am barren. I will never carry a living child. I thought I would never be a mother." Pale faced and tight lipped, tears rolled down Lady Annabel's face. "Then one day Agnes approached me. She said she had heard from her sister of our plight, and she could arrange for us to adopt a healthy child. The months passed. I gave up all hope, until one day she came to me again. She said she'd found a mother who didn't want her child, and for a fee, I could have her. And so the arrangements were made. I pretended to be pregnant and kept to the house. Then one day she came with the baby, and I was overjoyed. I was less pleased when she insisted that we also take her daughter in as nursemaid. Annie, Annibiah, is a difficult woman. I found out she had been dismissed for theft by several previous employers, even spent a while in gaol. But when challenged over her attitude and some petty pilfering, she threatened to tell everyone that I had brought a child, 'like a sack of potatoes at the market'. She said that Vicky would be taken away. I couldn't bear that, so we were stuck with her. I didn't even dare tell Cyril of her threats." She looked at him, eyes full of love and sorrow "I knew that you would be angry dearest. I knew that you would dismiss her on the spot. I couldn't risk that."

Sir Cyril squeezed his wife's hand, returning her fond gaze. He took up the tale. "After her encounter with you Nesta, I told her that I had had enough. Then the whole sorry tale came out, and Annabel explained about Annie's blackmailing ways. I planned for us to go away. To live in London for a while until the fuss had died down. I gave Annie her notice that day. When you came in Nesta and told us that my wife and baby had gone, I thought it was Annie. That she had somehow persuaded Annabel to go. It was only later in the woods when I recognised Doris Bates that I realised that they had been taken against their will. When I saw she was going to stab you Edward, I dived in. Made a bit of a mess of it, I'm afraid." He said wryly.

"And saved my life!" said Edward warmly. Watching Samuel from the corner of his eye, he could see that he was increasingly agitated. Smiling reassuringly, he continued. "Then Samuel chased Miss Bates up the hillside and rescued little Victoria. Miss Bates fell to her death."

"Undoubtedly she fell. What with the snow and the wind, it was slippery as anything that night. We're just lucky that Samuel here was able to rescue little Vicky. For that we will always be grateful, and I wanted to reward you." Sir Cyril said warmly handing over a heavy purse. "It's little enough compared to what you did for us, but we hope it will make things easier when your own little one arrives."

Samuel shook his head in distain. "No. I ain't taking no money from you. That's my niece you've got there. I ain't daft, I figured out whose babe you've brought. My niece! You can't buy a child like that. And you can't buy my silence neither. She were stolen, she ain't for sale"

"She was our daughter, Samuel. And I'm content for Lady Annabel and Sir Cyril to raise her. To give her things that I can never give my other daughters" Mary's voice was filled with emotion. It had taken many long, sleepless nights of tossing and turning and talking it over with Thomas before finally they had reached the painful decision to let their daughter go to where she was already so wanted, so loved. "What have we to offer? A crowded house, barely enough food, heaven knows the gale ain't doing as well as we'd hoped. They can offer her so much more. And as long as we all keep quiet, they'll be staying in the forest, so we can watch her grow. This is for the best. If we can accept it, so can you, Samuel. Now you swallow your pride, and you take that money. You'll be needing it when the bairn comes."

The final two days passed in a rush. Finally, in one last frantic whirl of activity, Sir Cyril and his family left. Nesta found herself sat in the kitchen alone. It was the first time since that dreadful snow-filled night up on the high pasture lands that she had found the time to sit and think. Despite having the two maids sent by Alfred to help out, having Sir Cyril and Lady Annabel to nurse, and Victoria to care for, had created a lot of extra work for Nesta. The two maids had been helpful, but they lacked initiative and required direction, so Nesta had found it easier to set them to the mundane cleaning tasks, while she took on the nursing of Sir Cyril and Lady Annabel herself. However, being busy had had its advantages; Nesta had simply not had the time to relive the horrors of that cold snowy night on the hillside. Exhaustion began to get the better of her, and closing her eyes, she began to drift off into an uneasy sleep. Her head on the table, her mind filled with troubling images, the race up the hillside through the dark trees, Edward nearly being stabbed and falling to the ground, the blood spreading across Sir Cyril's chest. And most terrible of all, the last dreadful scream of Doris Bates falling down the cliff and onto the rocks below, her body limp and broken.

She was woken up by Edward shaking her shoulder.

"Are you alright Nesta?" he asked, full of concern "you were crying out."

"I'm sorry Sir. I guess I was just having a nightmare. What must you think of me, falling asleep at the kitchen table like this!"

"I'd think that you have worked incredibly hard the last few weeks, organising those two maids of Sir Cyril's, looking after him and Lady Annabel, and making sure that despite all the upheaval the house has continued to run smoothly. That and you've had a terrible shock. I know that I have. I would never have dreamed that Miss Bates was capable of those terrible things. That she should stab Sir Cyril. And her own sister! I should have seen it. I should have prevented it somehow." Edward said sadly, sitting down at the table beside Nesta.

"I know Sir. I just keep thinking of the way she was that night. Like she was half mad, standing there holding the baby with that knife. That horrible sharp knife. I just keep thinking that she will come back. Come back and hurt us somehow." She said looking apprehensively at the large wicker armchair that continued to dominate the kitchen. "I keep looking at her chair, and her room, and.... sorry Sir, I'm just being fanciful. I must be more tired than I thought."

"No." Said Edward, "I know what you mean. However, one thing we can sort easily." And with that he strode over to the armchair, picked it up, and carried it outside. Shutting the kitchen door firmly behind him, he returned to the table. "There. That feels better. We'll burn it in the morning. I suddenly feel quite invigorated. Now I'm going to tackle her room this instant. I think I'll sleep better knowing whatever accursed spell she has put on us is truly broken."

Nesta reluctantly got to her feet, ignoring Edward's wave to indicate she should remain in the kitchen. "No Sir. I can't let you face that alone. Heaven knows what you might find up there."

Together they went upstairs to the small bedroom in the eaves. It was the mirror image of Nesta's room, except somehow, while Nesta's room felt wholesome, Miss Bates room was dark and oppressive, full of a brooding malign presence. The windows were dark with grime where she had never cleaned them, and there was an odd sour smell, as if she never opened the window to air the room or changed the linen on the bed. Bundling the bedding into a ball, Nesta carried the bedding and the clothing downstairs to burn in a great bonfire, along with the old armchair from the kitchen. While still of good quality, Nesta and the Doctor agreed that it was beyond saving, contaminated by its association with Miss Bates.

As Nesta left, Edward continued to look around. He had never ventured into Miss Bates room before, feeling as though it would be some kind of invasion of her privacy. Rows of shelves completely covered every available space, and these were covered in a range of oddments and trinkets. Looking at them carefully, Edward thought that they could not possibly have all rightfully belonged to Miss Bates. There were various hat pins in a large finely carved jewellery box. A few rings, some large old-fashioned broaches, and even a pocket watch with seals sat on the shelves. One or two items he recognized as belonging to Dr Thomas, well to him now he supposed, taken for her own by Miss Bates, rather than being consigned to storage.

Edward was still exploring the shelves. "I think it wasn't just Agnes who liked to blackmail people. The things in this room, it's as if Miss Bates was at it as well." He said to Nesta. Suddenly, amongst the various items of men's and women's jewellery, hats, and ornaments, he spotted a diary, which he picked up to take downstairs and read later.

It was too late, and too wet, to make a bonfire that night. So it was not until the following morning that they finally set the whole lot ablaze. Clothes and bedding were piled onto and around the large wicker armchair from the kitchen at the bottom of the garden. Carefully lighting the fire, Edward stood back with Nesta, watching the fire slowly catch, and gather strength as it devoured Miss Bates possessions. A cloud that had hung over them since the awful night on hillside began to lift, as though they had finally managed to exorcise her malign spirit. Together they stood side by side in companionable silence, remembering the upheaval of the past few months until eventually, once the fire had burnt down to smouldering embers, they went inside. They sat together in the kitchen.

Nesta took up her embroidery, carefully sewing a neat border onto table cloth which she intended to be a Christmas present for her mother. Edward retrieved the journal from his pocket and began to read. It was a diary, written in a firm, round hand. Flicking through the pages, it was clear that Miss Bates had been using knowledge gained by eavesdropping on consultations with Dr Thomas to blackmail his patients. However, like her sister, Miss Bates preferred to take treasured possessions in payment, rather than money. She didn't sell these oddments, she just hoarded them. Keeping them on shelves so that she could see them. Handle them. Gloat over them. Edward felt slightly unclean, as if he was listening in on a person's private conversations as he read the journal, but he just couldn't stop. Through the diary he felt that he started to know Miss Bates in a way that he never had as her employer. Page after page he read, page after page of Miss Bates ranting about perceived slights, and seeking revenge in the cruellest and most inventive of ways. Often her ire was directed towards her sister Agnes, who it seemed she both loved and hated in equal measure. Desperate for her approval, yet she constantly strove to outdo her, to be more successful. Flicking forward to the approximate date when Agnes died, it seemed that after a particularly vicious argument, Miss Bates had decided to kill her sister. The last line on the page read:

The bitch has done it again. She promised not to, but she took the baby anyway.

Turning over to the next page, Edward was chilled to read the following entry, made with a slightly less steady hand which simply said:

I've done it. She's dead. A knife to the back, just as she deserved.

At that point, sick to his stomach of the bile and self-justification that had been poured into the pages, Edward closed the book. He got up from his chair, walked to the range, and threw the book onto the flames. As the pages curled and flames licked along the pages, Edward felt as if a heavy weight had been lifted. The spectre of Miss Bates was finally completely exorcised from the house.

Edward had spoken to both Sir Cyril, and Dr Rudge, the coroner. Following Samuel's account of that last night on Purple Hill, they had agreed to record that Agnes had been killed by her sister, who had subsequently fallen to her death. No record would be made of the abduction of Victoria and Lady Annabel, and the wounding of Sir Cyril would but put down to him attempting to apprehend a villain, a poacher on his land who had escaped. Edward, aided by Alfred and Rose, began the painstaking process of tracking down the rightful owners of the various articles that Miss Bates had taken over the years, and discreetly returning them. The upstairs bedroom would be cleaned, renewed and refreshed. In agreement with Nesta, he had decided to leave the room empty for a short while, reluctant as he was to bring an outsider into his home.

In time he was sure he would find a new maid to come and work alongside Nesta, but for now they were content just the two of them.

Printed in Great Britain
by Amazon